The Sunny Spaces

A Novel of Romance, Inspiration, and Restoration

ANN ANTOGNOLI

May God bless you with the
courage always to forgive and
to fly in the sunny spaces.

Ann Antognoli

Printed by Create Space, Charleston, SC

Available from Amazon.com and other book stores

ISBN-10: 0996024115
ISBN-13: 978-0996024112

FOR DAVID
a Catskill eagle

Give not thyself up, then, to fire, lest it invert thee, deaden thee; as for the time it did me. There is a wisdom that is woe; but there is a woe that is madness. And there is a Catskill eagle in some souls that can alike dive into the blackest gorges, and soar out of them again and become invisible in the sunny spaces. And even if he for ever flies within the gorge, that gorge is in the mountains; so that even in his lowest swoop the mountain eagle is still higher than other birds upon the plain, even though they soar.

Herman Melville
Moby Dick
Chapter XCVI

CHAPTER ONE

ROLLING on his side, he reached to pull the pretty dark haired woman lying next to him closer. She laughed as she played with his thick head of hair. Her eyes grew large with anticipation when he leaned in to kiss her. Catching him off guard, she placed her hands on his chest and pushed him away. She whispered, "I'm sorry, I don't do recreational sex."

A slight jolt woke him, but he kept his eyes closed for several moments hoping to hold on to some essence of her.

Several times during the past year, he experienced this phenomenon. He would be in a deep sleep. The attractive woman would lie next to him, but before he could coax her, she would refuse his overture. She expected a commitment to love, something he resisted for the last ten years. Still, this dream that left him unsatisfied was much more preferable than the Vietnam War nightmares that haunted him just as regularly.

Fully awake, Dr. James T. O'Brien stretched his arms toward the ceiling. He held the position for several moments then lowered his arms and covered his face with his hands. I wonder what the weather's like, he thought. He rolled out of bed and stretched again. Peering into the still dark early morning sky, he thought, I'm not fighting an airport today. Brushing his cheek with the back of his hand, he mumbled, "I'll shave later."

He showered, packed his bags, and tossed his luggage into the trunk of his rented gray Lexus. Before he checked out of the Philadelphia hotel, he grabbed a cup of coffee and a bagel.

Although he made it a practice to expect the unexpected, he hadn't expected that the past week would be plagued with one problem after another. Exasperated with disorganized school officials who took part in a three day seminar, he was tired and would rather head home to Emerson-Thoreau University in Pennsylvania, where he enjoyed his work as the president of the college. Relieved that the lack-luster week was behind him, an ominous weekend threatened. First his brother called with a tempting invitation he was obliged to refuse.

"Are you ready for some serious golfing? Tee off 's 7:00 A.M. on one of Florida's premier courses."

"Sorry to break your heart, Sean. I'm on my way to Western Pennsylvania as we speak."

"No! That's the wrong direction, Jimmy. Make a u-turn right now. Drive south!"

"I was supposed to be free this weekend, but each year my frat brother asks me to give a commencement speech to his graduates. How many times could I tell him no?" With more enthusiasm, he suggested, "Call Mikey. He golfs better than all of us. He especially loves golfing with you."

"Everyone in the free world loves golfing with me. It's the only time they win."

"True," O'Brien said. "If Mike can't make it, call Pat. Do the poor guy a favor and get him away from that lunatic he married. I promise to golf with you in two weeks, okay?"

"Hope you enjoy your weekend as much as I plan to enjoy mine," Sean said.

"Stop rubbing it in, you sadist."

Sean laughed and said, "I'll give Mike a call."

There were a hundred activities he'd rather do this weekend than give a speech, but he thought about Joe Colao's tenacity, his pitch that last time: "The year 2000 is a great year to give a commencement speech, Jim. Think of the symbolism, how memorable it will be for those graduating seniors. I promise not to beg for another millennium."

Something about Joe's last plea stirred O'Brien finally to commit. Maybe it was his decades of dedication to the students and faculty in his school, his tireless efforts as an enlightened superintendent, and his unwavering loyalty and friendship during all the years he declined the invitation to speak. Grabbing Joe in a friendly head lock, he conceded, "Damn, you're persistent. Give me the date, time, and location." Gently shoving him away,

2

he said, "The only reason I'm doing this is to sit at Maggie's table and eat that delicious lasagna she makes." He pointed his finger and offered a friendly warning. "Make sure there's enough for both of us!"

***

He pulled into the Marriott Hotel parking lot, stepped out of the car, and drew in a couple of deep breaths of fresh air. The decision to get off the turnpike and travel an unhurried drive through Pennsylvania's picturesque back roads and quiet mountainous twists and turns proved relaxing. It was a welcome relief after being cooped up for days with Ph. D.'s who dropped more crap than a flock of chickens running loose in a laxative factory. The clear sky and brisk air helped take the edge off the disappointing early morning phone calls, first from Sean and soon after, from Joe, bearing more bad news that threatened to mar the weekend festivities.

"My two sons have the flu. It's spreading fast." Sounding harried, he said, "Under normal circumstances, we'd be able to maneuver around the chaos, but the doctor quarantined us. I'm going to escape tonight, but by Monday, guaranteed I'll be in bed with a temp of one hundred and five." Unable to hide his disappointment, he said, "I finally collar you, and I have to banish you to a hotel across town. Maggie's so sick; she doesn't even have the strength to make the lasagna and package it for you to go."

"Listen. Stuff happens. Tell Maggie I understand." Feeling a twinge of jealousy, he wondered what it was like to share a life with a good wife and kids. He philosophized, "We fill our lives with so much frivolity, but taking care of kids always pays the best dividends." He paused. "Make sure you stay healthy, buddy. It's bad enough that I can't have the pleasure of socializing with your beautiful wife and kids, but at least let me enjoy your friendship tonight."

"Thanks, Jim. I know it's not *The Today Show* or *Sixty Minutes*, but your appearance is important to us."

"Those shows lend me a level of credibility and make me a pseudo-celebrity, but the one thing they can never do is attest to my capacity to be a good friend to someone who has always been a good friend to me. We're on tonight!"

CHAPTER TWO

MID-LIFE crises and mid-section bulges plagued other men in their mid-forties, but he was handsome by most standards and maintained a high level of physical agility and strength. He stood close to six feet tall and laughed modestly when men decades younger marveled at his vitality and strength. Complementing his physical prowess were his intellectual and contemplative pursuits. Despite popularity, he wisely took care to nurture a small, close circle of good friends.

Sean, his older brother and closest confidante, never missed an opportunity to tease him mercilessly: "Hey Jimmy, you're not an Irishman like the rest of us. Mom and Dad found you down on the streets of Athens after some jealous god tossed you off Mt. Olympus!"

It was common for him to attract people with his warm, penetrating, dark brown eyes. His equally dark brown hair with several renegade strands of gray was always neatly combed but never stiff. Consideration, inherent to his character, allowed him to find common ground with the most belligerent individuals and factions. Although more reserved than his four brothers, he wielded a quick wit and loved to laugh. He possessed that rare quality allowing individuals to feel special simply by associating with him even if for a brief time.

***

The sight of an army jeep parked next to him in the hotel parking lot spun him back twenty-seven years earlier. His high-spirited demeanor was dramatically altered after he enlisted in the Marines. Contrary to news reports that the war was winding down, he was deployed to a heavy combat zone in the Mekong Delta. Back then, he was filled with the kind of enthusiasm and idealism that accompanies youth. He thought of the strong-willed eighteen year-old who embraced blind patriotism rather than his father's wisdom.

Hearing that his brother enlisted, Sean ran home and found O'Brien sprawled on his bed reading a magazine. In one angry swoop, he slapped him hard in the head and yelled, "What the hell were you thinking?" His voice was cold and mean. "One hand grenade can blow your ass to Saigon and leave your brainless head in the rice paddies of Cambodia!" Squeezing O'Brien's face, he said with a sneer, "I guess you didn't stop to think about Mom and Dad when you signed up to save the world, huh tough guy?" Shoving him hard back onto the bed, Sean left the room, slamming the door behind him.

Before the family gathered around the supper table that evening, O'Brien's father, a man of few words, sat across from him. Staring at his son, he asked, "Why didn't you talk to me, Jimmy?"

Without hesitation, he told his father the truth. "I knew you'd talk me out of it, Dad." With confidence, he offered a true, but still romantic defense of his rash decision. "Geez, Dad. Is it a crime to want to defend the freedoms that we have here? We're able to go to church, go to grocery stores and buy any food we want. We can even make fun of our president, and no one comes in the night to herd us into some camp and kill us like animals."

By now the whole family filled the table. Furrowing his brow and lowering his head, his father placed his thumb and index finger on the bridge of his nose. After several seconds, he lifted his head. Locking eyes with his son full of life and promise, he said, "You're going to learn that not all wars are about freedom, Jimmy." He turned to all his sons sitting around the table, penetrating them like bullets that would not mistake their mark. With authority, he said, "Sacrificing one son for this war—this debauchery—is enough. If you get drafted, then I'll say good-bye, but not one second sooner." He set his gaze on O'Brien. Wanting to tell him that men never seem to rest easy after killing in a war, he instead palmed both hands on the table and said, "I wish to God you would have talked to me first, son."

He rose from his seat. Eyes cast downward; he walked into the study and closed the door. No one in the family dared disturb him there. O'Brien would remember the dispirited look on his father's face for the rest of his life.

***

He remembered how he trudged for days through muddy fields that were obliged to accept incessant rain that poured on already saturated ground. He mastered the art of standing motionless for hours in swamps that were unforgiving of missteps; he watched helplessly as soldiers were dragged under in seconds and rendered lifeless. He heard stories of Vietnamese children saddled with grenades, children designed as weapons that sought and destroyed unsuspecting American soldiers. The tales taught him to be skeptical of crying toddlers who ran up to him seeking comfort. He learned that graves weren't always serene parcels of land marked with polished stones that bore the names of the people he loved and lost.

When his tour of duty ended, the only way he could survive the war events incongruous with his wholesome upbringing was to suppress his memories of the sewage and sludge that became the mass grave of his best military combat friends. No matter how hard he tried though, he couldn't stop the one scene that always played in slow motion, over and over in his mind, the same several seconds when he watched in horror as his friends blew up into a thousand pieces just yards away from him. Trying in vain to rescue them, he frantically dove into the mud, flailing like a man on fire. Each time he dove in, the wet, thick earth sucked him under. The last time he dove into the mire, he stayed under until he dizzied and felt his lungs would burst, but still he couldn't even succeed in retrieving pieces of them. Fighting his way back to the land of the living, the next fifteen seconds were so alien to his character that he would sever his soul from any kind of meaningful peace for the next twenty-seven years. So when he was honorably discharged, he had difficulty reconciling the fact that his actions were less than honorable, and he was in one piece, able to come home and live, laugh, and love, while his friends were blown to bits and pieces and remained buried beneath that formless sludge forever.

No matter how celebratory the welcome home party was, after the music stopped and the conversations waned, and days and weeks crept by, O'Brien's family and friends couldn't help but notice that he was too sullen, and he was too reserved. He drank too much liquor and excused himself from raucous family dinners. He didn't sing along with Crosby, Stills, Nash, and Young anymore. Gradually forging a poised outward appearance, benign sounds and sights like a firecracker on the Fourth of July or a father lifting a crying child to comfort it would stir his buried personal history of the fifteen seconds of irrationality in a war he tried to forget. The violent and obscene images of his war activities filled his mind like scorpions stinging on a hot, humid day.

At one point, the shadows of death penetrated so dark and deep that he even made a desperate attempt to find absolution for his war crimes by driving to Mexico in his royal blue Mustang. He intentionally sought out a priest who couldn't understand English; one who would be unable to discern the burden of evil that he wanted to unload in the secrecy of a confessional box. He wanted the priest to perform the magic that only those in the priesthood that stretched as far back as the apostle Peter were able to perform. They had the power to make his offenses vanish, to make them go 'poof,' just like his friends disappeared a thousand times in his dreams. Always that same loud "CRACK!" and he'd watch, paralyzed with terror, as they disappeared into the murky, black sea. But he knew well that sins don't vanish. All the while he was searching for magic; he knew he really needed a miracle. He hoodwinked the unsuspecting priest, and he tried to hoodwink himself, but he knew that it was impossible to hoodwink God.

The geographical and chronological distance from Vietnam, and the success he subsequently earned in the legal and educational fields over the next two decades made O'Brien proficient at assigning his unresolved war dilemma to a charnel house deep within him. Although less frequently, unsettling events in life would cause the demons there to stir. Despite his ability to laugh, to learn, and to love adequately, something intimate, something at the core of love was held captive in that cold, dead place. He resigned himself to the reality that he was unable to release it on his own. Something or someone who expected more than just adequate from him would have to help him exorcise the guilt he carried. Until that day of emancipation, he would have to mask his grimy interior, what he perceived embodied his essence.

***

He gave his head a quick shake to pre-empt the war memories. He leaned on his car for a few more leisurely moments soaking in the warmth of the sun, a rare commodity all week in Philadelphia. Not in any hurry to enter the confines of another hotel room, his mind wandered to a time where he was called to do a kindness for another friend. That particular engagement was unexpected and more somber than the ceremony he planned to attend with his friend Joe.

Over a decade and a half ago, a phone call from a family friend interrupted his routine business day. The friend requested that O'Brien serve as a pall bearer for his father, Paul, who passed away just a day before. While he was successful in controlling his demons, he expected the minister's sermon to compel him and other mourners to address their own long-standing trespasses against humanity and God. Aware of the emotional distress the general call to self-evaluate would most likely cause, he prepared himself the best way he could.

He offered Paul's family his condolences and joined other mourners to listen to the eulogy. There was nothing unusual about the minister first recounting Paul's spiritual evolution, but when he spoke in more general terms, O'Brien felt uneasy and shifted in his seat.

"People generally waste precious time confined in self-ordained prisons because they don't know how to ask or refuse to ask for forgiveness," the minister instructed.

He recalled the familiar story of how decades prior to his death, Paul served a prison term for selling contaminated drugs to an adolescent seeking a thrill. The youngster subsequently died because of the drug contamination. While in prison, Paul suffered the anguish of being away from his family and friends. To compound the pain, when his father was dying, Paul was denied precious, quality time with him, to tell his father that he loved him, to plant a kiss on his father's warm forehead before he said good-bye forever. Paul's absence was conspicuous at his father's funeral. His confinement and suffering brought him to the realization that he caused inestimable suffering for his own innocent family as well as for the family of the boy he killed.

"How does one who is responsible for this magnitude of destruction ever find peace?" the minister asked. "Peace can only be born out of one's willingness to accept responsibility for and assign purpose to the suffering he causes and endures. In Paul's case, his suffering finally brought him to the awareness that he could never replace what he destroyed. He had cut short a life, fragmented at least two families, and undermined his own promise for doing good works in the world. He would forever owe the world reparation for his sin."

Scanning the congregation, the minister said, "This is the way we must all approach God. We must face Him with a clear understanding of our trespasses, with a genuinely contrite heart, and a willingness to make reparation. Only then will Heaven accept our act of contrition and release us from the bondage of sin. God's grace freed Paul to become one of the community's most involved and beloved advocates for youth reform. He was a gifted organizer who designed innovative programs for juvenile offenders, programs that served as models across the state."

The sermon did its job by rousing the guilt feelings that lay dormant. The preacher's words forced O'Brien to admit that instead of suffering purposefully, he lived comfortably numb. Feeling constricted, he loosened his tie and thought, if I wielded the power, I'd rip the guilt out of every pore of my body and soul, burn it, reduce it to ashes, climb the highest mountain, and scatter the ashes in the wind. As far as reparation for my sins, to whom do I make reparation? To the Vietnamese people? To the American people? To the families of the friends I watched get blown to bits and sink into that obscure pit? Wasn't being a decent human being all these years reparation enough?

That night, after Paul's funeral, he found himself alone in his room. One unvarnished truth hounded him: I know what I did, and God knows what I did. He had been less than forthright about his war transgressions. If he wanted to end the guilt of his past threatening to spread like gangrene through his body—a lifetime of good works— attacking every good thing he ever accomplished in his life, he had to find a way to come clean.

Wearing success well, he was growing weary of his counterfeit character. For too long, he yearned for the confidence and peace that accompanied authenticity. Like legions of other sinners, he would have preferred to reach into the past and change the several seconds of bad judgment that eternity recorded in his name. The minister's recollection of Paul's transformation renewed him with courage. He made up his mind *again* to make a good act of contrition, but years passed before he found himself face to face with a force that exacted truth from him.

CHAPTER THREE

DESPITE bouts with guilt and pangs of hypocrisy, O'Brien enjoyed his ephemeral success whenever opportunities arose. He was relatively young when he earned a law degree that placed him in close proximity to well-connected segments of society. He recalled how there was no hesitation on his part to say yes when the head of a well-to-do law firm invited him and several other lawyers to spend a week-long excursion in Italy. They stayed at his villa where they indulged in all the comfort and conveniences that wealth could lavish on them. The highlight of the trip was a visit to the Vatican. The tycoon had long boasted a personal friendship with the Pope, and he promised that they were going to have the good fortune to mingle in the garden where the Bishop of Rome was known to make impromptu appearances.

The holiday in Rome proved even more gratifying than the wealthy lawyer promised. The day they visited the Vatican, the sun burned brightly, high in the azure blue sky. A cool, crisp breeze rippled through the garden carrying with it the fragrance of lilacs nestled close to a wrought iron fence lined with white roses. Members of the group snapped pictures of the garden and each other as if they knew some day in the near future they would need to furnish proof for skeptics back home that they indeed were privy to the Pope. They engaged in casual conversations until someone noticed a figure mingling among them, subtle as a butterfly lights on petals in a garden of flowers. A gentle, unseen force prompted the visitors to stop what they were doing and turn in the Pope's direction. Some close to him respectfully knelt down and kissed his ring.

O'Brien felt a cold sweat creep over every inch of his skin. His strict Catholic upbringing caused the darkness in his heart instinctively to retreat from the light that moved toward him. Trying to avoid the Pontiff altogether, he inconspicuously moved toward the door that led to a corridor where the restrooms were located, but Providence preempted his plan. As his friends laughed and drank wine, their spirits lifted by the extraordinary encounter, grace guided the Pontiff in a different direction. The Shepherd sensed a troubled soul and fortuitously made his way toward O'Brien, reached out and touched his shoulder. He inquired in broken English.

"Is your trip going well?"

"More than just well, Holy Father," O'Brien said, wiping his forehead with his handkerchief and struggling to maintain composure.

"You look pale. Do you not feel well?"

"Actually, I do feel a little lightheaded," he admitted.

"Come this way," the Pope said, motioning with his hand. "Maybe it will help if you can rest in one of my favorite rooms."

The Pontiff guided him to a sunroom off of the garden that lent more privacy for discussions and meditations. Sitting across from each other in matching purple chairs, the Pope teased, "Most people walk toward me;" the Pope pointed at him, "but you were quite different. You walked away. But I see now that you were ill."

In this room, O'Brien sat for several moments gazing at the brilliant colored flowers, listening to the soothing waterfall, and feeling the warmth of the sun on his clammy skin. Shaking his head, he lifted his hands and covered his face for a moment. He brought his hands back down and grasped the arms of his chair to steady himself.

"I was trying to avoid you, Holy Father."

He continued to stare at the holy man sitting across from him. Feeling relief that his fugitive status from grace was about to end, he confessed, "I've spent most of my life dodging God's judgment."

"*Owszem,*" (indeed), the Pope acknowledged in his native Polish.

There was an awkward silence between them as the soft sound of laughter from the outer garden intermittently filtered into the room, and the soothing sound of the waterfall splashed on the rocks. Lost and bewildered, O'Brien shook his head.

"It would take a lifetime to separate myself from the horror of my actions."

"Then we are fortunate that God always gives each one a lifetime," the Pope consoled.

O'Brien's eyes canvassed the tranquil room for a few seconds before his eyes settled on the Pope. "I really don't know how or where to begin. The Vietnam War was over a long time ago, Holy Father, but it will never be over for me. No matter what I do. No matter where I go. No matter what I accomplish, what I did is always right here," he said, tapping his temple with his index finger. "If I give it this much," he held his thumb and index finger close together, "it will tear me apart; it will consume me."

The Pontiff nodded. Cognizant of the emotional turmoil the penitent before him exuded, he stood and extended both his hands toward O'Brien's head. "Do you mind?"

With complete submission and in a barely audible voice, O'Brien said, "Please."

Laying his hands on O'Brien's head, the Pope prayed with two thousand years of authority:

"God, the Father of mercies, through the death and resurrection of his Son has reconciled the world to himself and has sent the Holy Spirit among us for the forgiveness of sins. Through the ministry of the Church may God give you pardon and peace, and absolve you from your sins in the name of the Father, and of the Son, and of the Holy Spirit."

O'Brien was surprised that the Pontiff didn't ask him to recite a litany of his sins. He didn't even ask me for my plan to make reparation, he thought. He intuitively recognized a man fragmented, wandering in spiritual desolation, contrite, yet unable to find a valid way to reconcile with the goodness of God and the world, so the good Shepherd simply reached out and freed him from the hellish confinement he forged for himself.

As O'Brien blinked back tears and ran his handkerchief over his face, the Pope smiled and clapped his hands with joy.

"And now the mercy of God frees you to love yourself and others as He loves us."

Despite the Pontiff's generous gift of forgiveness without the benefit of explanation of the sins he forgave, O'Brien needed the Pope to know: "My friends are buried in filthy Vietnamese sludge, and other innocent people are dead because of me, Holy Father." Shaking his head and keeping his stare at one distant point, he said, "All these years, it was so much easier to pursue the immediate world in front of me. I even succeeded," his voice oozed sarcasm. "I acquired money, fame, and golden opinions from my peers. I tried desperately never to look back, and certainly never to look inward, but truth . . . " his voice cracked, "truth hounded me and never let me forget my inhumanity."

The Pontiff placed his hand on O'Brien's shoulder. Before he walked outside to socialize with the others and then excuse himself to his private quarters, he recited several lines from a poem that O'Brien later learned was Matthew Arnold's "Dover Beach."

"Always remember that God puts us where He wants us. Be wise enough to know that our earthly world that '*lies* before us like a land of dreams, hath really neither joy, nor love, nor light, nor certitude, nor peace, nor help for pain.'" With a final, clear directive, the Pope said, "Go now to love and serve the Lord. It is in service that all wise men find peace."

O'Brien walked out into the garden where the laughter seemed lighter. He drew in a deep breath and felt more alive as he exhaled slowly. He stood back watching the Pope transform in little ways the lives that he touched for a brief moment. When the Pontiff excused himself, O'Brien's friends called to him with benign envy. "You lucky devil! What'd the Pope say to you all that time?"

Joining his friends at the table, he asked, "Besides appointing me to head the Vatican Bank?"

Between snorts and condescending laughs, they said, "Come on! What'd he say?"

"He talked about love. He talked about treasures that last. Not fortune and fame, but the kind of peace that only truth lends to life."

Lifting their glasses to toast everything from the Holy Father to the gondolas that filled the canals in Venice, they cheered in unison, "To love!"

CHAPTER FOUR

SNAPPING his eyes shut at the recollection of the years that passed since that day of spiritual emancipation in the Vatican garden, O'Brien turned his thoughts to the speech he would present to the graduating Class of 2000. From the back seat of his car, he grabbed his smaller suitcase of personal items in one hand, and he slung his suit over his shoulder with the other hand. With a brisk stride, he entered the hotel lobby. He stopped at the front desk to check in and pick up his key.

Keeping an eye out for the hotel's anticipated guest, the young man at the desk immediately recognized the college president and said, "The manager will be right with you, sir."

Within minutes, the manager entered the lobby, welcomed him, and handed O'Brien a copy of the itinerary for the evening. O'Brien asked several questions for clarification and thanked the manager and the clerk for their consideration.

Beaming with pride, the desk clerk said, "If there's anything you need, sir, just call the front desk. I'm here until ten."

O'Brien nodded. "Thank you."

***

He entered the room and emptied his pockets onto the chest of drawers. He hung his suit in the closet, sat on the bed, eased back and rested his head on a couple of propped pillows. Planning only an overnight stay, the room was more than adequate to meet his needs. In the early years of his extensive travels, some rooms offered few amenities. Now, as a recognized expert on education reform, he often enjoyed suites designed for royalty. He found in the end that it wasn't the room that initiated good or bad memories; it was the people with whom he surrounded himself. Right now, he felt quite alone.

Lonely times like this triggered thoughts of his life, after the Vatican trip in the early years of his brief marriage. He shared his world with a woman who seemed to delight in accompanying him on his travels. She found ways to quench her curiosity until his work day closed and evening drew them together in friendship and love. They shared the same law profession, but she didn't appreciate courtroom drama the way he did. She'd often ask him, "Don't the games people play in the pursuit of justice wear you down? They unnerve me."

Even though she possessed a brilliant legal mind, she claimed, "I can't wait to be a full-time mother." She'd laugh and tell him, "You know what they say about the hand that rocks the cradle."

"If motherhood is a means to rule the world, you may want to engage in a less demanding route to power," he teased, embracing her.

For more salient reasons, O'Brien shared his wife's desire to have a baby. Weary of his war experiences with children, he welcomed the prospect of nurturing a child. Sometimes curious to him though, was his wife's lack of interest about his stint in Vietnam. She would read the stories and see the movies that depicted Vietnamese children strapped with grenades whose purpose was to seek and destroy American soldiers, yet she never once questioned him about his personal experiences, and he gladly never broached the topic. When he would wake from a nightmare sweating profusely, she never moved beyond consoling him. She never prodded for any specifics about his part in the war, and it made it easier for him to avoid feeling guilty for not volunteering what he desperately tried to forget. Some secrets are best kept between God and oneself, he reasoned in silence.

He remembered the evening when he and his wife were at a party to celebrate the opening of a friend's art exhibit, and how she casually informed him that the head of one of the most prestigious law firms in New York City had only minutes prior offered her a job in his firm. Knowing how she felt about the justice system and her desire to become a mother, he expected to hear her laugh with disdain at the thought of working for the ruthless, overbearing magnate. But she didn't laugh. He was both shocked and bewildered that she seriously considered the offer. Later that evening, O'Brien questioned her more.

"Isn't this career move an abrupt three hundred, sixty degree turn?"

She was distant. Her response was curt. "I need a change."

"We all can benefit from change," he acknowledged, "but don't you think a change of this magnitude warrants some discussion? It would be nice to review our options."

"I know what I want," she said, her mind made up.

He still believed love meant sacrificing, and he wanted her to be happy, so he made the necessary adjustments to accommodate her new career. Two months later, he flew home from San Francisco a day early to surprise her with good news. The board of trustees of a small college in Boston asked him to manage the school on a permanent basis after he and a team of lawyers saved the school from financial ruin. His first concern was the ability for his wife to work for the Boston branch of her present law firm. When O'Brien opened the door to his Manhattan apartment, he heard unfamiliar laughter coming from his bedroom. His wife's boss, the same one at the party who tempted her to join his firm, was in O'Brien's bed holding O'Brien's wife.

Paralyzed by his presence, they clung to each other like two stunned animals caught in a trap. Before either of them could jump out of bed, O'Brien flung her robe at her and issued a cold command. "Get out before I get back!"

The next day she called and said, "You have a right to be angry, but our marriage wasn't working for me."

"I thought our marriage was supposed to work for both of us."

Neither spoke for several seconds when she broke the ice cold silence saying, "Maybe it's better for everyone if you move to Boston alone."

He subdued his heart drowning in desolation long enough to say with rancor, "At least Boston will ensure that I never see your face or hear your voice again!"

The old war demons of bloodied rice fields and eye deep mud, coupled now with meaninglessness and lack of order and values in his life, he felt himself being drawn into a familiar state of despair. Then, perhaps stimulated by years of family support and extensive education, although he did not completely understand his feelings, he sought the advice of an analyst he had come to respect after working with him on one of his court cases. After several sessions with a counselor, he began to regain some sense of balance and purpose in his life. He moved to Boston, and he immersed himself in his work. It wasn't long before his innovative ideas on education reform caught the attention of the education gurus around the country.

He remained at the college for several years during which time he earned a Ph.D. in education and administration. His love of learning allowed him to lose himself in the pursuit of sound education practices which made him a man in high demand. He just didn't have any inclination to lose himself again in something as elusive as love.

O'Brien's mother, whose heart ached for her son's loss, never missed an opportunity to bolster his spirit. She reminded him that genuine love had a way of drawing people together, and when he least expected it, love would find him.

"Listen to your heart, Jimmy. Never be afraid to love. There's a wonderful woman waiting to love a good man like you."

He'd playfully give her a gentle bear hug and whisper, "You're the only woman I need in my life."

***

Laying his arm across his forehead, he thought about where people's choices lead them. He recalled how two years after his marriage ended; his ex-wife was losing her battle with cancer. To make matters worse, her affair with her boss ended badly, and the sweet law career that he promised soon soured. She sent O'Brien a note and asked him to meet with her. She wanted to apologize, and she needed his forgiveness. Accompanied by a nearly forgotten nausea, his initial thought was nothing on God's earth will draw me to your bed!

Later that evening, he relaxed on his patio nursing a glass of "Ars Poetica" red wine. He reminisced about his own improbable reconciliation in the Vatican garden and his struggle to come to terms with his wife's deceit. His heart mellowed as he contemplated sins and the art of forgiveness. He concluded about his ex-wife: If she knew the story of my own dark soul, she might think it more worthwhile on her death-bed to request something more substantial than this sinner's forgiveness. Besides, if God forgave my war sins, who am I to bind her to her betrayal through eternity?

When he walked into her hospital room the next day, her shallow, strained breathing caught his attention. He waited while the nurse made adjustments with the machines attached to the frail body lying in the bed.

After the nurse quietly left the room, he bent down and planted a gentle kiss on his ex-wife's forehead. She opened her eyes and yielded a weak smile of appreciation. He did all the talking.

"I understand how easy it is for us to lose our way." With a warm gaze, he said, "God knows, I've made more wrong turns in my life than I care to remember." His eyes locked on hers. "What happened to us wasn't entirely your fault."

She closed her eyes for several seconds then opened them. They were moist with gratitude.

Gently brushing the corner of her eye with a tissue, he said, "Don't do that. It's okay. *We're* okay." He moved some strands of hair from her forehead. When she opened her hand, he gently took hold. Playing with her fingers for several moments, he said, "I always regretted walking away angry." He raised his eyes to meet hers and whispered, "Thank you for giving me a chance to come back and make things right." He sat by her side for over an hour before he planted a soft kiss on her cheek. Caressing her hand, he assured her, "I'm holding on to the good memories."

Her eyes glistened and relaxed. There was a peace about her before she closed her eyes to rest. It was the last time he saw the woman who broke his heart.

CHAPTER FIVE

"THANK God for better days," he said to the ceiling. He sat up and reached for his phone to touch base with several contacts across the country for up-coming events. The last call was to notify Joe Colao that he was in town and would be at the reception in time to review the procedures for the ceremony. Joe was apologetic.

"I can't believe you're in a hotel when you deserve our signature hospitality."

O'Brien laughed. "It actually feels good to hear you apologize to me for a change."

"Most of the city officials will be at the reception. It's scheduled for five o'clock this evening. Wait until you see the spread there!"

"If Maggie didn't cook it, it doesn't count."

"Go ahead. Make me feel guiltier than I already feel. Look at the bright side, Jim. The food at the reception will only have salt and pepper sprinkled on it; right now Maggie's food has influenza germs masquerading as garnishing."

"Wow! Yet another eloquent example of your ability to persuade."

"Yeah. My ability to persuade is legendary. It only took me . . . what . . . ten years to talk you into this engagement? Then invisible organisms threaten to upstage everything in a few hours."

"Think like a postman, Joey. Neither rain, nor sleet, nor flu . . . nor anything like that, will waylay us tonight."

Joe laughed. "Do you have the itinerary?"

"Got it this morning. When I'm done, your wife won't recognize you when you get home."

After telling Joe about the week from hell, he teased him one more time. "I hope your audio's working. Then again, no matter how bad your system sounds tonight, it can't be worse than last week. That dull Philly crowd made me feel like I was adlibbing in a high school talent show."

"We tested it, but I'll check it one more time; my professional life is in your hands."

O'Brien let out a hearty laugh. "What power the gods bestow upon me. Listen to the doctor. Swallow a bottle of Tums if you have to, and I'll see you at the reception."

Falling back on the bed, he closed his eyes. As he drifted, an inner voice gnawed at him to unpack. He did a slow, sloppy sit-up. Hoisting the bag carrying his personal toiletries onto the bed, he accounted for all of the items that he usually used on any given trip: toothpaste, aftershave, and deodorant were there, but where was the razor? He pawed through the bag again, but to no avail. This time he checked the whole bag and side pockets with eagle-like precision, as though looking in the same places over again might make it appear.

"Damn! I forgot the razor," he mumbled.

Cupping his face in his hands, he felt the scruff across his cheeks and chin. "I need a shave!"

It would be easy enough to secure a hotel razor or ask the young hotel clerk to purchase one for him from a nearby store, but he didn't want to risk using a blade that would nick his face. He recalled seeing a Wal-Mart close to the hotel. With both sets of fingers massaging his forehead, he said with frustration, "And I thought this week couldn't get any worse!" A hectic excursion in a busy Wal-Mart store mixed in the brew of mounting discontent wasn't exactly the panacea he envisioned before his speech tonight.

"No sense in dwelling on it," he muttered. "I may as well get it done."

He grabbed his blazer and shoved his hotel-key and wallet into the pocket and walked out the door.

***

Traffic was light for a Friday afternoon, but the Wal-Mart parking lot was packed. He drove around the lot several times searching for a convenient parking space. As frustration mounted, he spotted a woman about to back out of a tight space. He put his blinker on and waited. He pulled in cautiously because the space was even tighter than he realized. The car was so far from the store that his brisk walk to the entrance felt like a workout. Once he entered, in a matter of seconds, he disappeared in the flurry of humanity. To his relief, he located the razor kit with ease. Carrying the single item, the next leg of his journey involved one of the great paradoxes of life: the express check-out line. Taking his place behind several customers who casually disregarded the "twenty items or less" law, he waited patiently for his turn. When he approached the cashier, she was pleasant.

"Ten dollars and sixty cents, please."

Instinctively, he put his hand in his pocket to grab his wallet, but his pocket was empty. Minor panic struck him until he remembered how he shoved his wallet into his blazer pocket, but eager to get in and out of the store, he left his blazer on the front seat of the car.

Attempting to camouflage his embarrassment, he offered a longer than necessary explanation. "I guess I was in such a hurry that I forgot to grab my wallet." Watching the express line grow longer each second he delayed, he said, "I'm staying at the hotel across the street. I'm scheduled to speak tonight at the high school. I'm a little disorganized." Backing away from the cashier, he said, "I'm sorry for the trouble I caused you."

Showing what sympathy she could, the cashier said, "How about if I hold the razor for you while you go get your wallet?"

"Thank you. I'll be right back."

At least I won't have to waste more time walking through the store to pull the razor from the shelf again, he thought. He glanced upward questioning some higher power how long he would have to contend with the dark cloud looming over his head. He yanked his keys from his pocket and hastened toward the exit.

"Dr. O'Brien!" a woman's voice called.

He stopped. Standing motionless for a second, confusion—who knows me in New Castle, and frustration—what now, crossed his mind.

He turned to see a pretty, dark-haired woman who had been standing in line two person's behind him wave him back to the checkout. He walked back toward her, still wondering how she knew his name. He detected an unmistakable glint in her eye as he gave her a quick once-over.

"I'll buy that razor for you," she said.

In a gesture of sympathy, the other customers allowed the woman to move past them to make the transaction.

Pulling her credit card from her purse, she looked up at him and teased, "Yesterday's news featured a less wooly replica of you on the front page."

Ringing up the purchase, the amiable cashier said, "Hey Mr. Guest Speaker; it's turning out to be your lucky day!"

Keeping his eyes steady on the woman making the purchase, he said, "It seems that way."

Swiping her credit card, the woman looked sideways at him and light-heartedly admonished, "Just make sure you tell all those die-hard conservative friends of yours that not all bailouts are bad."

Her playful, verbal assault amused the customers who patiently stood in line as the cashier placed the razor in a bag and handed it to the woman. Her generosity and playful mockery of his political affiliation eased some of his previous embarrassment.

As she pushed her cart toward the exit, the woman told him, "I hope my having fun at your expense back there didn't embarrass you. To be honest, that's probably the most fun any of us will ever have in a Wal-Mart."

When they reached the exit, she stopped and held the razor with both hands and presented it to him with exaggerated importance. It was as though she were entrusting the crown jewels of Saudi Arabia on a silk pillow into his care. Playing along, he took a step back, offered a slight nod, and whispered, "Thank you." He breathed deep and exhaled before saying, "I really do appreciate your kindness. Up until the moment you called my name, this week couldn't end too soon."

Offering a blasé nod, she pretended to show little sympathy for his plight. She reached out and gave his chin a light touch with her index finger. "Ouch!" she said, as though his whiskers wounded her. Pointing to his chin, she said, "Those whiskers are almost as dangerous as some of your conservative notions."

Her fun-loving nature suggested she was open for an invitation to discuss what she thought she knew about his political views. One thing was certain, she captured his attention, and he didn't want to let her go just yet.

***

About five foot-four, she was personable and affectionate. She had pretty olive skin. Her dark brown hair was all one length, straight and shiny, and it hung past her chin, turning under at her shoulders. She had a habit of pushing one side of her hair behind her ear so that it didn't distract her when she talked. Her nose was more prominent, yet symmetrical with her large, dark brown eyes and high cheekbones. This beauty can't be over forty, he thought. She was in shape and shapely, quite the contrast from the manufactured beauties he often encountered that relied on a myriad of products. Everything about her was natural and approachable. I bet she's Mediterranean, maybe Italian or Greek, he thought. At times she was playfully aggressive, animated, and comical. He laughed thinking that these personality traits likely made her an easy target for family and friends to imitate and tease.

Before he invited her to share a cup of coffee, he glanced at her hand to see if she was married. Great! No ring! What are the chances that this beautiful creature is available? To be sure, he made a safe overture.

"Will your husband disfigure my face or break my legs if I offer to buy you a cup of coffee and humbly explain my brand of conservatism?"

For a brief moment, he detected an aura of sadness about her, but in seconds her eyes danced, and an inviting smile formed on her lips.

"My husband wouldn't mind . . ."

His heart sank. Working hard to conceal his disappointment, he barely heard her add, ". . . even if he were alive."

Realizing the impact of what she said, he winced. His voice soft and low, he whispered, "I'm sorry."

She nodded and looked down as she hung her purse over her shoulder.

He wanted her to laugh again, so he devilishly laid blame for conjuring memories of her husband on the bad week that dogged him.

"Now do you believe how disastrous my week has been up until I met you? I think those Philadelphia superintendents have a vendetta against me for questioning their organization skills." Exercising more creativity, he added, "I didn't mean to make you feel bad, but those people probably unleashed a militia of demons riding on dark clouds that are stalking me from town to town to trip up my physical and social well-being." He raised his right hand to heaven. "Honest! I'm convinced that as we speak, they're gathered in a wooded area in Philly, if you can find any vegetation in Philly, where some high priestess, who pretends to be an educator, is sticking pins in a rag doll that resembles me!"

She shook her head and laughed. Holding up her hand, the palm facing him, she said, "Stop right there. I bought you the razor, but I'm not buying that story. I don't believe in witchcraft, but I do have an Italian friend named Angelina who's convinced she has the ability to exorcise the 'evil eye' from people who believe they've been cursed." She held up her phone. "Do you want me to call Angelina for you?" she teased in a sultry voice.

"Only if her last name is Jolie."

She pulled back, feigning insult. "Oh, I forgot! You're one of those quasi-conservative men who preach 'family values' but gravitate toward uninhibited women who deep throat kiss their brothers on the red carpet and carry the blood of their current boyfriends in vials around their necks." Her eyes grew large as she threw up her hands. "I can't compete with that kind of vamp; so coffee with me might prove disappointing."

Pretending to block her insult, he raised both hands in front of his chest, palms facing her.

"Wait a minute," he said, laughing. "Somehow this conversation took a wrong turn."

Her wit and assertiveness were refreshing. He enjoyed the prospect of having a lively conversation with an attractive woman who wasn't afraid to challenge him. He placed the palm of his left hand on his chest and kept the other hand up to indicate he wanted to arrest her false, albeit humorous, idea about his taste in women.

"I'm just a nice guy who believes that my luck will change if you have a cup of coffee with me in that restaurant."

They stood in the parking lot where shoppers steadily moved past them; cars drifted in and out of parking spaces, and there was an occasional screech of tires from the near accidents that happen around so many distractions in large parking areas.

"Okay," she said with mock resignation. "First, let me check my wallet to see if I can afford a discussion with you."

"This one's on me," he reassured her.

Sighing with exaggerated relief, she said, "Maybe now I'll learn how an intelligent man could write a book that actually quotes Melville's *Catskill eagle* at the same time he supports mean-spirited politicians who believe everyone is going to hell except them."

"Wow! You complimented and insulted me without taking a breath. Do you always talk in mini dissertations?"

Embarrassed at her tendency to be long-winded, she answered the shortest way she knew how. "No!"

"Ah ha! So you *are* capable of brevity." Before she could spike the verbal ball back into his court, he pointed to the restaurant. "I'll meet you over there in a few minutes. I need your name and number just in case a business call delays me."

"I bet that phone of yours has more numbers stored in it than a math book."

"Maybe my business phone, but my personal phone only includes 911, family, and friends." He closed one eye and said, "Where do you think you belong?"

She raised her eyebrows. "Where do *you* think I belong?"

"Both," he said, with confidence.

She let out a laugh. "How many people rate both phones?"

He locked eyes with her and said, "My family, 911, and some *special* friends."

"Really?" she asked, eyeing him with a combination of surprise and suspicion. "My name is Ava—724-555-0805."

CHAPTER SIX

SPOTTING O'Brien standing at the entrance of the restaurant, she waved. She turned to the waitress and gave her an enthusiastic hug. He relaxed into a carefree gait as he approached her.

"Do you hug all the hired help?"

"She's one of my former students. She was kind enough to prepare this table for us. I like the sunlight streaming through the window, and it doesn't have as many distractions." She stirred sugar in her tea and looked up. "I hope you don't mind all the sunshine." She narrowed her eyes and teased, "I ordered the black coffee because I knew you wouldn't be long."

He immediately made himself comfortable, tore open a packet of sugar, stirred it in his coffee, and said, "I'm a man of my word, but I wish I had your confidence that my phone wouldn't ring at the most inopportune times." Looking across at her, he said, "Before this hour is up, I hope I give you reasons to be kinder to conservatives."

She smiled and said, "You already have."

He wiped his brow with his hand. Playing with his spoon, he asked, "You're a teacher?"

She nodded.

"What subject?"

"Senior English."

A few moments earlier he teased her for stringing ideas together as though life was about to silence her forever. Now that they carved out time to talk, her tacit responses forced him to prod. There was a reluctance to reveal information about herself. He caught himself staring at her wondering, what makes this beauty tick?

"What's the most difficult part of your day?"

She raised her cup of tea to her lips; she took a sip and held it there for several seconds before answering. "Six o'clock in the evening."

The deliberation in her responses was missing in their initial encounter. She was operating on a five second delay, this one apparently serving to conceal unmistakable sadness that her wit and humor camouflaged so well in the store. His confused look signaled that she had misunderstood his question. He inquired about the hardest part of her work day; she cited the hardest part of her whole day. The misunderstanding afforded him an opportunity to glimpse a sad interior that she invited few to share.

"What makes six o'clock more difficult than three o'clock or eight o'clock?"

His demeanor was benign; all the more reason why she was angry with herself for allowing foolish expectations to raise passion in her. She reminded herself that he was just passing through. In one hour he would thank her for making his afternoon more pleasant than his morning had been. He would speak to an adoring crowd and then disappear into his elitist world. The likelihood of ever seeing Dr. James O'Brien again after today was slim. But she knew why he mattered to her. After three years of feeling life had sucked her dry and discarded her, he made her glad to be alive.

"Did you forget the question?" he teased.

"No. I don't forget easily."

There was an edge to her voice as she spoke with candor. "Six o'clock is when I sit down to eat supper. It's the routine activities that conjure the most haunting and poignant memories. I cook, eat, do the dishes, and wrap the leftovers." Her face grew expressionless. "Three years ago my husband and two children sat around the table with me." She looked down at her teacup. With resignation in her voice, she said, "When the quiet begins to sear my soul, I visit relatives, read student essays, and volunteer."

An uncomfortable silence fell between them. The music in the restaurant seemed to amplify. Other conversations became more distinguishable and intrusive. In a gesture of respect and good service, the waitress approached the table to ask if Ava wanted refills. They both thanked her. Again, Ava lifted her teacup and pressed it to her quivering lips. The mini-bio-sketch instantly replayed in her head as the ramblings of a pathetic, lonely widow. He must think I'm stupid and silly. What am I even doing here with this man?

O'Brien's instincts told him that her pain was deep and tender, yet she masked her grief well. He canvassed her hair and face until she glanced upward.

"I'm a good listener," he said.

Her eyes dropped again.

His voice soft and low, he asked, "What happened, Ava?"

He said her name so sweetly, as if he really knew her. She blinked back tears. He wants to know, what happened? I'm forty-three years-old, and I don't want to be a widow, and I don't want to cry any more, and I don't want to be lonely anymore. Biting her lip, she struggled to find a way to deflect his kind curiosity. How do I begin to tell this man about all the pain I caused so many people?

She raised her eyes and peered over her cup of tea. Forcing a smile, she said, "I thought this meeting of the minds was your opportunity to defend conservatism."

Despite the awkward moments and her immediate unwillingness to talk about her family, he knew intuitively that he had connected with her on an emotional level. Rather than pursue a discussion wrought with emotion, he decided to lighten the mood. He leaned across the table without invading her space. Narrowing one eye, he said, "No. What I actually proposed was a humble defense of *my brand* of conservatism."

Pretending to be more relaxed, she bent her head back and forced a chuckle. "I stand corrected. I do recall those exact words."

Thankful that he willingly shifted the topic from her family's deaths; she settled back in her chair and looked at him with a renewed sense of confidence.

"So what makes your heart flutter, Dr. O'Brien?"

Surprised at the first thought that entered his head, he was about to tell her, *you* make my heart flutter. His heart had been fluttering from the moment he met her. He entertained the possibility that this chance encounter could be the beginning of a substantive relationship. The gentle, but constant magnetic force between them was all the more reason why, until he learned more about her, he would put a brake on his desire for her. He guided the conversation toward less personal subjects like politics and education.

"I enjoy learning, and I like aspects of law. I'm fortunate my position at the university satisfies many of my interests."

"You certainly are well-received in education," she said.

During the next hour, they talked about the size of government, welfare reform, health care, religion in politics, and of course, education reform. He told her, "Despite our differences in political philosophies, I want you to know that I care deeply about the marginalized people in the world." He explained, "I wrote my book in part to fulfill the university's expectation that each faculty member and administrator publish some form of personal treatise and to offer evidence of reaching out, maybe more for myself rather than for others who would never really know me, to bolster my own self-doubts of my depth of feeling for humanity." He ended emphatically stating his position: "Just because I hold conservative views, don't make the mistake of thinking I belong to some fanatic religious group that wants to cast people into hell." He tapped his index finger on the back of her hand. "I'm well aware that in the sight of heaven, I may be the one most deserving of hell."

He checked his watch. Although commitments constrained him, he lingered. As he brought his coffee to his lips, he reached across the table and tapped her finger again. "Be my guest tonight. We can have a late dinner and spend the rest of the night getting to know each other better."

Put off by his suggestion, she glanced off toward other diners in the area.

"Is something wrong?" he asked, confused by her reaction.

Her eyes shifted back to him. Unable to mask her disappointment, she managed a fake smile. "It took you longer than most to go in for the kill." She grabbed her purse. "Don't worry; I have my car. Other men usually call me a cab ten seconds after I tell them I'm not the least bit interested in being their prey for the evening."

"Prey?" he repeated, with a muddled look.

"I'm not into casual sex," she told him, with cold detachment.

Staggered by her indictment, he pulled back. The shock on his face sent a shiver up her spine. Oh God! What did I just do?

He watched as she dissolved into embarrassment. He studied her for several more seconds before leaning toward her with an unmistakable touch of arrogance mixed with sympathy.

"Do you honestly believe I'm preying on you right now?"

Mortified at misreading his intention, her voice froze in her throat. Struggling to speak in a barely audible voice, she said, "I didn't mean to insult you."

She bent her head down, covered her face with one hand, and closed her eyes. His silence intensified his stare. Raising her head and making eye contact, she said, "It was an arrogant and presumptuous thing for me to say."

The embarrassment at assuming that he wanted to carry their chance encounter to an intimate level rose in her like an ocean flooding a cabin on a sinking ship. Grateful that the waitress brought the check, she began to choreograph a less awkward goodbye after her less than eloquent mini-tutorial about dating sex-crazed men. *There aren't many more ways I could ruin this platonic encounter that would be the envy of most women, but I'm not going to stick around to find out. It's only a matter of time before he walks out on me.*

Feeling trapped and ill at ease, she managed gracefully to retreat from his graduation invitation. Her nephew was one of the graduates, and her original plan was to join other members of her family to celebrate. *After this fiasco,* she concluded, *I'm standing in the shadows and forgoing the reception. There's no way I can face this man again.*

"I have several friends whose children are graduating tonight," she told him. "They'll be eager to tell me about your performance over breakfast." Her face still flush, she smiled and said, "Thank you for the coffee and the conversation."

Fumbling through her purse for her keys, she reminded him of the obvious. "Don't forget to shave those whiskers."

He nodded. Before she turned to leave, he reminded her of the not so obvious. "You're wrong about me, Ava."

Letting out a long sigh, she said, "Look. I actually cross the street when I see most men coming. They're not even subtle about what they believe they're entitled to after a dinner. They assume I'm tired of playing solitaire, and . . ."

She couldn't believe she reinforced her original insult: *He targeted her as an easy playmate.*

Holding up his hand, he said, "Don't explain. Just know that was never my intent."

She felt the warmth of fresh embarrassment creep over her. "I'm going to leave with the shred of dignity I have left." Pushing one side of her hair back behind her ear, she said, "I'll be thinking of you tonight."

His eyes followed her as she hurried toward the exit. She wove through the parking lot, slipped into her car, and drove out of sight. He stood at the entrance of the restaurant and felt queasy. I can't believe I let her walk away, he thought. He pushed the door open and made a silent vow: I'm not leaving New Castle without talking to her again.

**

Back in the hotel room, he revised parts of his speech before tucking it in the breast pocket of his suit. He stripped to his waist and grabbed the razor. Handling it with more reverence than it deserved, he removed it from the package. He lathered his cheeks and chin and with precision, cut down the prickly whiskers that had grown rampant for a day and a half. As he guided the razor over his coarse chin, he laughed inwardly remembering how Ava feigned injury when she grazed his chin with her finger. He rinsed the last vestiges of growth down the drain, splashed water on his face, and patted it dry. A pretty clean shave, he thought. He dried the razor and placed it in its plastic cradle just as carefully as he removed it. He shook his head at his maudlin behavior toward this common tool, yet here he was, treating an ordinary razor from Wal-Mart as though it held the significance of a Babe Ruth rookie card.

I'd sacrifice Babe Ruth and a couple of Honus Wagners for an evening with that creature, he laughed to himself.

"What the hell," he said aloud. "Two more strikes before I'm out, so let's give her another try."

The phone rang, but no one answered. At least I won't have to endure another direct rejection. So with no real consideration as to what he would say to a machine that would capture his words for posterity, at the tone, he told her: "When you asked me what made my heart flutter, I should have been more honest. You make my heart flutter. My mission is to convince you to have dinner with me tonight. If my mission fails, this tape won't self-destruct in five seconds, but a part of my heart will." He rolled his eyes and thought, I can't believe I did that.

Mindful of the time, he jumped into the shower and reveled in the hot, pulsating water that cascaded over his body. The evening with Ava was tentative, but he planned to make the evening memorable for Joe Colao and the graduating Class of 2000.

CHAPTER SEVEN

THE reception was festive; people mingled warm and friendly. Standing next to a table laden with pastas and cheeses, O'Brien motioned for Joe to join him.

"I'm telling you, Colao! If you guys guzzle food like this on a regular basis, expect some weight watcher company to target the city for a diet commercial."

As they canvassed the tables, he picked on a variety of shrimp and filled a small plate with fruit. He turned to Joe and shook his head. "Chances are I'll leave here with more rolls on me than a bakery."

"Tell me about it," Joe said, patting his slightly protruding stomach. "Ever since Maggie's sabbatical, I've been ballooning out of shape."

"Running helps," O'Brien teased.

"You want to talk running? Try running north, east, south, and west with three kids who have activities in different parts of town all at four in the afternoon. Did I mention on the same day? Then add a wife with culinary skills. That will curb your arrogance."

He brushed imaginary dust off Joe's shoulder and said, "Not arrogance. It's called envy." Pointing his index finger at his friend, he said, "You're living a life most men dream of living."

Joe laughed. "You're not immune. Your turn will come."

O'Brien glanced around the room. Spotting the mayor engaged in a spirited conversation with an attractive woman who arrived late to the reception, he said, "Do you suppose she knows her way around the kitchen?"

"Vikki? You sure have good taste." With a wry grin, he added, "But a frozen dinner would be healthier for you, buddy." Narrowing his eyes, he said, "She's more than devoted to her husband, Jake Coury. You don't want to mess with Jake. He's one of our judges." Joe directed O'Brien toward the trio and tapped Judge Coury on the shoulder. "Excuse me, Jake. I'd like you to meet Dr. O'Brien."

Extending a hearty handshake, Judge Coury said, "It's nice finally to meet you. You've been a topic in our household for weeks. We read your book." The judge playfully added, "My sister maintains that you're an aberration, a lost character from *The Wizard of Oz.*" He shook his head and mischievously warned, "She's eager to congratulate you tonight for being the only conservative that has a brain, a heart, and the courage to use them both." Lifting his hands up in front of his chest to block a possible assault, he said, "Her words, not mine!"

Laughing, the mayor said, "She's a force to reckon with. Remember the last teacher strike when she cornered me and told me to stop riding the fence and decide if I'm for or against unions? She looked at me with those huge, Bambi eyes and scolded, 'Read Pope Leo's *Rerum Novarum*, Ed!' She got so mad at me when I laughed and told her I'm thrilled she thinks I have the intellectual capacity to understand a church encyclical on fair wages, but my eighth grade son has to help me understand the *News's* editorial page." The mayor shook his head. "I ducked really fast." He looked at O'Brien and teased, "It's not too late to hire a body guard."

"Don't believe one word these guys say about my sister-in-law," Vikki countered. "They know she's smart and fair." Her eyes shifted to the mayor. "As I recall, she talked you into doing the right thing in that strike, Ed, and your involvement was instrumental in the fair settlement, not to mention your re-election."

The men nodded.

Laughing, O'Brien said, "Maybe I should be concerned about this trend. I met a woman in Wal-Mart this afternoon, and she wasn't impressed with my conservative views either." He draped his arm around Joe's shoulders. "Just to be on the safe side, I better make this guy stand in front of me tonight to catch any slings and arrows that might come my way."

"No slings and arrows from the Coury family," the judge promised. "We're eager to hear your speech and my son's speech. He's the salutatorian."

Before O'Brien could respond, someone pulled Judge Coury away. A pall fell over Joe's face as the judge walked toward a group of men in the middle of the room.

"Now there's a case study on how to handle tragedy with style and grace."

"Tragedy? They're the most vivacious people I've met all day."

Joe's voice carried fresh disbelief as he recounted the accident. "His sister's whole family was killed in seconds. To make matters worse, she was driving." Shaking his head, he said, "I used to throw words like *tragedy* and *nightmare* around so casually. The day Ava buried her family seared the meaning of those words in my heart."

"I met an *Ava* this afternoon," O'Brien said.

"No kidding! There's only one Ava in this city. She emerged with some broken bones, but her family . . . " He stared at Jake from across the room. "They have one helluvah strong family, but how does anyone bury two beautiful kids and—" Before the superintendent could finish his sentence, someone signaled it was time to make their way to the high school to begin the ceremony.

O'Brien thought; she played me. She planned to attend the ceremony all along. Although Joe's recollection filled him with sympathy, he couldn't mask his elation at the prospect of seeing her again. She had to be the same 'Ava.' She was a widow; she said she used to have a husband and children. He approached Judge Coury before he departed.

"Excuse me, Judge. Joe just informed me that Ava Panetta is your sister." Shooting a broad smile, he said, "This may sound ironic, but I already had the pleasure of meeting her this afternoon." He confessed, "She was kind enough to bail me out at Wal-Mart. We had coffee and talked politics for over an hour." His eyes widened as he beamed with admiration. "She certainly knows how to challenge a person's ideas." Admitting defeat, he said, "I tried to convince her to have a late dinner with me after the graduation ceremony, but unfortunately she declined."

The judge asked with amusement, "Ava bailed you out?" His broad shoulders shook as he laughed. "You didn't do us any favor, Dr. O'Brien. She'll be difficult to live with for some time." Raising his bottle of water to congratulate him, he said, "My kid sister isn't easily impressed. The mere fact that you held her interest long enough to drink a cup of coffee is impressive." Narrowing his eyes, he said, "You don't strike me as the kind of guy who gives up easily."

O'Brien countered, "Is the judge suggesting that it would be in my best interest to persist?"

Judge Coury unexpectedly grew serious. "Honestly, I have only one interest and that's my sister's happiness." With little posturing, he confided, "Look, Dr. O'Brien. My sister is a wonderful person. In the blink of an eye the cosmos sucker punched her whole world, and she was left reeling." He blinked back tears. "Only God knows how she bears her grief." He laughed with sarcasm. "Really nice men try to woo her, but she shows little interest. If she had coffee with you and discussed politics with you, well . . ." He looked off to the side and swept his handkerchief across his eyes.

"Ava's fortunate to have a brother who cares deeply for her."

"We're fortunate to have a close extended family," the judge countered.

To impress upon O'Brien how concerned he was about his sister's welfare, Judge Coury made a rare plea. "I don't make it a practice to discuss Ava with potential suitors, but I'm asking you man to man. Make sure she doesn't get hurt."

O'Brien nodded. "You have my word."

***

The band played "Pomp and Circumstance" as the graduates marched into the auditorium. After the invocation, the salutatorian and valedictorian addressed the audience. O'Brien noted that Ava's nephew, Charley Coury, delivered his speech well. His animated gestures, some of the same ones that characterized his aunt, left little doubt that talking with their hands was a family trait.

Armed with a well-crafted introduction, Superintendent Colao presented his renowned friend to the audience. O'Brien stood at the podium and received the applause.

He cautioned, "People usually wait to hear what I have to say before they decide to applaud. Before I'm done, some of you may be inclined to run me out of town."

His humor delighted the audience. He acknowledged the parents, faculty, and civic leaders in attendance. He fixed his eyes on the graduates.

"Congratulations Class of 2000!"

The audience granted enthusiastic applause. He paused for several seconds before beginning his speech.

"We all know what practice means. We know that 'practice makes perfect.' For instance, if you practice football three hours a night, chances are you'll end up with a championship team or at least a respectable team. If you practice your part in the play each evening, the better you'll be as an actor, and the better the play will be on opening night. If you study for a test in homeroom . . ." He waited for the spatters of laughter to die down. "You'll receive a higher score, and you'll also make your school statistics look better.

"Practice not only makes each individual more skillful, it also affects in a positive way those with whom each individual interacts. When one player strives to be good, the team is better; when one actor strives to be good, the play is better; when one student strives to be smarter, the class is better; when one member of the family strives to be more loving, it makes the whole family more loving and stronger; and when we practice being good people, the better we become as individuals and as a society.

"So if you want to be happy and successful in life, continue to practice reading, writing, arithmetic, and whatever other talents that you possess. But keep in mind that acquiring knowledge and being talented are only parts of the formula for happiness and success. Knowledge plus talent are powerful only if you apply them properly. And if you want to achieve genuine contentment, if you want to achieve some measure of *meaningful* success, you first need to practice being a good person."

His straightforward, spontaneous style engaged the audience. Despite an occasional buzz from the audio system, the graduates remained respectfully attentive when he talked of success.

"While some may argue that to achieve one's goal is the measure of success, consider Adolph Hitler. He almost achieved an Aryan race. He most definitely was happy about it, and he certainly is well known. Fidel Castro's dream was to be a ball player. Although he wasn't good enough to play major league ball, his back-up plan was a huge success. He channeled his talent into oppressing people!" There was a spatter of uneasy laughter. "He continues to rule Cuba long after those who attempted to assassinate him have been reduced to skeletons.

"So if achieving one's goal is the measure of success, we can argue that Hitler was a success and Castro continues to be a success story. People like them possess intelligence, charisma, and power. They amass fortunes. They revel in fame." He paused. "I submit that we need to embrace a definition of success that moves us beyond the pursuit of fame, fortune, and power."

Aware that the school's basketball program dominated other teams in Pennsylvania, he elicited a reaction when he asked, "Does anyone here know anything about basketball?"

The auditorium erupted in applause. Some students raised their hands above their heads signaling victory. He nodded approval.

"The best definition for success that I encountered came from a man who knew he had only months to live. When reporters asked the youthful but gravely ill Jim Valvano, coach of the North Carolina State basketball team, to define his idea of success, he eloquently stated, 'The goal of life is to be able to sit in a room all by yourself and enjoy the company.'

"Did you ever notice that people who genuinely like who they are rarely cause other people grief? They don't abuse animals. They don't bully people smaller or weaker than they are. They rarely gossip. They don't cause unnecessary family drama. They don't undermine their colleagues in the workplace, and they don't hang people from trees if others hold contrary religious and political beliefs. Coach Valvano agreed with the philosopher Blaise Pascal who said, 'All men's miseries derive from not being able to sit in a quiet room alone.'

"So the goal of academic excellence is not simply to make honor roll. Academic excellence is the pursuit of knowledge and using that knowledge to transform us into good, thoughtful people with strong character. Academic excellence demands that we use whatever knowledge and talent we possess in just, skillful, and magnanimous ways.

"While awards may be a fine way for a collective society to acknowledge the extra-ordinary effort of individuals, we should never allow awards to be our main motivation to achieve. If we don't consistently practice having the courage to stand up to minor injustices in our daily lives, don't expect to be courageous in the face of major injustices that confront us at home and in the world. Wise men in ancient as well as modern times have urged us to practice doing what we can with what we have where we are to the best of our ability. When we practice being good, it might not make us perfect people, but it certainly will make us better people, people who respect ourselves enough to respect others the same way."

He scratched his temple with his index finger and spoke off-the-cuff. "I was driving to New Castle behind a car that toted a bumper sticker that read, 'My Child is An Honor Student!'" With animated enthusiasm, he said,

"I had to fight the urge to flag the car down and ask the driver: Does your child have the honorable character to go along with that fine distinction?" His voice inflections and gestures drew laughter.

"If students simply maintain good grades and win awards, yet their actions lack justice, skill, and magnanimity, there is no honor!" He interrupted his speech to ask a silly question.

"How many of you are looking forward to Christmas?"

The graduates cheered.

"Even though it's rather warm outside, and we're looking forward to summer vacation, I'd like to remind you of a Christmas story that teaches 'We are what we habitually do' and 'We owe the world; the world doesn't owe us.'

"When a baby who promised the world peace was born in Bethlehem, wise men pursued the star that marked his location. Since the text doesn't limit the number of wise men to three, let's assume that scores of wise men traveled across the treacherous terrain searching for peace. They carried saddlebags filled with treasures they used to barter for food, shelter, and entertainment. After months of hardships, it became apparent the journey wasn't for the faint hearted. Frankly, finding this baby proved more daunting than the wise men imagined. As weeks turned into months and months turned into years, most of the wise men became weak-minded and spiritually bankrupt. The thrill that captivated them in the beginning soon turned to drudgery. Each new day filled with obstacles swayed them to settle for the easier, ephemeral treasures at their fingertips. Out of many who began the journey, only a few remained true to the original goal."

O'Brien shook his head and said, "Then something foreign to us happened. No one clapped for the few wise men who finally achieved their goal. No one presented them with medals and plaques. As backwards as it sounds, those who succeeded emptied their saddle bags; they gave all that they possessed to the baby!"

He shot a broad smile and asked, "Did the wise men believe the baby ripped them off? Not on your life! By staying the course, they acquired more than fame and fortune. They found knowledge, peace, and love. Those acquisitions equipped them to go home a different way, a better way, both geographically and spiritually. When the wise men achieved their goal, despite the absence of accolades, it made them stronger, better people."

With an air of whimsy, he asked, "Have you ever gotten lost?"

41

There was a ripple of applause. O'Brien scratched his head with his index finger again. "No doubt it's a recorded fact somewhere on the planet that if women were on those camels wandering in the desert, they would have stopped at the first oasis they came to and asked for directions. They would have arrived in three days instead of three years!"

The audience roared with laughter confirming his assertion.

"Whether you journey for three days or three years, achieving your goal is important, but never allow the goal to get in the way of living a good life. For instance, it's not difficult to imagine that some wise men with good intentions got lost, ran out of money, fell ill, or simply had to address immediate problems that legitimately cut their journey short."

O'Brien noted with sarcasm, "By the typical definition of success, anyone who failed to arrive at the manger would be failures!" He paused before suggesting, "Maybe appearances are deceiving. Maybe some of our failed attempts carry more success than the eye can see."

He paused to think of his own life and the years he wasted along the way not trusting or loving the way he should have.

"The journey of the wise men reminds us that achieving academic, professional, and social successes may be worthy pursuits, but ignoring life, ignoring the needs of people around us, treating the weakest among us as though they are obstacles as we journey toward our goals is not.

"Even if the world fails to recognize your achievements, like the wise men, you have to stay the course. Like the wise men, you may carry in your saddle bags all the worldly possessions that define success, but understand that how you travel toward your goal, what you do or fail to do along the way, is what brings contentment and peace. And while some may believe it's foolish to be just, kind, generous, compassionate, and good, remember that despite public acclaim, your journey will only be genuinely successful if you can 'find yourself alone in a room and enjoy the company.'"

The audience's mood was appreciative and receptive.

"So if you want to be successful, work hard! If you want to achieve goodness and peace, be a wise man and be prepared to offer the world your best gifts. When you journey as wise men, the world will become a better place to be for each of us and for all of us.

"Again, congratulations Class of 2000!"

As a thunderous ovation exploded in the auditorium, Ava stood motionless, her back up against the rear wall. Emotionally charged by his sympathetic characterization of the weary wise men, his realistic account of their hardships was a stark reminder of her own Sisyphean journey searching for some measure of purpose and peace after burying her family. She pressed a tissue to the corner of one eye and then the other. She breathed in deeply and held it for as long as she could, not wanting to exhale for fear the dream she fostered in her heart—that he would treat her poor judgment that caused so much pain with the same kind consideration he afforded the wise men who lost their way. I wonder if I really made his heart flutter, she thought with a twinge of happiness. Her eyes scanned the jubilant audience as a burning mist blurred her vision. I wonder what his heart will do when he learns I killed my family.

CHAPTER EIGHT

A lull in the post graduation festivities allowed O'Brien to break away from enthusiastic photo shoots long enough to seek out the Courys to congratulate them on the speech their son delivered. They were talking when Vikki playfully gave a heads up to O'Brien.

"Remember that attractive lady that bailed you out at Wal-Mart? She's headed our way. If she doesn't stop to politic with everyone she knows, she'll be behind you in three seconds."

O'Brien turned to see Ava surfing through the crowded room. An older gentleman grabbed her arm. Visibly surprised to see him, she embraced and kissed him. They talked briefly before she turned and advanced closer to her family. He perused her from head to toe as family and friends detained her several more times. Her plain, sleeveless, short, black dress accentuated her attractive, tanned legs. Her high-heeled black sandals made her legs look longer than they really were. A single layer of ruffles circled the back of her neck and meandered to the front and cascaded down to expose a small part of her cleavage. The solitary diamond necklace that lay exquisitely on her chest matched her diamond earrings.

After being swept in different directions and showering affection on family and friends along the way, she gently undulated toward him. Like a scintillating bottle carrying a mysterious message floats almost still in calm water close to shore, he reached out and grabbed her. He pulled her close and bent his head down to whisper.

"I thought I'd never get a second chance."

"We all need second chances," she whispered back.

He held her hand and gently pulled her toward a quiet corner of the room when several graduates separated them to pose for one last picture. The stragglers signaled the end of the formal event. Joe extended both arms high above his head and called out, "Touch down!" Shaking O'Brien's hand, he said, "Tonight was such a success; you own me!"

Nodding modestly, O'Brien said, "Success isn't how hard they clap; it's in the application."

"I know. I was a captive listener. It's about being a *wise guy*, right? Well, this wise guy wants you to grab a drink with us," Joe said, laughing.

"Drinking with wise guys can prove dangerous." He turned to Ava. "Count me in only if this lovely lady bails me out at a decent hour."

"You're beginning to appreciate that concept, aren't you, Dr. O'Brien?" Ava teased. She clapped her hands to attract the attention of several friends standing close by. "Gather round and witness the first stages of a staunch conservative getting hooked on big bad bailouts!"

Closing one eye and leaning toward her, he whispered, "I'll admit that I'm getting hooked, but it's not on bailouts."

Joe and some others pleaded, "Come on, Ava. We can't have a party without you!"

O'Brien raised his eyebrows. "It seems that you're quite a popular lady."

"Don't be silly. They just want to be with you."

"I understand how they feel, because I just want to be with *you*."

Her eyes widened. Caught off guard by his candid comment, she hesitated for several seconds then held up her index finger. "Don't go away. I'd like to say goodnight to my brother and his family."

She talked with Jake and Vikki for several minutes. Jake held her head and kissed her first on one cheek and then the other. Vikki wrapped her arms around Ava's neck and hugged her tight. Ava turned and joined the party.

***

The small gathering dispersed after an hour. Joe gave O'Brien a playful right jab on the shoulder and teased, "It's been a long time since I felt like a third wheel. You made me look so good tonight; I'll reciprocate the best way I know how." He slapped O'Brien on the back. "Make sure Ava gets home okay, and I'll go home and take care of my sick wife and kids."

O'Brien nodded. He glanced at Ava standing in a group. "She certainly makes Western Pennsylvania more appealing."

"No doubt! That girl is golden," Joe said.

O'Brien shook Joe's hand and hugged him. "If you need me for anything else, I mean *anything;* let me know. I promise it won't take me a decade to respond."

Joe eyed Ava talking with the mayor at the bar. He turned to O'Brien and said facetiously, "Something tells me I'm destined to see you more than once a year at a reunion."

"Only if I'm lucky," O'Brien countered.

"Be on notice, buddy. She's right up there with Maggie and Vikki. You might say they're the triumvirate of the kitchen kingdom! Flex those abs while you can."

With playful irritation, he threw Joe a condescending look and said, "Let me take care of my abs. You go home and take care of Maggie and the kids."

***

Joining Ava at the bar, he said, "I'm going to be brave and try this again, okay?"

"Try what?" she asked.

"I know it's late, but can we find a quiet place to talk?" He quickly held up one hand and stressed, "*Just talk.*"

She nodded and laughed. "At the risk of you getting the wrong idea, I'm going to be brave and make *this* suggestion. Right now, the quietest place I know is my house." She tempted him. "I even have some Arabic food for you to sample. I baked bread this morning, so it's fresh!"

Mildly shocked, he pulled back slowly, stared at her for a moment and said, "I'd love to sample your Arabic cuisine, but . . ." He wore a puzzled look.

"But what?" she asked, wondering what he was really thinking.

His eyes teased as an impish smile played on his lips. "I've known women that use their mouth-watering, edible delights to trap unsuspecting, lonely men like me who travel all over the country, into stationery bliss." He cocked his head, pointed at her and asked, "Is that what you're doing?"

Her eyes danced with his as she stood still and absorbed his gentle, fun-loving retaliation of her earlier rash assessment of his intentions.

"Okay, I deserved that. Now we'll both have to trust that each of us is a nice person who simply wants to share an enjoyable evening with the other." She assured him, "This evening is about friendship and food. If the stronger seasonings don't appeal to you, I won't let you starve. I'll buy you a couple of fast-food sandwiches designed to pacify unsophisticated taste buds."

Feigning insult, he pointed out, "My discriminating palate is sophisticated enough to handle your culinary skills, so don't you worry about my taste buds. Besides, whatever you have waiting for me, I claim it as my consolation prize for sweating half the evening wondering if I was ever going to see you again."

Ava chuckled. "I'll overlook that misguided notion of entitlement because I really did give you a rough time this afternoon, didn't I?" She straightened his tie and gave it a gentle pat. "I promise to make the evening more pleasant."

His eyes canvassed her face. "You've already accomplished your goal."

***

The moon hung low as the fountain in the center of the pond forced soft ripples to split beams of light dancing on the surface. A light-gray cobblestone ranch sat back from the road. She invited him in, and he immediately noticed a fresh, clean, neatness and order to the rooms. His Irish grandmother always told him that you can tell what a person holds important and dear by what she keeps in her house and how she keeps it.

He made himself comfortable as she walked into the kitchen and immediately began to assemble several plates of food. She stopped what she was doing in the kitchen to turn on the CD player in the living room. Crosby, Stills, Nash, and Young's *Déjà Vu* filtered through the rooms.

"Can I get you something to drink?"

He waved and said, "I'm fine."

She talked to him as she moved back and forth from the kitchen to the dining room to set the table. "I know you were teasing earlier, but I do know women who bring men home after brief encounters." She stopped and made eye contact. "I've never been one of them." She continued to ready the table with silverware and told him, "Jake said he talked to you earlier this evening at the reception. He likes you."

As he listened to her, he observed everything he could about her. She set the table with bright green and yellow floral print plates. Bright green cloth napkins matched the green in the dishes, and she folded the napkins neatly around the silverware. There was a small, fresh bouquet of flowers in the center of the table, and she used clear stemmed glasses for the drinks.

She held up a jug of wine. "Would you like a glass of my brother's homemade remedy for all ailments under the sun?"

His eyes lit up. "What kind of Irishman would I be if I declined that kind of offer?"

"You must be starved," she said, apologizing for the delay.

"Don't worry about me. I ate quite a bit at the reception." He let out a laugh. "It was more like a food fest catered for gluttons."

He watched her move from the kitchen to the dining room. Unable to restrain himself any longer, he asked, "You knew all along that you'd be at the ceremony tonight, didn't you?"

She carried a basket of bread to the table, smiled at him and nodded. Her cheeks flushed soft pink when she admitted, "I almost didn't show up because of my foolishness in the restaurant. My brother called me from the reception and convinced me that you simply wanted to have dinner and enjoy my company." She ran her hand through her hair pushing it back off her face. "Not to mention that he paid you a large sum of money to be nice to me because I'm ugly."

He let out a laugh. "I hope your brother judges cases better than he judges beauty. Does he always talk to you like that?"

"No." She paused as though she were in serious thought. "Sometimes he says mean things to me."

He laughed at her ability to make fun of herself and her brother with such ease. "So my shameless phone message had no bearing on your decision to show up tonight?"

She leaned over his shoulder and poured water into his glass; she gently tugged his earlobe. "You know, I just might take a page out of the Watergate scandal and hold on to that tape. If it's as original as you claim, it might make me a wealthy woman some day."

He turned to face her and began to mimic Richard Nixon. "Make no mistake about it; tapes can be incriminating." He shook his imaginary jowls. "But understand if that tape gets accidentally erased, and that can easily happen, you know . . . it's . . . not . . . my . . . fault!"

Ava suppressed her laughter. She narrowed her eyes and countered, "If anyone erases that tape, I'll . . . hunt . . . him . . . down!"

He smiled and reassured her. "I promise if anything happens to that tape, I'll make sure you receive an equally shameless message to replace it."

"Some *firsts* can't be duplicated, Dr. O'Brien. I prefer to cherish the original!"

He nodded as he filled his plate with appetizers.

"It's nice to enjoy the company of a thoughtful man for a few hours, even if you're just passing . . ." She tried to act natural, but she was filled with more emotion than she expected.

He drank some wine and eyed her. "Just passing through?" he finished her thought.

"New Castle is hardly on anyone's ten top places in the world to vacation," she said, with soft sarcasm.

"That may be true, but you underestimate the power of vanity. Remember, you're holding incriminating evidence. I have to keep coming back to make sure you never go to *Enquire Magazine* with that tape of me begging you for a date."

She ignored his silliness. "The truth is I was spoiled. I actually had something special in my life." As though she were trying to convince herself, she said, "Even though I feel so disconnected and empty most of the time, I won't let myself settle for less than what I had." She looked across the room and lost herself for several moments in the pictures displayed on a small desk. "Even if it means I'll live the rest of my life alone," she said with resignation in her voice.

O'Brien stared at her. He wondered when, if ever, a woman was this open and honest with him about what she expected out of life.

Her eyes shifted back to him. More upbeat, she said, "I have to admit that I was aware you were coming to New Castle. I'm also familiar with your work in education." She tilted her head. "Your face was a little wild and wooly in the store, but I recognized you right away." She lifted her wine glass and said with soft enthusiasm, "I even studied your book." With impish accusation in her voice, she said, "There's an outlying chance you could be a sociopath and a liar." She sipped her wine. "But everything in your book indicates that you're an intelligent, kind, and thoughtful man. So right now, I feel like a groupie taking advantage of you, but Jake's the one who convinced me that I misjudged you. Besides," she said with nonchalance, "I figured if I said or did anything stupid tonight, I'd never have to face you again."

He bent his head back and eyed her. "So when you walked away in the restaurant, after stuttering and stammering that apology, you had no intention of talking to me tonight until your brother convinced you I wasn't a lecher?"

She gave him a cryptic smile.

He picked up his wine and drank. He swirled the wine in the glass and looked up at her. "I'll try to say this with humility. Most people can't see past my celebrity. I try to understand, because it comes with the territory." He pointed at her. "You say you're a groupie, but you're unimpressed with the peripheral that swirls around me." He shook his head. "Other people read my book; you *studied* the ideas in my book." He placed the glass on the table. "I appreciate that." He paused. "Especially after your brother told me that you're not easily impressed."

"Jake's right. But it could be a flaw on my part. Sometimes I expect too much from people, maybe even the world." She acknowledged, "I did like your book. But I actually didn't get impressed until page ninety-six."

"Memorizing the page numbers is impressive. Now, if only *I* could remember what I said on page ninety-six."

Her eyes were transfixed on her wine glass; her voice was strong and direct. "You alluded to Melville's *Catskill eagle*." She lifted the glass to her lips and sipped. Her eyes caught his. "Anyone who understands the *Catskill eagle,* anyone who understands what strength it takes to fly in a deep, dark gorge in the mountain, then has the faith and courage to soar out into the sunny spaces again . . ." Her face glowed with sincerity. "That's the exact moment you impressed me!"

For the next hour, they ate and talked about their families, literature, and philosophy. As he helped clear the table, he asked, "Do you do everything as well as you cook?"

Before she answered his question, she handed him a selection of pastries on a hard plastic plate. Not intending to be seductive, she kissed away some icing from her index finger and said, "I believe I do some things even better." From the corner of her eye, she caught his wide-eyed stare. She placed her hands on her hips, turned, and stared back at him. "What I *mean* is I'm an excellent seamstress; I love to inspire my students, and up until tonight, I prided myself on my ability to speak concisely and clearly." She wagged her finger close to his face. "You have an overactive imagination!"

He set the plate of cookies on the dining room table. Pretending to pout, he said, "My imagination was sweeter than that icing you licked off your finger, but rest assured, your cold clarification neutralized my mind's palate."

She looked up at the ceiling and let out a laugh. "Are you the same guy who tried to convince me several hours ago that he's not a debaucher of women?"

A wistful smile crossed his lips as he plucked a cookie from the plastic plate. He held up his hands in surrender and forged a safe passage to the living room couch. Bending his head back, he patted the seat next to him. "Let's talk about those other things that you do so well."

***

The clock on the living room mantle struck twelve as they browsed some favorite pictures and mementoes. The shelves of the built-in bookcase displayed generations of family photographs. As Ava explained how her maternal grandmother and grandfather raised their children in Cuba, Beethoven's "Song of Joy" from the CD player filled the quiet moments. She picked up a picture of her mother and beamed.

"She would tell us stories of her teen years. She loved to run and dance along the shoreline. The white, clean beaches extended for miles, and when she reached into the recesses of her youth, she'd take a deep breath and hold it, as though she could still smell the aroma of the warm breeze that pushed off the ocean as she stood in awe of it."

There was an aura of peace about Ava when she explained, "One of my fondest memories was listening to my mother describe the parade the villagers had for the Virgin Mary during the May Day celebration. They'd carry the life-sized statue of the Madonna for miles along the coastline singing one hymn after another, and then they'd circle back to the church. They'd still be singing as they entered the church to celebrate Mass."

She returned her mother's picture to its rightful place on the shelf. "When my father sailed from Lebanon to Cuba, he met and fell in love with my mother. After an appropriate courtship, they married." She stared at the picture for several seconds then turned to O'Brien. "Life is exciting and frightening with its twists and turns and contingencies."

O'Brien leaned back and gazed at her with admiration as she, with more levity and animation, imitated her father offering her mother a series of choices: "'We could make our home in Cuba, move to Lebanon where I still have many cousins, or seek adventure in America.' And here I stand!" She shook her head still amazed. "Every time I think about my mother and father's love story, I still marvel at her fearless spirit. She left all that she knew and loved to sail to a distant land where she needed to learn a new language and needed to embrace new customs and traditions." Ava laughed at herself. "If my mother would have chosen Cuba, I'd probably be enamored with Che Guevera. If she would have chosen Lebanon, I'd probably be a Middle Eastern militant with some famous terrorist's picture on my bookshelf."

"I don't know," O'Brien said, scratching his head. "You remind me more of an Anwar Sadat who had the wisdom and the guts to show up at the Camp David Accords."

"Thank you for that compliment. Jake's convinced that if I were raised in the Middle East, I would have been stoned to death before I was twenty-five." She laughed when she talked about Jake. "Do you know that he was always thankful that I wasn't old enough to attend Kent State University during the Vietnam War protests? To this day, he's convinced that they'd be singing 'Five Dead in Ohio' if I were a student at Kent when they demonstrated against the war that day."

O'Brien sat captivated by her stories and even more so by the story teller. Each characterization of the people in the photos accentuated an undeniable pride in her heritage.

Ava pointed to his empty glass. "More wine?"

"It's one of the best I've tasted, but I'd like to avoid a private invitation to the Judge's courtroom. I have a self-imposed two drink limit when I know I have to drive. Contrary to what your brother told you about paying me to be with you, the truth is that he threatened to fit me with a cement suit if I messed up tonight."

"Why are you laughing, Dr. O'Brien? Do you think Jake was kidding?"

Raising both hands high in submission, he said, "No. Honest. I have no intention of getting that man angry with me. He's an inch taller than me!"

She moved to a nook where one wall had three framed photographs of a teenage boy in a football uniform. "This is Lucas," she said with admiration. "He's Leila's twin." She pointed to an opposite wall that displayed framed pictures of a handsome lean man dancing with a beautiful long haired young lady with dark hair and dark eyes. She wore a royal blue prom gown, and she was a mirror image of her mother. Ava's eyes moistened. "And this handsome man with Leila is George Elias Panetta."

Ava didn't have to tell him who Eli was.

"Are you okay?"

She nodded and continued to talk about the people who used to fill her world with love, people whose leaving shattered her heart and sense of being.

As he listened to her stories, he thought how learning about Ava was like taking part in a rare archeological expedition. With each artifact of her life that she invited him to inspect, the more he gleaned her profound essence. There was a depth to her that he wanted to dig into. He had an eye for quality, but even though he couldn't define it, he perceived quality was standing before him. He made up his mind that it would not escape him again.

***

She invited O'Brien to canvass the rooms while she retrieved the plastic plate of desserts from the dining room table. A vintage Muhammad Ali *I Am the Greatest* album cover displayed on the highest bookshelf in the living room caught his eye. A focal point in the dining room was a large charcoal drawing that depicted the crucified Christ. It was designed in prisms that split the light into components of various degrees of shading. He never encountered a piece like it before.

"This is a unique work of art."

Ava nodded. "Everyone I know comments on that drawing."

"Does it have a story?"

"It sure does," she said with pride.

"I was helping Eli's sister clean out their deceased aunt's apartment when I asked her what she wanted to do with this drawing lumped in with items designated for Goodwill. She told me she planned to haul it away with everything else. She said, 'If you want it, it's yours.' That very evening Eli hung the drawing right there on that wall for me."

There was one more picture that attracted his attention: a small framed photograph of a beach with the words, "Ava Loves Eli" scrawled large across the sand. At first she was reluctant to talk about the photo, but his eyes remained fixed on it. She picked up the picture and held it to her heart. She glanced down at the frame and then she looked up and her eyes met his.

"Eli and I were able to vacation in San Diego for five days when a stroke of luck had Luke and Leila scheduled to be at summer camp for football and cheerleading at the same time. We stayed at the Hotel Del

Coronado, right on the beach." She shook her head. "Mother Nature reminded us that *Lady Luck* is finicky. It rained three out of the five days that we were there. As luck would have it, the day we were to fly home, it proved to be the best day of the vacation, sunny, blue skies with billowy clouds, and warm." Her next recollection made her smile. "While Eli was in the shower singing one Motown tune after another, I managed to sneak down to the beach and etch in the sand 'AVA LOVES ELI.' We left San Diego a couple of hours later." With sadness in her eyes, she said, "I took the picture to make him happy, but he always felt bad because he didn't get a chance to write, 'ELI LOVES AVA TOO.'"

O'Brien selected another cookie from the plastic plate, and a familiar face emerged. He pointed to the dish. "Does this dynamic duo mean something special to you?"

She tossed her head back and laughed. "Actually, that Raggedy Ann and Andy plate is super special! I hope it doesn't defy your sophisticated sensibilities to eat off of a child's worn plate?"

"Are you kidding? Who could possibly harbor ill will toward Raggedy Ann and Andy? Besides, I told you how refreshing it is to be with someone who treats me like an equal."

Unable to resist challenging his attitude on equality, Ava asked, "Do you really believe that I'm your equal, or is it just nice for Chanticleer every-once–in-a-while to fly down from his perch and flatter Lady Pertelote, you know, make her believe that she's his equal?"

"Ohhh! That hurt!" More serious, he said, "No doubt, you're *better* than I am. Still, I hope you understand what I mean."

She nodded.

"Actually, I envy Andy's enduring relationship with Ann," he mused.

"It's funny. You're the second intelligent person to speak philosophically about this little kid's dish." She traced the outer rim of the plate with her index finger and said, "This was Leila's favorite dish. For the first five years of her life she wouldn't eat unless the food was on this plate." Ava shook her head as she reminisced. "Even when we ate in restaurants, I had to tuck this plate in the diaper bag and carry it with me."

She recalled how one evening, long past the time Leila had grown out of her affinity for the plate, their parish priest stopped by as the family dined at supper.

"Eli insisted that he share the meal with us. I grabbed Leila's dish somewhat as a joke, and told him, 'You get the Raggedy Ann and Andy plate because you're special!' When I noticed the priest's eyes tear up, I asked him why he was so emotional. His answer revealed a quality about human nature that we hadn't considered. He told us, 'When you allow a visitor such as me to eat from an everyday family dish like this child's plate, it signals I'm not a guest anymore. I'm no longer someone you believe you have to impress. This dish makes me feel accepted and loved, like one of the family.'"

O'Brien narrowed his eyes and said, "So let me understand you correctly. Anyone who gets to eat from Leila's Raggedy Ann and Andy dish can assume that you accept and love him?"

His inference, his desire to be accepted and loved warmed her heart. She masked her pleasure by narrowing her eyes. She countered, "That's what the wise priest maintains."

With an air of self-confidence, he raised one eyebrow and fixed his eyes on her. He selected a cookie from the Raggedy Ann and Andy plate and pressed his lips around it and slowly drew it into his mouth in increments. "Mmm! Mmm! I really like your—"

Her eyes widened. Before she could reprimand him, he tilted his head, grinned and said, "I'm beginning to think *you're* the one who has a one track mind, Ms. Panetta. All *I* did was show appreciation for your priest's line of reasoning."

She shook her head and laughed. "Yeah, I guess I read you wrong again."

***

They sat on the living room couch and talked for several minutes more. Ava glanced at the clock on the mantle above the fireplace then turned to him and asked, "Have I sufficiently bored you with my autobiographical tour, Mr. President?"

With his hands clasped behind his head, he emphatically shook his head and then moved his hand in a circular motion for her to keep the stories coming.

"It's one o'clock in the morning. I don't believe my stories will help you function well on your early morning trip home," she said, bending down to pick up a napkin.

"Please don't worry about me. I'm where I want to be."

"You're waiting to hear what happened to everyone, aren't you?" she asked, putting him on the spot.

"I'd like to know what happened so that I can understand where your head and heart are," he said, trying not to sound curious or macabre.

Ava bent her head back and let out a sarcastic laugh. She stood and walked to the dining room table, sat, and motioned for him to sit across from her. The ceiling light she dimmed while they ate their meal was still on, and the light dramatized the angles and shading of the prisms in the crucifix, *the artwork* that she rescued from the trash. He placed both elbows on the table and then rested his chin in the middle of his clasped hands. He looked like he was praying.

Her eyes rested on his face for several seconds. She studied the lines that ran across his forehead, marks more from fatigue than age. Knowing she had his undivided attention, she pushed one side of her hair back behind her ear, hesitated, and asked, "Do you really want to know where my head and heart are?"

He nodded.

She nodded in return and let out a soft sigh. "If my heart were simply broken, some day a knight in shining armor could carry me away to a better place. He might even be able to perform magic to make me forget." Disillusioned with life, she added, "I have no words to describe how often I feel purposeless and hauntingly alone." She shrugged and said, "I know it's wrong, but sometimes it's just easier, safer for me not to love again. Life snatches away the people you love and leaves you reeling." Struggling to hold back tears, she said, "I've learned to fear losing." With a forced nonchalance, she said, "My heart is shattered into a million slivered pieces that cut into my very being every time I hear one of my children's favorite songs or when I see lovers hugging, laughing, and sharing." Her face carried a hint of defiance when she said, "My head and heart? They tell me that there's nothing, *not a single thing* in God's universe that can put Humpty Dumpty back together again." Her eyes dropped to her glass of wine. She quickly added, "But it's all my fault."

She reached for a clean napkin lying next to the bottle of wine and pressed the corners of her eyes. "The fact that you understand the *Catskill eagle* makes me believe you might understand more than most what it means to lose the people you love and be trapped in a world devoid of their light."

More composed, she asked again: "Are you really sure you want to hear all the gory details?"

He nodded. "I want to know *you*."

Gently biting her bottom lip, she said, "Okay. It's important to know that I was married to one of the nicest men on the face of the earth. Eli and I had our differences, but we shared a common bond of ethics and values. We respected and supported each other. We married after graduating from college." With a hint of pride, she added, "We stayed happily married for eighteen years." She looked down and swirled the wine in her glass. Her voice weighed heavy with sorrow when she said, "He was my best friend." She looked up, offered a shy smile, and said, "Being pregnant with the twins caused excitement in both our families, but the pregnancy took a physical toll on me." Her smile faded when she said, "I wasn't able to have any more children. Eli wanted four kids, but he was happy with Luke and Leila. We grew closer during the rough times, and we couldn't imagine living life without each other. We finally got to the point where the twins were looking at colleges, and we were selfishly looking forward to an empty nest."

She poured wine into her glass and sipped on it. Picking at the tablecloth, she said, "We visited Eli's elderly mother on a Sunday afternoon. Leila complained first because she wanted to stay home and go to the movies with her friends. Luke just wanted to stay home to be antisocial. I insisted in a heavy-handed way that they learn to be appreciative that they still had a grandmother to visit and that we were going to visit as a family.

"We shopped, ate supper, and did chores around my mother-in-law's house. We actually had a nice time, but it was getting late. I knew Eli was exhausted, so I offered to drive home to give him a chance to rest. It was an unusually dark night, and it began to rain. About half way through the trip, Luke began his litany of complaints."

Ava mimicked her son saying, "'Mom, do you always have to drive like an old lady? Flash bulletin! Americans have a legal right to pass cars on the highway. Come on Mom! Wake Dad up! By the time we get home, I'll have three social security checks waiting for me in the mailbox!'"

Luke must have had his mother's caustic sense of humor, O'Brien thought. Ava took another sip of wine. She asked, "Can I get you something else to drink?"

"No. I'm good."

Cupping her wine glass in her hands, she said, "I tried to be patient with Luke. I told him I was driving the speed limit, and it was difficult to see. I reminded him that he wasn't the only one who was tired. Leila and Eli were asleep because they worked hard, and I suggested that he do the same, or I wasn't going to let him live long enough to collect social security checks." She cast her eyes downward and shook her head with shame and regret. "I can't believe I'm telling . . ." She looked up at him. "I never told anyone those were some of the last horrible words my son heard me say to him."

Choking back tears, she said, "If I weren't so angry, I would have laughed at what he said next to taunt me." Her voice cracked as she mimicked Luke muttering in disgust, "'God, Mom! A man with empty eye sockets drives in the dark better than you.'" Her eyes moistened, but she quickly wiped them with her hands. "Frustrated with the driving conditions and angry with Luke's incessant whining, I screamed at him and told him to shut up or I would throw him out of the car and make him walk the rest of the way home. My outburst woke Eli and Leila. Eli turned and glared at Luke." Her eyes were still misty as a half smile crossed her lips. "One look from Eli was all it took to derail Luke and Leila's attempts to disrupt." Sniffing softly, she said, "But something went wrong."

O'Brien could see the agitation in Ava's eyes before she snapped them shut for several seconds. She fought back tears.

Speaking more rapidly, she said, "A semi pulled up beside me and seemed to linger longer than it needed to. It kicked up water and dirt that splashed on my windshield. At the same time, I was distracted by what I thought was an object that flew from the back seat toward the windshield."

Her hands lay flat on the table as she stared at O'Brien. An aura of disbelief possessed her as she recalled, "I turned my head toward Eli. It was only for a split second. The next thing I knew, the car was grating along the guard rail. I panicked. I gave the wheel a sharp turn to get back onto the road." Her voice carried self-recrimination when she said, "But I lost control." She was silent for several seconds. Sighing heavily, she said, "The car hit a cement abutment then flipped into a ravine." She shook her head. "I thought the car was never going to stop tumbling. When it did finally stop, everything in front of me was black except for intermittent flashes of red light that allowed me to see just a few seconds at a time Leila's head in my lap. I rocked Leila and kept telling her I wouldn't let anything hurt her."

Ava's eyes stared past him. Her senses shut down. There was a vulnerability about her that made him reach across the table to touch her hand. In an instant, his touch jolted her back to the present. She gently pushed his hand away. With futility in her eyes and voice, she asked, "Why did God make me live without them? I wanted to die, too." Staring at him, she said, "I was so mean to Luke, and I lied to Leila." Picking at the table cloth again, her voice cracked. "I was holding my baby girl's beautiful head in my lap, and I wouldn't let them take her from me." She put her hands over her mouth and whispered, "I tried so hard to stop the blood" Closing her eyes, she cried, "There was so much blood!"

When she slowly dropped her hands from her face, he watched the horror consume her as she explained, "Leila's throat had a deep gash; it was mangled, and the blood . . ." She stared in cold, dead silence, hoping that if she paused long enough, the story might end differently, but the story always ended the same way. "I just sat there and watched my baby's blood drain out of her. No matter what I did, I couldn't stop the blood." Looking at him, she pleaded, "Why couldn't I at least stop the blood?"

She sat quiet and still and stared like a stone statue.

He instinctively reached across the table and held her hand. He knew it would be a Herculean task to bring the pieces of her heart back together, and he knew he was no Hercules, but this time he told himself, I'm not letting go!

She used her free hand to wipe her tears. Regaining composure, she gently tried to pull her hand away from his, but his grasp was firm. She whispered, "I'm okay."

Depleted of emotion to the core of her soul, her voice was cool and detached when she said, "Now you know where my head and heart are."

Her words hung heavy in the dim dining room light as she excused herself for several minutes. The house was silent except for an occasional deep moan from a bullfrog calling in the night and the refrigerator freezer whirring on and off in the kitchen. O'Brien was sitting on the sofa when she returned to the living room and said, "It's late. You need to get some rest before you drive home in the morning."

Studying her with concern, he asked, "Will you be okay tonight?"

She said, "This story is who I am."

He understood her feelings, but he stopped short of telling her that this story is only part of who she was. Instead, he told her, "I'll be leaving the hotel around nine in the morning. That will give me plenty of time to get home, rest, and prepare for some meetings coming up in the middle of the week." Standing close to the door, he said, "I hate leaving you like this."

His smile was warm and sympathetic. "I don't mind sticking around . . . to talk."

"I've talked enough," she said, feeling flush.

Reaching for her hand as she walked him to his car, he asked, "Is breakfast in the hotel out of the question?"

His invitation surprised her. After the debacle in the restaurant and the melodrama over the past hour, she had given him ample reason to walk away, but he persisted with overtures toward her. Overcome with trepidation, she crossed her arms and held them tight to her chest.

"It's easier for me to say good-bye tonight than have to say good-bye to you next week, or next month after I fall . . ." Her eyes shifted toward the fountain in the center of the pond. She listened to the water splashing and followed the ripples as they gently drifted to shore.

The thought of her entertaining the idea of falling in love with him sent a surge through his body. He gently held her chin and turned her head toward him to force eye contact.

"I know you've been through hell the past couple of years, but please believe me when I tell you there's an attraction here, and I feel compelled to pursue it."

She smiled and placed her hand on his cheek. Her smile warmed his heart.

"You need another shave," she said.

Pressing his cheek on her hand, he coaxed, "What I need is you sitting across that breakfast table from me tomorrow morning."

She instinctively leaned in closer. She could feel his warm breath on her shoulder, and the scent of him awakened a desire that she thought she buried in another life.

"I don't know about breakfast in the morning," she said soft and low, "but I do know that I'll treasure tonight."

As he drove away, images of her flooded his mind.

CHAPTER NINE

AFTER a restless night, Ava awoke eager to raise the luminescent window shades that blocked the bright beams of morning sunlight that carried hope. She showered and dressed by seven. Just as she grabbed the teakettle, an early morning phone call from Jake startled her.

"I know the rooster hasn't crowed, but do you want us to pick you up for breakfast? The whole family's craving waffles. Vikki said Aunt Halima suggested it yesterday." With mock wonderment in his voice, he mused, "Why I just found out about the plan three minutes ago is another Coury family mystery! Are you in?"

"I don't know," she said.

"Ava, it's breakfast, not a commitment to scale Mt. Everest. Do you have other plans?"

"Dr. O'Brien was here until one in the morning. He asked me to have breakfast with him at the hotel before he leaves. I don't know what to do."

"No kidding!" Calling to his wife, he said, "Hey Vikki, Dr. O'Brien asked Ava to have breakfast."

Ava heard Vikki say, "I don't know why you're surprised. He didn't exactly hide the fact that he's attracted to her."

"I'm so afraid, Jake. Isn't he out of my league? What if I fall in love with him and then he gets bored and never comes back?"

"Ava, listen to me. You're intelligent. You're damn attractive, and you have depth of feeling. There's not a man on earth that is out of your league. Go slow, and see what happens."

"But what if I fall in love and he leaves?"

"What if you let him walk away without ever finding out if he loves you too? Will you be any less lonely or your heart less broken?"

Sighing, she said, "Vikki is the luckiest lady in the world."

"I'll hold the phone toward Vikki; do me a favor and say that louder."

She chuckled. "I'll let you know what happens."

***

She drove across town and waited for O'Brien in the hotel dining room. He had taken his luggage to the car earlier and planned to grab a bagel and a cup of coffee before he began his trek home. When he rounded the corner, he spotted Ava sitting at a table with streaks of sunlight filtering through a nearby window. His heart began to race. The dining room was empty except for her, so he strode confidently toward her holding his chest. Since they were alone, he spoke louder than he would have, and he was more animated.

"Wow! You keep surprising me, pretty lady. I don't know how much more my heart can take."

Wiping her fingers with a napkin, she said, "Then maybe I should stop accommodating you, for medicinal reasons of course."

"No. Don't do that. I'd rather die a happy man."

Motioning for him to sit, she said, "I know some people who manage to be both healthy and happy."

He nodded. "How'd you make out last night?" he asked.

"I've survived worse."

"I have some meetings this week; then I fly to Chicago on Wednesday. I should be able to catch a flight to Pittsburgh for Friday evening." He looked up from his calendar. "If it's okay with you, I can rent a car and drive back here Friday night and stay until Sunday afternoon."

He talked in casual comfort as Ava visualized beautiful women across the country whom he probably delighted with similar overtures. Less self-assured since the accident, she knew her brother was right. She was fast falling in love, and she needed to find out if O'Brien felt the same way. Before he solidified his plans, she prodded him to learn more of his intentions.

"Look, Jim; let's be realistic. Long distance relationships are next to impossible to maintain. That's why they rarely work. Frankly, after everything I've told you about myself, you have to know that I'm not like some of your other lady friends. I can't compete with them, nor do I want to compete with them." She looked past him to the empty chairs in the dining room. There was a hint of distress in her voice when she said, "I don't want to lose . . ."

She wasn't as confident in her honesty as she thought she could be. He listened to her concerns and tried to alleviate them with some straightforward talk of his own.

"I appreciate your unfettered and unfiltered honesty, Ava. They're qualities that I find lacking in most women I've known. What I don't appreciate is your constant effort to categorize me with all the other men you've known." Tilting his head to force eye contact, he said, "Give me a chance. You read my book. You probably know more about me than you know about some of your colleagues at school." Reaching for his coffee, he said, "You're also smart enough to know that I reserved some parts of my life to share with someone who actually cares about me and not my celebrity status." He shrugged. "I know you don't like the concept of 'celebrity,' but be honest; it's probably the initial quality that attracts people to me." He laughed with sarcasm. "I'm not knocking celebrity. It certainly has treated me well, but believe me; it's a world where people never really take the time to know the depth of a person." Moving his index finger back and forth from himself to her, he said, "We share an important quality. I don't appreciate losing either." Softening his voice, he said, "I can't guarantee that this relationship will work. Our worlds *are* somewhat different, but we have more in common than you think." He paused. "We've both been hurt, and . . ." looking down at the table, he said in a lower voice, "I know what it's like to be afraid." He looked up. "The money and fame wears thin when you're searching for substance." Wondering aloud, he said, "What happens when you get sick of my traveling, my being away from you? Then I'm afraid that I'll break one too many promises, when I'm expected to be at family gatherings and some unexpected problem holds me captive at the college, or in California, or one of the other fifty states." He looked at her in amazement. "Wow! I can't remember a time when I've been this open and honest about my fears to anyone, let alone a woman I just met less than twenty-four hours ago." Relying more on his heart than the skills of a motivational speaker, he assured her: "We're not kids, Ava. We know what we want and need, and frankly, there's something about this encounter that strikes me more as fate than accident."

Her eyes canvassed his face as he spoke. When he lifted his coffee mug, she said, "I'm going to say something that might make you feel bad or even get you angry, but I think it's important."

More playful, he countered, "At least I'm getting a warning." Sitting straight in his chair, he pooh-poohed her. "You've lambasted me from the moment I met you. You've ridiculed my political beliefs; you even tagged me as a sexual predator, but LOOK, Ava!" He raised his hands high over his head. "After all your cynical abuse, I'm still here." Leaning forward, he said, "That ought to count for something."

She laughed at his voice inflection and gesticulations. Looking down at her teacup and tracing the rim with her index finger, she said, "As much as I want to believe that you're attracted to me," she looked up, "I can't understand what I have that your long line of lady friends lack." Running her hand through her hair, she said, "I'll tell you what I absolutely cannot— no, I should say—*will not* do." She began to list all the disgraced politicians and sports figures who succumbed to infidelity. "They drag the women they say they love into the spotlight of ridicule and force them to stand there like frightened fays just so the sleaze balls can hold onto their power and fame. Nothing like a *celebrity* that believes the world is his private playground and women are his toys."

Shaking his head, partly out of frustration, partly out of shear amazement, he said, "You know there was a time that listening to a woman talk like you would have made me run faster than Jesse Owens facing down Adolph Hitler in the '36 Olympics. You said a mouthful. Let me address at least some of your concerns." He sat back in his chair and studied her face for several moments. There was slight irritation in his voice when he said, "First, there is no 'long line' of lady friends." Reaching for his coffee, he said, "I'll mention several factors that make you quite attractive, but understand my short list is by no means exhaustive. For starters, you made—no—let me change that to, you *make* my heart flutter. Second, your unwavering principles and overactive moral compass make you quite rare. As Hamlet states so well: You're '. . . to be picked one in ten thousand.'" Breaking into a broad smile, he pointed at her and said, "Now, if I'm honest about the third reason, you have to promise you won't walk out on me." He eyed her and said, "You are an amazingly attractive woman."

Feeling her face flush, she smiled and said, "I won't walk out, but I will tell you what I'm *really* afraid of."

Leaning forward and firmly planting the palm of his right hand on the table, he asked, "You mean that everything you've said up to this point hasn't been what you're REALLY afraid of?"

Ignoring his sarcasm, she said, "I'll be devastated if your third reason is your only reason." She looked away for several seconds then swung her eyes back to him. "When I was younger, I never used to be afraid to follow my heart. I was fortunate that the first man I loved really loved me enough to marry me." She closed her eyes and said, "I never experienced a broken heart in romance." She stared at him. "Now, I find myself overly concerned about becoming some man's toy, just another conquest that he brags about on the golf course or in the locker-room." Gently shaking her head, she said, "I know you can offer fame and fortune, but I only want to mean something special to someone again."

Futility blanketed his face as he glanced at his watch and took a final gulp of coffee. He quickly gathered his belongings for the ride home. From Ava's perspective, it took him longer than most suitors to reach the point of saturation with her deep-seated distrust of men who couldn't measure up to what she had with Eli. But before he stood to leave, he surprised her one more time. With a glint in his eye, he leaned back.

Imitating her, he said, "What I'm going to say may hurt your feelings, but now you need to know how I feel. Talking to you over breakfast this morning has made me realize that there actually might be benefits to staying a bachelor. But then I thrive on challenges, Ava. If I ever convince you to trust me enough to have an intimate relationship, I promise. . ." he placed his right hand on his heart and looked up with an impish twinkle in his eye to some unseen power, "not to talk about you on the golf course or in the locker room. No sir, Ms. Panetta!" He tapped the table with his right index finger with each word he uttered. "I pledge to you right now. If I get you to trust me, I intend to hire the Goodyear Blimp and notify the four corners of the earth! I may even throw in a few primetime commercials on that ludicrous liberal station that mesmerizes you." After he finished mocking her, and her laughter subsided, he stood. "I'll call you as soon as I get back to the university and know my schedule better."

Walking him to his car, Ava said, "You're probably tired from last night, so make sure you stay alert."

Pulling her close, he said, "I wanted to tell you this last night, but I didn't think you were in the mood to listen. Bad, unexplainable things happen to good people all the time, Ava. You were a wonderful and loving mother and wife. Everyone who knows you says your family loved each other, and that's a magnificent accomplishment. Some things that happen to us won't ever make sense." He cupped her face with his hands. "You are so much more than that tragic accident."

She leaned into him. He buried his face in her hair for several seconds. Looking up, she asked, "Does it bother you that we're moving fast?"

"Not at all. Age and distance will temper us." He massaged her shoulders and studied the gentle lines on her face. "You know what bothered me? Watching you walk away in that restaurant. I felt empty." Holding both her hands, he said, "I hope you never feel a need to walk away from me again."

CHAPTER TEN

THE more leisurely summer months cooperated with Ava and O'Brien. Even with his busy schedule, they managed to be together more than they thought possible. She grew confident in his loyalty, and he grew strength from her consistent faith-filled character. They found refuge in each other. The first time he kissed her on the lips, he aroused the magic that lay dormant in her for three years. There were times when O'Brien naturally attempted more intimacy than her emotions would allow, but he read her signals well and retreated. He afforded her the time and space she needed to anchor herself emotionally in their new relationship. When she apologized for her inability to surrender fully her marital vow to Eli, he lightened the mood by pointing to the curio cabinet filled with camels and challenged himself.

"I bet I can survive without sex longer than all those collective camels can survive without water!"

Some weekends he would travel to New Castle and stay in Ava's guest room; on opposite weekends, she would visit the university. They attended picnics, parties, and family gatherings together, and they blended well in each other's lives.

One early autumn picnic in particular turned into a milestone for them. The uneventful gathering took on an ominous tone when one of the wives turned a benign conversation on "Why Men Cheat" into a serious condemnation of men in general. Ava was adamant.

"Making love and engaging in sex are two distinct activities. If a person sleeps with everyone he or she is attracted to, then that person is no better than a dog in heat on the front lawn."

Some of the men began to bark and howl.

Ava said, "Come on guys! Don't you think there has to be something more significant than endocrine glands, body scent, and primordial instinct to bind two people together in a meaningful way?"

One husband dared to suggest, "What's meaningful to some may not be meaningful to others. People have different physical and psychological needs."

With contempt written across her face, Ava's friend Bethany scoffed. "I bet your wife is thrilled to hear you find casual sex can be therapeutic."

Bethany, who was married to a quiet, unassuming man, named Carl, prated loud and long on the subject. O'Brien steered clear of the conversation by talking sports with the men who also distanced themselves from the torrid topic. The men successfully dodged the fray until Bethany yelled across the patio.

"Hey, Dr. O'Brien! I bet your theory on why men cheat is enlightening."

Deflecting her attempt to drag him into the quagmire, he offered a benign response. "I can't believe you ladies think so poorly of half the human race."

"Well, half the human race knows full well that at any given time a man's animal instinct trumps his reason," Bethany said with a jeer.

Against his better judgment, he allowed the ladies to reel him closer to the eye of the stormy group discussion. Like college girls at a bonfire on a brisk Saturday night, they scooted close together to allow the 'Big Man on Campus' to squeeze in at their table. The teacher in him wanted to counter the irrational attitudes on relationships, but the man in him heard an inner voice whisper a warning: tread carefully.

"First, let me say men and women can be faithful if they choose to be."

"Oh come on! We're not talking about women right now," Bethany said.

Another husband offered O'Brien weak encouragement. "Good first move Dr. O., but they always set a trap that no man can escape."

As the comments grew more biting, he quickly regretted his involvement. Mindful of the friendly warnings from men who carried their own battle scars from previous discussions on the topic, he gently disputed the logic that men cheat mainly because they're biologically predisposed to answer a primordial physical need.

"I'd like to get serious for a moment because I believe we all have a stake in this."

"Not really," Bethany said with a snarl. "Only guys have *stakes* in this!"

A loud "Ohhh!" from the men rippled through the patio, and some of the women blushed, laughing softly.

Realizing that he'd have to choose his words more carefully, O'Brien playfully admonished the group. "Ladies and gentlemen, get your minds out of the gutter." When they were more attentive to him, he said, "While human beings can't deny an element of animal instinct in mating, we've come a long way in recognizing that humans have the capacity and willingness to use their minds, a characteristic that animals in general lack. Society sets up moral, ethical, and legal rules and traditions that keep our animal instincts in check, and most human beings, both men and women, reasonably see the benefit of those laws and traditions and live by them. Reason over-rides natural instincts."

One husband yelled out, "That makes sense! My instincts tell me to go hunting, but I go to work instead. I know if I lose my job, I'm deader meat than what I hunt!"

Laughter rose from the gathering.

"Most of us agree with you, Mike." Turning to the women at the table, O'Brien said, "We rely on our intellect rather than our instinct because we don't want to lose our jobs or our wives and families. To believe that men follow women mindlessly like roosters follow hens simply because they want to satisfy their instincts becomes insulting when we discredit the capacity for human beings to choose fidelity because it's actually in our best interest, in our family's best interest, and in society's best interest."

Teeming with confidence from the other men who drew closer to the table to offer their newfound champion moral support, he bolstered his argument.

"If we study the habits of men who cheat," he jabbed the air with his finger, "and I might humbly add some women cheat, too, we can probably trace their dalliances to a host of social and emotional reasons that have little connection to basic instinct."

O'Brien remained conciliatory to both male and female camps until he made his last fateful observation: "To say unequivocally that all men act on their animal instincts and have intercourse with any woman who gives them the look, well, ladies, look at your husbands. Do you believe that they've cheated or they will cheat on you in the future?"

The men mumbled, "Don't look at us! We got the memo."

Bethany's husband, Carl, simply flipped the sirloins and tried to diffuse the conversation by innocently calling out, "Who's hungry for one of my steaks?"

For several seconds, his ill-chosen words shocked the rowdy gathering into a fumbling silence until Mike, imitating a cave man, yelled out, "Carl's the man! We mere men have to talk *singular*." He pounded his chest and said, "But the god of steaks is talking *plural*!"

Bethany glared at Mike. She turned to Carl and barked, "You're not funny either!"

An unnatural silence fell over the picnic until O'Brien coaxed, "Come on, ladies; lighten up. At least let me wrap up the discussion before we," he looked around and asked the guys, "is 'eat' a safe word?"

A light-hearted groan filled the air.

Palming the table with both hands, he said, "Be realistic. If wives believe husbands are cheating on them, what does that say about the women who stay with these cheating men?"

Dumbfounded by his question, Bethany turned and shot O'Brien a venomous look that baffled him.

On the way home, Ava explained that Bethany had suspicions of quiet, unassuming Carl, and that his more intellectual discussion probably chafed the scabs of some unattended marital wounds. It also didn't help to imply that wives who tolerate their cheating husbands are akin to prostitutes.

"That woman is absolutely bizarre with her paranoid belief that all men cheat," he said, unable to mask his irritation. "I never heard such a Neanderthal view of men. The only thing missing from that picnic was the Beverly Hillbillies playing a washboard." Still vexed by Bethany's behavior, he asked, "If she really believes her husband is cheating, why does she invite ridicule by publically insinuating that every other man is unfaithful?"

"I guess misery loves company," Ava suggested.

"I think your friend, and I use that term loosely, was consciously trying to undermine the other solid relationships gathered at that picnic, and I especially feel targeted," he complained.

Still bothered by what he perceived to be the unfair implication of the absurd discussion, he pulled Ava by the arm and asked, "Do you buy into Bethany's theory?"

The delay in her response irritated him.

"Ava, what do you think I'm doing when I'm away from you?"

A wry smile crossed her lips. "You're making a mountain out of a molehill, Jim."

With an edge in his voice, he insisted, "You didn't answer my question."

"Do you know that close to forty percent of the high school seniors that I teach every year come from broken homes? People declare their love; they flash huge diamonds on their fingers, they go into debt orchestrating lavish weddings that shout how much they can't live without each other on one day; then the next day, they come home, and they say they need to find themselves, and the marriage is over. It's life."

Ava's harsh assessment of relationships caught him off guard. She was the one who enjoyed a faithful marriage for eighteen years, but she was right. He held that same negative belief about relationships ever since his own marriage ended. Still, he was angry and hurt, maybe because he wanted her to recognize something more unique in him, in *their* relationship. He knew it would only exacerbate the situation if he pursued the conversation while he felt beleaguered. Maybe he *was* making a mountain out of a molehill. He begged off the rest of the evening and quietly withdrew into the guest bedroom, took a long, hot shower, and rolled into bed. His low lit lamp invited Ava to come in and console him.

After she too had showered, she wrapped a light blanket around herself and retreated to the living room to curl up on the couch and reflect. She closed her eyes and memories of the first time she made love to O'Brien, only a month ago, flooded her mind. He flew to California several times a year, and in the last week of August before his college was in full session, he had to attend a conference in San Diego. He invited Ava to travel with him before her school year began in a week. She was hesitant at first. She knew she loved him, yet she still felt twinges of guilt, unable to separate herself from the strong marital bond with Eli. O'Brien was sensitive to the conflict that waged within her, and he gave her the space she needed to feel comfortable loving him. He booked adjoining rooms to make it easier for them to interact, yet still offer her the privacy she needed. They stayed at the Hotel Del Coronado, and it conjured memories of when she and Eli vacationed there.

She thought of that particular evening, after they returned from the banquet that signaled the end of the seminar. She scampered around the room to ready herself so they could walk on the beach and watch a fireworks display that the hotel provided to kick off a citywide celebration of the arts. A conspicuous envelope lying on her pillow caught her eye. Curious, she opened it. She slowly pulled out a photograph of the beach. In the sand, scrawled in huge letters, were the words: "ELI LOVES AVA TOO."

She remembered how she stared at the picture, first in shock, then in sheer wonder. He went out of his way to ease the regret of a dead man, she thought. Her body quivered as she drew the picture to her heart. She touched the door that separated them and thought, my love for Eli doesn't threaten him.

Of all O'Brien's kindnesses and considerations, this act of symbolic closure was the single drop of consideration that fell upon her heart and made it overflow with love for him. Her head and heart aligned, and all guilt of loving him slipped away. She pushed open the door that separated them. He was lying on his back resting across the bed. She gently climbed up next to him and opened the top of his robe to expose his chest. He kept his eyes closed, but she could feel his heart pounding as she glided her index finger over his bare chest until she spelled out, "AVA LOVES JIM."

He opened his eyes and stared up at her with wide-eyed wonder and anticipation.

"Are you sure?" he asked, not able to believe what his senses were telling him.

She nodded.

He gently slipped her robe from her body and pulled her toward him. He brushed his lips on her ear and whispered words that he had never spoken to any other woman.

"I never thought I'd love someone as much as I love you."

They held each other close and became one for the first time. They caught glimpses of the brilliant fireworks display that filled the night sky as the sweet communion of their love began to drown the noise outside their window. Their bodies moved in rhythmic motion, as if choreographed to a symphony playing deep within them. It let loose a magic that loaned them, for a brief time, the power to quell the turmoil in the world.

Remembering the love she felt for him that night made her heart overflow with love for him all over again. She opened her eyes and thought of him now, lying in a room only a few feet away believing that she didn't trust him. She needed to tell him that it was herself that she didn't trust. It was a fear that kept creeping back like a dark spirit that invaded her happiness, making her question her ability to love and sustain him. Feelings of inadequacy caused her to dread the day that he'd tell her he wanted more in a partner than she was able to provide. She wanted him to know her insecurity, but she didn't know how to express it without sounding accusatory.

He heard her tiptoe into the bedroom. His eyes were closed, but he wasn't asleep. He was remembering the first time he stopped by the roadside to pick wild flowers for her on one of his trips to New Castle. As he picked daisies and some white flowers that had a sweet fragrance, he stopped dead in his tracks. The only other time I ever picked wild flowers for a woman was for my mother, he thought. Three days before he was to ship out for basic training, he stopped his car and gathered a bunch of pretty flowers for his mother to give her a special memory of him. His brothers teased him, and it became one of those archived family stories that the O'Briens drudged up at every family gathering. His mother dried the flowers and displayed them for years after he came home from the war. He wouldn't be surprised if she still preserved them somewhere in her house. He told her, "You're the only girl I'd ever stop and pick flowers for, Mom."

Remembering the sensation of guilt he felt, helped him understand Ava's feelings of disloyalty the first time she held him, the first time she kissed him, and the first time she made love with him.

Ava sat on the edge of the bed as he pretended to be asleep. She gently used her index finger to brush his hair away from his forehead.

"All I want is to know you love only me," she whispered.

A few seconds passed with no response. She slipped her robe from her body and draped it over a chair. Careful not to wake him, she lay on her side of the bed. Several minutes passed when O'Brien rolled toward her and began to nuzzle his nose on her neck between her chin and her ear. The stubble from his day-old beard tickled her as he moved his face back and forth sniffing her like an animal sniffs a prospective mate. He whispered one thing before he fell asleep holding her secure in his arms.

"Get this through your head, Ava. My instincts and my intellect draw me to you. I want and love only you."

CHAPTER ELEVEN

AFTER several months of courtship, there was little the lovers didn't know of each other. Ava especially developed a heightened sensitivity toward O'Brien's feelings and moods. She appreciated his easy-going and affable personality, but there were times when she detected a look of doubt in his eyes, especially after they made love, and it worried her. Although he managed to dispel her feelings of inadequacy, she wondered if he harbored feelings of inadequacy of his own. She would initiate conversations designed to probe the heart and soul, but he always stopped short of inviting her to that place that held him hostage.

"Those professors discussed some interesting topics tonight," she said, after coming home from a university event. She sat at one end of the couch in his den as he entered the room bare-chested and sporting his favorite cut-off sweat pants. He lay on the couch and rested his head on her lap. He kept his eyes closed, but she wanted to talk. Moving his hair off his forehead, she glided her fingertips over his face and cheeks, down to his chin and across his lips, and back up to his forehead. She wanted him to initiate the discussion, but he stayed quiet.

"What's your take on 'Why People Argue'?"

"I haven't given it much thought," he mumbled.

Gently poking him in the chest, she said, "You just don't want to talk to me."

He struggled to subdue a smile.

"We never argue," she said.

"Is that a bad thing?" he mused, keeping his eyes closed.

"I don't know. Sometimes when people disagree, it gives them a chance to air some negative feelings. It's a way to identify weaknesses and work to strengthen them. A person can have character flaws, and a partner will still love him. Love looks past all the garbage." She rattled off a list of his positive qualities: "You're kind, intelligent . . ."

He lifted his hand and moved it in a slow rotating motion to egg her on. He knew it was only a matter of time before the word 'but' would stop him cold. Then BAM! She said it!

"*But* what's going to happen when I say something stupid or do something that causes you grief?"

Opening his eyes wide in mock surprise, he asked, "You mean like the evening you skewered Henry Morgan in front of the whole board of trustees the first time you met him?"

Pulling back and narrowing her eyes, she said, "That can't possibly be your best example, Jim! Henry told a horrible racial joke. He intentionally included the Arabs to insult me. Every single one of those professors was a coward for laughing when each one should have walked away."

Heaving his body up from her lap, he said, "Ava! Henry was wrong, but you divulged information that I shared in confidence. My God! What if Lucy would have heard you? It's bad enough that she heard about it." Looking at her crosswise, he asked, "Do you even remember what you told him in front of all those people?"

Surprised by his vehemence, she said, "Obviously not as well as you do."

"Well let me refresh your memory, sweetheart."

Doing his best to mimic her voice inflection, he spewed her words: "'Frankly, Dr. Morgan, you're fortunate to live in the United States of America where you're free to flaunt mean spiritedness and talk about Arab women in a derogatory way. If you lived in an Arab nation, your testicles wouldn't be fondled by the latest tramp that attracts you; they'd be hanging from a Ramadan tree!'" Giving her a look of rebuke, he leaned back on the couch and closed his eyes. "As I recall, we had a spat that evening."

Chuckling at his imitation of her, she leaned in and tucked her shoulder under his arm. Playing with the soft curly hair on his chest, she asked, "You know what the worst part of that evening was? You used arrogance masqueraded as kindness to teach me that I didn't know anything about Ramadan."

"Your paranoia is unbecoming, Ava."

"Yeah, right, Dr. O'Brien! It's all my imagination," she said, gently playing time on his chest. "Now let me see if I can capture that teachable moment." Mimicking the deep, irritated voice he used that night, she said, "'Just so you're aware, Ava, there is no such thing as a Ramadan tree!'" Grabbing his earlobe with her lips, she whispered, "You thought I was dumb, didn't you?"

Pulling his head away from her, he said, "Not at all. You were perhaps theatrical and tactless. Never dumb."

Sitting up, he put his head in his hands and rubbed his whole head hard for a couple of seconds. "I'm going upstairs to get some rest. If you're as smart as we both know you are, you'll let me go in peace."

Ignoring his friendly warning, she turned out all the lights and followed him. When she entered the room and sat and stared at him, he startled her by slamming shut the book he was reading.

"Okay! Make this easy on me and tell me what you're after."

Unsure at first if this was the best time to pursue her intuition; his eyes revealed she was dangerously close to some kind of disclosure. She saw the look time and again in the eyes of students who suffered abuse or unwanted pregnancy. She'd be counseling them, and she'd see that same frightened visage possess them right before they couldn't hold back any longer the horror that bound them in shame and fear.

"I really don't know," she said, her voice soft and steady. "There seems to be a part of you that's off limits, and I guess I want you to take me there so that I can help make it better."

Shielding himself with an angry rebuff, he said, "Everyone has places that he or she would rather forget, let alone share. You of all people know that."

Undaunted, she persisted. "That's true, but I've always shared my fears with you. I even told you a detailed account of the accident, how I blamed myself. I wanted you to know all of me."

In every intimate relationship with a woman, he dreaded this day, but no woman ever ventured this close to delving deep in him. Ava was the only one who waded past the superficial and knocked on the door of his essence. Now she was insisting that he open it. He wondered if she could still love him if she knew what he did long ago in the marshes a world away. His thoughts wandered to the Vatican garden where the Bishop of Rome pursued him and cleansed him of his sins. Now she pursued him. Confessing before the God of creation seemed so much easier than confessing to her, he thought. Maybe it's because God forgave him so much easier than he believed Ava would.

He clenched her shoulders. With desperation in his voice, he said, "I don't think you really want to know everything about the man you love, Ava."

"I already know what kind of man you are. It hurts me that you still don't know what kind of woman I am."

"I'm lugging some pretty heavy and horrific baggage. Do you really want to add it to this head of yours that already houses more than its fair share of ugliness?"

Pulling away, she said, "Look! I told you before that I don't even believe in love at first sight, but I loved you the moment I saw you. I expressed my love for you faster than I ever dreamed I could, and I've been faithful to you. Remember what it felt like in those early months when I didn't trust you?" Her eyes welled up. "Now, I find out that you're the one who doesn't trust me!"

Before he could turn away, she said, "I'm not the one you caught screwing an old man for his money. I didn't screw around with the men who offered to comfort me after Eli died, even though I was so alone and lonely that I may as well have been dead. I loved Eli and was faithful to him for eighteen years, and I love you, and I will be faithful to you forever. That's what I want from you. I've never kept what I wanted from you a secret. I told you what I wanted the first morning we had breakfast." She threw her arms up in frustration. "Frankly, if I didn't see the distrust in your eyes every time we make love, then you could keep your secret buried forever for all I care. I see it in your eyes, Jim, and it hurts." She wiped her eyes with the back of her hand.

Staring at her, he thought of the inadequacy she felt all those months believing someday he would tell her that she wasn't good enough for him. Fear seized him. What if the full knowledge of my character proves not good enough for her, he thought.

Standing paralyzed for several seconds, she witnessed tears well up in O'Brien's eyes. Detecting a slight tremor in his body before he retreated to the bathroom, she thought, what darkness is he harboring that causes him to cry? Her own heart filled with fear as she waited for him to return.

He sat in a chair across the room from her so that she wouldn't be able to touch him. Making direct eye contact, he said, "Remember when I told you that I was fortunate to have the Pope absolve me of my sins?"

Ava nodded.

"Well, I didn't approach him. He did what you're doing now. He spotted me trying to avoid him." Letting out a sarcastic laugh, he said, "Your knight in shining armor was trying to run away from God." He shook his head. "You know, he forgave me before he even heard my sins, just like you're willing to do." With a beleaguered look, he rubbed his forehead. "But you need proof that I trust you, and the only way I can prove that I trust you is to tell you something about me that I've kept buried for over twenty-five years. And Ava. . ." he hesitated, "after you hear what I have to say, you won't ever be able to look at me with respect again."

He lowered his head to stop his eyes from watering. Looking up, he stared at her for several seconds. He perceived it to be the last time she would look at him with love in her eyes, and he wanted to mark it indelibly in his mind. He took a deep breath. Like a man on the run who finally gets captured, he exhaled with relief that the fear holding him hostage for so long, that impeded his ability to love fully, was about to be expelled from him. He told her what she deserved to know.

"When I was in Vietnam . . ." Hesitating for a second, he cleared his throat with a light cough, and said, "I shot and killed . . ." Correcting himself, he said, "No! I *murdered* a mother and the baby that she was holding in her arms."

A deafening silence enveloped them. O'Brien searched her face to detect signs of appall or disgust, but she hid well the hot, stinging sensation that raced up her spine. Ava fixed her eyes on him and looked puzzled. The silence thickened. She wondered how he carried this burden with him for decades, harboring the fear of being exposed as an example of what most Americans came to believe was synonymous with the worst evils of the Vietnam War, a "baby-killer." The inhuman act, taken at face value, was enough to ostracize any individual from the realm of humanity. Still, he managed to live a successful life that gathered honor and respect from all who knew him.

She moved to the edge of the bed closer to where he was sitting. She narrowed her eyes and shivered. She controlled her fear as she tried to make sense of the revelation. She searched for words that would comfort him.

"I love you for the man you are, not the eighteen year-old kid who the army trained to kill in a war."

Shaking his head, he said, "Please. Don't start making excuses for me. I *am* that eighteen year-old man who murdered an innocent woman and child because I was angry and afraid." Covering his mouth with his hands, he whispered, "I've seen what the darkest part of my nature is capable of doing, and I'm so sorry, Ava. I never meant for you to have to see it, too."

She stared back at him with equal intensity. She wanted to acknowledge the horror of his actions, yet she wanted to place the horror in context with why it happened.

"You say you *murdered* people. What you didn't tell me is why." Struggling to remain calm, she said, "There's a difference between murdering people for sport and killing people because it's a war and that's what soldiers do." Her voice shook when she whispered, "Why did you kill them, Jim?"

He stared at her for several seconds. More like a plea, he said, "I've never told anyone the story. Isn't it enough for you to know that I murdered a woman and a child?" His eyes wandered across the room out over the balcony into the night sky, then turned back to her. He said, "How can you hear the whole story, Ava, when you can't even say *woman* and *baby*? For God's sake. You're simply dismissing them as faceless, nameless creatures!"

Insisting that she wouldn't understand angered her. Eyeing him with determination, she said, "You're right, Jim. Help me understand. If you won't allow me to make excuses for you, then I need to know what happened and why it happened. No matter what becomes of us now, when your story is over, at least you won't have to live your life tiptoeing around a quarter of a century secret."

"What will happen to you if I break your heart?"

"What will happen to you when you see me stealing looks wondering if you're really a monster?"

His eyes weighed heavy with sadness. He covered his face for several seconds. Lowering his arms to his side, he told Ava the story that changed his life forever.

***

"It rained nonstop for two and a half days. Four of us were trudging through miles of sludge along a river trying to catch up with our scattered platoon. We approached a hut; the others were ahead of me. I was several yards behind them. A man was coaxing a toddler into our path. A woman held a baby and didn't act alarmed. She didn't cry; she didn't try to protect the kid from slipping in the sludge that could easily drag him under in a split second. I yelled, 'Don't touch the kid!' Donny called back. 'He's gonna go under. He'll suffocate.'

"'Don't touch the kid!' I screamed louder, but Donny grabbed his arm. There were explosions. They all blew up! The kid . . . the man . . . Donny . . . everyone! Pieces of them . . . flesh flew everywhere.'"

O'Brien wiped his eyes and stared past Ava as though he were catapulted to the death trap he desperately tried to forget. Looking dazed, he said, "I tried frantically to pick up whatever pieces of them that I could grab. One second I held a severed hand. The next second I seized a leg . . . a hand . . . an arm . . . a head . . . legs . . . another head!" He shook his head. "Oh God, Ava!" Bewildered, he said, "All parts, but no people. Parts of my friends slipped out of my hands and sank into the mud. I yelled at the lady to help me, but she wouldn't move. I screamed, 'Why didn't you stop him? Why didn't you try to save your own kid?' You killed them all! You killed my friends!' I kept saying it over and over and over . . ."

He paused. Filled with regret, he wanted what he was about to say to be different than it was a thousand times in his nightmares. "I aimed my rifle and shot once at her." Finding it more difficult to verbalize, he whispered with deeper remorse. "Then I shot the baby."

His eyes were transfixed on Ava, but his senses were in another place and time. Ending his story, he said, "My whole body groaned so loud that I thought the Viet Cong would hear me and kill me. I slid into a shallow part of the mud and thought I'd vomit forever. Members of another platoon found me. I told them what happened, and they assumed that someone other than I shot the lady and the baby before the others blew up, because no one asked me any questions after that." He bent his head down to his knees and held it in his hands. Barely audible, he said, "My God! What did I do?" He admitted, "I was so afraid to die, and I didn't know what to do."

Ava moved toward him, but he pushed her away. She moved toward him again, and he pushed her away again. She moved toward him a third time, but before he could push her away, she pushed back at his arm that blocked her. She rocked him in her arms for several seconds.

"Listen to me, Jim. For God's sake, listen to me! You were an eighteen year-old kid, just a little older than Luke. You watched your friends get blown up by a child that was turned into a human weapon."

"You can't make this right," he said, shaking his head. "Nothing can make this right."

"This may sound cold, but they all probably had hand grenades attached to their bodies," she told him.

Holding both her shoulders and gently reproaching her, he said, "Listen to yourself. Don't let your love condone my sin. I don't want your love to excuse my subhuman behavior. I need your love in spite of my behavior." He shook his head. "We can try to parse words to high heaven and back, but a woman and her baby are still dead because of me."

Confounded by his self-recrimination, she said, "Can you at least acknowledge that sometimes parsing words may be a worthwhile defense mechanism that prevents us from judging, convicting, and imprisoning ourselves for crimes that we had little control over?"

"Ava, the truth is I should have acted differently. This sin will always be an albatross that hangs on my soul."

"Do you remember what you told me in the parking lot the day after I told you about the accident? You told me that the accident wasn't my fault, that I was a wonderful mother and wife. You told me that the accident wasn't who I was, that I was the sum of my experiences. I really want to believe you meant what you said." She whispered, "Did you mean what you said?"

He nodded.

"If you meant it, then isn't the same true for you?"

"Not quite."

With frustration, she stood and looked down at him. She yelled, "You want me to face reality? Fine! I don't want to believe that someone I love is capable of killing a *woman* let alone a *child*. There! I said the words you wanted me to say. Now why can't you admit that war forces good people to act less than human?" Resentment oozed from her when she said, "Other people don't go to war. They'll never have to agonize over the prospect of killing women and children with grenades attached to them to save their own lives and their friends' lives." Her tone turned to mockery. "What they do instead is lie for their own gain. They cheat on their spouses because they're bored and tired of commitment. They ruin reputations; they pass unjust laws, and they ravage the environment to quench their selfish thirst for wealth, recreation, and amusement. The difference is that these nickel and dime sinners sleep better at night than the soldiers who kill, because it's their nature to lie, cheat, and desecrate." The edge in her voice softened. "Most soldiers are forced to act against their nature and kill human beings who in a different time or place they would be treating to a beer and sharing universal family concerns." Her voice was filled with wonderment when she said, "For over two decades you have been making reparation for your war crime. Look how many kids' lives you saved and made better over the years at the university. Doesn't that count for something?"

Closing his eyes, he whispered, "I love you for defending me, but we can't change the facts." He stood. Holding her head, he said, "I'm not concerned with other people's sins right now. I want you to love me, but you need to love me for who I am, not for who you want me to be. If you want to compare me to every other sinner, then understand that there were some heroes in the war." With deep remorse in his voice, he said, "I wasn't one of them."

She pulled away from him. Frustration mounted at her inability to console him. Crying, she said, "What do you want from me? Now I know you killed a woman! I know you killed a baby! I know you're not perfect!" Turning her back to him to wipe her face and blow her nose, she told him, "I know what it's like to wonder if someone will ever love me after he finds out that I was responsible for the death of innocent people." She turned and pointed at him in defiance. "You say we can't change the facts? Well, what if you don't even have the correct facts, Jim? You admit that everything happened in split seconds; you were in shock."

To prove her point, she fired one question after another at him: "What would have happened if you weren't lagging yards behind your friends? Would you have instinctively grabbed the little boy you warned Donny not to touch?" She backed further away from him. "What about the soldiers who found you? If that woman were still alive, how many of *those* soldiers may have been blown up and buried in the sludge because you didn't kill her?" With an intense stare, she said, "Sometimes that's why I get so afraid of life. It only takes one second here, another second there. Someone is a hero; someone is a coward. Someone is losing her family; someone is beginning a wonderful love affair." Moving closer, she said, "After making reparation for twenty-five years, don't you believe it's time to let God judge if you murdered an innocent woman and her baby or if you killed people in a war that would have killed you and other soldiers if they had the chance?"

Emotionally spent, she rested her hand on his chest. In a low, soft voice, she asked, "Don't you think I know that we both caused pain? I know that our demons will always haunt us. Isn't it enough that we're sorry, that we're trying to be good people?" With a heavy sigh, she offered one last consolation. "Every time we made stupid mistakes and even when we made some big ones, my mother always reminded us that after God destroyed the world with a flood, He gave it a rainbow. God gives us new beginnings, Jim. Look what you've done with your life since that horrible war."

O'Brien was overwhelmed by her ferocious defense of him. Although his revelation forced her one more time to face the harsh reality that decent people bear suffering so long and heavy for their split seconds of inattentiveness and bad judgment, she embraced him with unwavering loyalty. She pushed him back on the bed so they could rest in each other's arms.

"Are you going to be okay?" he whispered.

"I'll be okay if you'll be okay."

"This is the closest I've ever been to paradise without dying."

They both lay holding each other for several quiet minutes. Breaking the silence, he said, "I don't know why your family had to die. I don't know why I wasn't buried in that earth a world away, and I don't know how you have the capacity for so much understanding, forgiveness, and love. One thing I do know; I dreaded losing you." Caressing her cheek, he said, "After everything you've learned about me tonight, your love still insists on elevating me to a place where I will never have a right to be."

"You're wrong, Jim. God gives us the right to love, and love obligates us to soar."

CHAPTER TWELVE

OVER the next several months, Ava and O'Brien learned more about each other's family and friends through the stories they shared. One particular childhood memory exhibited Ava's inherent fun-loving nature. Her animated recollection caused him to laugh so hard he held his side so it wouldn't hurt. More than once, he begged time out to wipe tears of laughter from his face and catch his breath.

"The moment I woke up on my sixth birthday," Ava told him, "I pranced around the house like I was Cleopatra, Queen of the Nile." Faking child-like, snobbish self-importance, she said, "I had every expectation of enjoying a fairytale birthday party in the evening where I'd ascend to my rightful place as center of the Coury universe. I expected all people and all activities to revolve around me!" She bobbed her head and said, "Then that asshole Oswald assassinated President Kennedy!" Jabbing her finger in the air, she said, "Not only did the assassination interrupt my mother's soap opera, it was like a flash of asteroids bombarded earth and smashed my fairytale world to bits. My mother wailed, 'Charley, come quick! Someone shot President Kennedy!' So began the trail of tears that led well into the late evening. Forget about being the center of the universe for a day. They all forgot to sing even one note of 'Happy Birthday' to me. My aunts and uncles, aided and abetted by my own mother and father, preempted my birthday celebration by hurling unsubstantiated accusations at Vice President Lyndon Johnson. Some relatives were convinced Johnson conspired to kill the young, first Catholic president so he could be president; other relatives, equally devoid of evidence, insisted that the mafia eliminated the president. One thing was a given, my family inadvertently taught me to loathe Oswald for making me forever share my birthday with the tragedy of the century."

Coughing to catch his breath, O'Brien said, "I've heard of people holding grudges, babe, but you really need to let this one go."

Staring wide eyed at him, she said, "Easy for you to say!" Swirling the wine in her glass, she said, "Ever since that birthday, each year my family gathers to celebrate my birth, and each year more than one person in the tribe announces, "Today's the day that asshole Oswald killed Kennedy.'" Letting out a laugh, she said, "When I was growing up, I actually believed that 'asshole' was Oswald's first name. I was probably in an eighth grade history class when I stumbled across the fact that Oswald's real name was Lee Harvey Oswald!"

O'Brien laughed. As if Oswald's legacy wasn't steeped in enough societal damnation, he pictured Ava as a defiant little girl heaping her brand of disdain on him, too. He held his hand up to catch his breath when Ava started to imitate her aunt's emotional reaction the next day when Jack Ruby shot and killed Oswald on the courthouse steps.

Unable to squelch her own laughter, with histrionic bent, she demonstrated her aunt's irrational fervor. "She lifted her hands to high heaven and praised God like she was swept up at one of those revival meetings where the spirit yanks your body from you for several minutes, and some unseen force twists and turns it senseless into contortions and tongues unintelligible to earthbound beings. She jumped up and down and did everything but roll on the ground! She wanted to send Ruby a thank you note, a bouquet of flowers, a loaf of Syrian bread . . . " Ava dabbed her eyes with a napkin. "My father finally convinced her not to be too quick to canonize Jack Ruby for blowing Oswald away. He talked her down in Arabic, but we kids understood: 'Now we'll never know if that asshole Oswald had any accomplices.'" Ava cleared her throat. More serious, she said, "As I grew older, I found it regrettable that the authorities never had an opportunity to question Oswald. The n*ot knowing* in life is a difficult place to be."

***

Knowing that Ava's birthday coincided with Thanksgiving weekend, the O'Brien clan began to apply friendly pressure, suggesting it was time O'Brien formally introduced her to the whole family. She met some family members who attended a college function, but to most of the O'Briens, she was just a name. Anxious to meet his parents, the holiday presented an ideal time to acclimate herself to the O'Brien personalities that she had come to know through the tales he told over the past several months.

When she visited the university a month before Thanksgiving, she still hadn't finalized plans to travel to Florida where the O'Brien family gathered each year to celebrate holidays with their parents. The weekend plans at Emerson-Thoreau included a rendezvous with friends in a local restaurant. They took advantage of the unseasonably warm weather and waited on the patio for their friends to arrive. Ava appreciated the loving way O'Brien talked about his mother.

"I watched my mother's heart break the day I told her my marriage was over." Sighing, he said, "She feels sorry for me." A waiter carrying a tray of hors d'oeuvres approached them. He grabbed one, but Ava passed. "My brothers get mad at her because she insists that I stay in the most convenient room in the house when we congregate. Then to add insult to injury, she gives me more coffee, more ice-cream, bigger pieces of pie, and the biggest steaks." Shaking his head and laughing, he told her, "You should hear my brother Sean whine. He teases her saying, 'Stop feeling sorry for him, Mom. He can buy all our houses with one check.' Her cold response is always, 'Houses are just made of wood.'" He looked past Ava to a pool of water with lilies floating on the surface. Not quite understanding his mother's affinity for treating him like an *at risk* child after all the years of professional success, he sounded apologetic. "Her favoritism toward me is so overt, she doesn't even pretend anymore." Stepping backward and wielding an imaginary sword that cut through the air, he said, "My Mom fights anyone who says anything negative about me with the mettle of Prince Hector of Troy." He looked at her wide-eyed and smiled. "Before you came into my life, they all viewed me as a lost cause in matters of love."

Ava played with his fingers and laughed. She understood his mother's over-protective nature toward the son she perceived to be wounded.

"My mother treated Jake like he was a Saudi king, and my mother-in-law always doted on Eli." Rolling her eyes, she said, "What is it that makes me attract mamma's boys?" She didn't wait for an answer, but asked, "Do you think she'll like me?"

"There's no doubt in my mind that she'll like you."

Lifting her hand to his lips to kiss it, he said, "You're talking about a lady who has been praying for the last ten years that I find a woman who loves me and not my money."

Shooting an impish grin, she asked, "How can you be sure that I don't love your money?"

"For starters, painful as it is to recall, you made me wait for months before I could make love with you. That's not on anyone's top ten ways to tap into a man's bank account. If all you want is my money, you need to manipulate better. Ask for diamonds and rubies instead of books and back rubs. Then you could finagle an exotic trip or two instead of acting like your English classes can't live without you for a couple of days. Honestly, Ava! If you really wanted my money, you could talk me into flying to Vegas, tonight, get me drunk and talk me into getting married in one of those chapels where Elvis could be my best man. Do I really need to belabor the point?" Frowning, he said, "Then again . . ."

"Then again what?" she asked, pulling back.

"Well, there might be slight reason for concern, but with some luck, we can deflect the problem."

She rolled her eyes. "Just a second ago you told me, 'There's no doubt in my mind she'll like you!'" she exaggerated his exact words. Eyeing him, she said, "Now, all of a sudden we have a slight problem, and I need *luck* to deflect the problem?"

"Shhh," he whispered. Pulling her close to muffle her voice, he said, "I can't help what Sean told them. He meant well, but he was a little off on the particulars."

Her eyes narrowed when she asked, "How difficult is it to describe me? Exactly what 'particulars' did Sean get wrong? Does your family know he never even met me?"

He placed his finger on his lips to quiet her. "He told everyone that you were a fifty year-old widow who—"

"Fifty? I'm not fifty! Isn't Sean the one who's close to fifty?"

"Yeah, but instead of telling them that you're a Maronite Catholic, he told them you were something like a Moslem."

"He told your Catholic mother that I was 'something like a Moslem'?"

She snapped her eyes shut for a second then opened them and locked eyes with his. "Your brother sounds like a pathological liar! He needs some serious counseling." Stretching to whisper in his ear, she said, "Then again, maybe Sean's not the O'Brien who has a problem at all. Maybe his little brother likes to harass people."

Raising his eyebrows in surprise, he asked, "When did you catch on?"

Shaking her head, she slipped her arms around his neck and said, "I have an idea. Let's forget our families and fly to Las Vegas tonight and get—"

Interrupting her, he said, "Gee, I'm sorry, sweetheart; I'd love to accommodate you, but we're meeting friends for dinner tonight," he pointed toward the entrance, "and I think they just walked through the door." He gave her a quick kiss on the lips. They laughed as they walked with their friends to the reserved table. The discussion quickly turned to university life, politics, and how the holiday season seemed to come more quickly every year.

***

Days later, he received a commitment from Ava to share her birthday and Thanksgiving with the O'Brien clan. While Ava was a woman easily satisfied with meaningful gifts, not necessarily expensive ones, he wanted to make his first birthday gift to her memorable. He had the money and creativity at his disposal, but she showed little interest in jewels or trips abroad. She enjoyed small bouquets of flowers from the grocery store, and she'd be more apt to join PETA in dowsing red paint on a mink coat than wear one. He remembered the day he suggested, "I'm going to blindfold you, put you on a jet, and make you wait to see where the plane lands." She threatened, "That plane better land somewhere in America, lover boy!"

He thought of the other gifts that held meaning, the razor kit that had long been rendered dispensable as a tool, but priceless in its emotional significance, on its way to elevation as a family heirloom. He thought of the 'ELI LOVES AVA TOO' photograph that he left on her pillow in San Diego. These mementos guided him in his quest to make her happy. He thought of the quirks that made Ava so different from other women. She had an affinity for placing everything meaningful to her in a frame, the generations of family photographs, and favorite passages from books and poems. She even managed to frame him with her love.

Inundated with university obligations during the week leading up to Thanksgiving, they decided to celebrate her birthday the Saturday after Thanksgiving. To add some intrigue, he called her during her lunch hour and gave her mysterious directives: "Be on the lookout for a notice to pick up a package at the post office. You'll have to sign for it. Promise me you won't open it. Pack it in your suitcase and bring it to Florida. I want you to open it in front of me on your birthday."

"Do you really believe that I can have a package in my possession without sneaking a peak at it?"

"I trust you, Ava. Promise me!"

"Okay, okay, I promise!"

On her way home from work, she stopped at the post office to check on the package. It was a small box that weighed next to nothing, easily able to fit into her mailbox, but O'Brien didn't want it to get lost or damaged. She gave the box a little shake, but to no avail. The contents would have to remain a mystery. She shoved the box in her purse and made one more stop. The first thing she did when she came in from the garage and walked into the kitchen was shake the package again. Okay, she thought. The safest place for this gift is in my purse. I don't want to forget it or lose it. What if it's a ring? No, it's too early for a commitment like that, she thought. She shook her head. Whatever it was, the presentation was memorable in itself.

CHAPTER THIRTEEN

IT took two days for all the O'Briens to congregate in the spacious, two-story, colonial house that overlooked the ocean. The O'Brien brothers and their families flew from across the country to join their mother and father who generally spent their winter months in the warm climate. For several days there was a display of food, family stories, laughter, and song that reaffirmed and strengthened family bonds. By Friday evening, family members made their rounds to say goodbye. Evident that they held deep love and appreciation for their brother, Jim, they took comfort in the knowledge that he had finally found the balance in his life that was missing all these years.

As Ava moved among O'Brien's family members, she gravitated toward his older brother Sean, who was gregarious, loud, and funny. They traded barbs and bantered throughout Thanksgiving evening. The ruckus they caused spread like a contagion, as they drew other more reserved family members into the fray. Any lingering concerns about being accepted into the clan vanished.

Before the family began to break up Friday evening, Sean grabbed Ava and hugged her. He proclaimed, "My brother is a fortunate man. Keep him happy, you hear?"

"I'll keep him happy on one condition," Ava said.

Sean looked at his brother and asked with mock surprise: "Already she's placing conditions on your happiness?"

He looked at Sean with mock helplessness and said, "She's a liberal. You know how difficult it is to talk sense to card carrying ACLU members? I've had my hands full ever since I met her."

"No sympathy from me, little brother. What did you expect to find in a

Wal-Mart store?" He draped his arm around Ava's shoulder and boasted, "Besides, I'm a card carrying member, too!" Eyeing O'Brien, he warned, "So watch it!"

By now, the family gathered around Sean, Ava, and O'Brien. Turning to Ava, Sean asked, "Out of curiosity, what's the condition that I have to agree to that ensures my brother's happiness?"

"Don't ruin any more Crosby, Stills, Nash, and Young songs when I'm around you," she told him.

Sean's eyes widened. "That's downright insulting! This woman thinks I butchered the songs." Grabbing Ava's arm, he said, "Come here! One more song before I hit the road. I'll let you sing with me to make sure it's good enough."

Ava shook her head and tried to pull away, but a soft rhythmic clapping rose louder as Sean turned his family into a singing Irish mob. He began to sing solo, "Wasted on the Way" and pulled Ava close, coaxing her to harmonize with him. As they sang the last lines, the water may not have carried them away, but the camaraderie did. Parents and children erupted into loud cheer. When they separated that evening, their hearts were full of gratitude and love for each other.

***

Standing by the hearth, she stared at the flickering embers carrying the last vestiges of heat in them. In the quiet of the empty house, thoughts of her own festive family Thanksgivings washed over her. She missed the warmth of knowing Eli, Luke, and Leila were safe and secure after the fanfare of the day found a place in their memories.

The melancholy sound of the ocean's ebb and flow just outside the door made her feel alien and awkward. Her heart and mind straddled two different worlds, one full of life, the other full of echoes of life. She struggled to ward off the guilt that staggered in the way of her newfound contentment in the face of all that was lost.

O'Brien studied her from across the room. He wondered if ghosts beckoned.

"Is there anything I can get you?"

His voice startled her. "I'm good," she said.

"Would you rather be alone?"

She shook her head.

He wrapped his arms around her. "I imagine holidays are difficult." She felt his warm breath on her cheek when he said, "If it's any consolation, you made Sean a happy Irishman tonight."

She smiled and asked, "Is he always that much fun?"

"He's certainly the life of all the O'Brien parties." He added, "You gave him more incentive tonight than the liquor he was drinking."

"Are you suggesting that I'm more potent than alcohol to an Irishman?" she countered with wide-eyed surprise.

Kissing the back of her neck, he said, "I won't presume to speak for all Irishmen, but I can say with certainty that you are this Irishman's aphrodisiac."

Playfully pushing him away, she asked, "How about if the sex crazed Irishman and his aphrodisiac ask his mother if she needs help in the kitchen?"

"How considerate of you, my exquisite *Love Potion*, but every year my mother hires someone to clean-up. Let's go out there anyway. I'm sure my mother and father would enjoy saying goodnight to you."

***

His father was tall and handsome, a retired lawyer who still enjoyed consulting on cases. His once dark head of hair had long since turned white. Full eyebrows matched his full head of hair. He had fair skin, the kind that could burn easily if left exposed even for a short time in the sunlight. In his late seventies, he continued to exhibit a sharp wit and wisdom on personal and general topics. Family and friends sought advice from the patriarch, because, like a well maintained library, he embodied a wealth of knowledge, insight, and experience into human nature.

His mother also aged well. An attractive woman in her seventies, she was mentally sharp and physically agile for her age. She was darker complexioned than her husband but still protected by wearing lightweight sweaters and jerseys with sleeves. Strands of her pixie hairdo, dyed the lightest brown, shimmered like gold in sunlight. Her dark eyes and thick long eyelashes mirrored O'Brien's eyes. This mother didn't need a certificate of birth to lay claim on her son. Although she spoke with a soft, accommodating demeanor, she was a strong-willed, rugged, independent woman who stood her ground.

A cool breeze rippled across the patio as the sound of waves assaulting the crags just beyond the house warned of a storm. O'Brien sat with his dad and talked about work and some stock investments, while his mother took

Ava's hand and guided her to a nearby flower garden illuminated by solar lights.

"I'm fortunate my children are good, successful people." Looking down as she walked, she said, "I still worry about each of them one time or another." Turning to Ava, she said, "My Jimmy tries to hide it, but I know he bears deep sorrow." She plucked a white rose and handed it to Ava. "I can tell you love my son. That makes me happy." Stirring warmth flowed from her as she wrapped her arm around Ava's waist. She felt a slight tremor move through the older woman's body.

To ease her concern, Ava confided, "He's an easy man to love." She glanced at O'Brien talking with his father. Turning to his mother, she said, "He brought meaning back into my life."

"I can't begin to imagine your loss and pain, Ava." She looked at her son. "He teases that you're liberal and he's conservative, but you have more in common than he admits. Jimmy doesn't let on because he never wants to worry me, but I know that he learned how difficult it is to make sense of life after he saw death in that war."

Ava smiled each time his mother used the words *my son*. The scenario was familiar. Her own mother protected Jake. Her mother-in-law hovered over Eli, and now O'Brien's mother laid claim to the son she worried over, prayed over, and whose heart was irrevocably tied to hers. Ava would trade all that she had in the world for one more chance to protect Luke the way these mothers protected their sons.

She told Ava, "He never was the same boy ever since he came home from the war. Whatever happened to him over there marred him; it broke his heart." Airing a hint of contempt, she added, "He had his heart broken in other ways, too." She patted Ava's hand. "Be patient with him, dear. Give him time to open up his heart."

Before she was able to address his mother's plea, O'Brien called out, "Hey, Mom, don't tell Ava too much about me. She'll expect me to live up to all the hype."

His mother quipped, "Just take care of each other. The hype takes care of itself." She glanced at Ava and winked.

Mr. O'Brien stood and yawned. "Time to say goodnight." Holding his hand, Mrs. O'Brien said, "I'm with you, dear." Turning to Ava and O'Brien, she said, "We'll see you two in the morning. And Ava, we'll celebrate a belated birthday breakfast."

After his parents retired to their bedroom, Ava turned and looked wide eyed at O'Brien.

"What's wrong?" he asked.

"I never opened my present!"

"Where is it? Do that right now."

She searched the den for her purse. Finding it underneath the coffee table, she retrieved the gift. She sauntered onto the patio and ripped the wrapping off the small box. Admiring the plain silver frame, her eyes grew large when she recognized a laminated *Republican* registration card cut up into several pieces strategically placed under the glass. Formatted next to it was an intact *Independent* registration card that had his name printed on it. He signed it, "Independently Yours!"

She knelt in front of him. "I don't know which is more profound, the concrete gift in my hand, or the idea that I influenced you," she said, fanning herself with the framed card.

He leaned forward in his chair, kissed her and said, "You influence me." He kissed her again and said, "You inspire me." He kissed her a third time and said, "You make my heart soar."

Grabbing her hand and tugging her toward the beach, he said, "Let's dodge the waves."

"Will you save me if a wild one threatens to carry me away?"

"Absolutely! I refuse to allow anyone or anything to carry you away from me."

They kicked off their shoes and crept close to the water's edge where the waves sweeping across the sand lapped at their ankles. She squealed with delight as one of the larger waves caught her off guard, grabbed her at the knees, and threatened to pull her down. He steadied her at the waist.

Holding hands, they strolled side by side up the coast for a quarter of a mile. When they turned for home, Ava slowed down and stopped. She stared up into the sky catching one or two stars twinkling around the clouds rolling in. He stood behind her, held her tight, and rested his chin on the top of her head.

"Do you think there's life on other planets?"

"I don't know," he whispered. "If there is, I hope they're more civilized than we are."

Bending her head down to kiss his hand, she said, "Stephen Hawking says that history proves alien visitors, whether they're conquistadors or extraterrestrials, usually invade and conquer."

He let out a laugh. "I can understand the conquistadors, but how does the brilliant physicist know so much about the conquering habits of extraterrestrials?"

Turning to face him, she rolled her eyes. "You know what he means. If aliens arrive where there's an existing settlement, chances are that alien group will conquer."

He narrowed his eyes. "In some ways you came to the O'Brien household as an alien. Do you plan to conquer?"

She peered into the heavens. Her answer was unexpected. "The only thing I want to conquer is my fear of losing you."

"I thought we were past that."

She turned and looked squarely at him. "Not other women. I'm skittish about losing people I love." Wide eyed and indignant, she pulled back from him and jabbed the air with her index finger. "Now you have to pay for calling me an alien."

"Are you threatening me?" Laughing, he pointed back and threw out a threat of his own. "Be nice to me or I'll tell my mom."

Placing her hands on her hips, she said, "Okay, smart aleck. That does it! I plan to hug and kiss all night long the first man who catches me on this beach."

She turned and bolted up the coast. He sprinted and caught up. Panting slightly, he grabbed her, lifted her in the air and swung her around. Enfolding her in a tight embrace, he planted a lingering kiss on her lips. Raising his hands high over his head, he declared, "I win!"

Wrapped in each others' arms, they stood on the patio listening to the waves crashing against the nearly invisible crags. The wind began to pick up, and wisps of cold mist sprayed their faces. Ava scampered to gather their shoes and her purse; he grabbed his phone. They climbed the stairs to the loft, a bedroom conveniently situated away from the main part of the house. O'Brien showered first and slid into bed. In a twilight sleep, he heard Ava's whispery sing-song voice call, "Jimmm."

He covered his face with his hands. What could she possibly need? He rolled out of bed and planted himself on the dry side of the shower door. "At your service, madam."

"Can you come in here?" she whispered.

He closed his eyes and placed his thumb and index finger at the bridge of his nose. Tapping on the shower door, he told her, "You watch too many movies. Romantic shower scenes aren't as easy as they look."

Her alluring voice teased over the cascading water. "Okay, hon. I won't take it personally. Maybe if you were ten years younger . . . ."

He relished her romantic preludes, but he wouldn't allow her to goad him into making love in the shower, especially not while his parents were sleeping in the same house.

"I'm exhausted, babe. Tomorrow."

Quiet filled the room. She turned off the shower and stood there for several seconds as the steam slowly escaped the stall. She popped open the shower door and reached for her towel. Within seconds, he swooped like a bird of prey and lifted her in his arms. He pressed his lips on her mouth to muffle her surprise. Together they clumsily dropped onto the bed. He whispered, "Didn't I tell you that your mouth was going to get you into trouble some day? Now keep your voice down and don't wake up the old people."

"I already woke up one old person," she said, struggling to stifle her laughter. "At least let me dry off."

Pressing his mouth on her ear and whispering in a steady, deliberate voice full of confidence and authority, he said, "Make note of this, Ava. I'm not that much older than you. After I'm done, you can marvel at how conscientious and with what precision older people perform their duties." Gliding his right hand over her wet, glistening body, he told her, "And all this water that you're so worried about drying off," he held his hand up above her head and flicked drops of water onto her face, "in a couple of seconds, these drops will turn to steam."

"I don't know, lover boy; a second ago you were snoring! Which of the muses inspired you?" she asked, her fingers playing with his hair.

"The god of champions inspired me, Ava." Holding her head with both hands and locking eyes, he said, "Let me introduce you to the first man who caught you on the beach. Now make good on your threat!"

***

Early Saturday morning they enjoyed a hearty breakfast on the patio. True to her word, Mrs. O'Brien offered kind birthday wishes and presented Ava with an Austrian crystal vase filled with red roses. As she watched his mother and father walk hand in hand along the shoreline, she wished aloud, "I hope I can do that with you thirty years from now."

"You did that with me last night."

She shot him a disconcerted look. "You know what I mean. I hope we can grow old together."

He wanted to reassure her, but they both learned in brutal ways that life holds no guarantees. Reaching across the table and playing with her fingers, he said, "I can't promise that we'll grow old together, but I can promise as long as we live, we will be best friends and exclusive lovers."

With a sweet sigh, she relaxed and stared out toward the ocean. Smiling, she asked, "Why didn't you say that in the first place?"

Heaving himself out of his chair and pulling her up, he stole a quick kiss and said, "Because I don't dwell on what I can't control. Now let's see if we can catch up to those two old people still holding hands."

***

Saturday evening, O'Brien reserved a table in one of the finest restaurants on the coast. Gently swirling the wine in his glass, he said, "I'm always on the lookout for unique gifts for you." He eyed her and grinned. "I saw one that I wasn't sure you'd want just yet."

Was he alluding to a ring, she thought. Then again, he could have been thinking of a Dalmatian named Spot. She played it safe.

"What could be more special than the birthday gift you gave me?" She raised her eyebrows, flashed a bright smile and boasted, "You're independently mine!"

"That's a fact, but I know I can do better."

More serious than she needed to be, she said, "It must be hard buying me gifts when you know the only gift I want is a Catskill eagle."

He knew what she meant. The irony was that to him, *she* was the *Catskill eagle.* She was the one who possessed the kind of love and courage needed to dive down deep into the dark gorge, and she was the one he trusted to show his soul how to fly out again into the sunny spaces. He knew there was no earthly possession purchased with mere money that could ever symbolize what her love meant to him.

CHAPTER FOURTEEN

ALREADY, it was the first Friday of December. The Thanksgiving holiday in Florida caused a delay in Ava's Christmas schedule. Each year she dovetailed Thanksgiving into Christmas, keeping her decorations up until the Epiphany. For an intense, fun-filled two weeks, aunts and cousins gathered on assigned dates to participate in a marathon Christmas cookie bake-off. She loved everything about the Christmas season: the snow, the carols, the movies, the shopping, and the nativity story. She even had an affinity for blizzards, as long as she didn't have to drive in them. Elation welled in her when the principal dismissed school early because the weather report warned of hazardous conditions, snow accumulating up to eight to twelve inches in several hours.

Inching her way home, the snow fell hard and steady. Relieved finally to pull into her garage and hear the door shut behind her, she slipped into her green velour leisure suit and filled the tea kettle to brew a cup of tea. She remembered an Irish professor's instructions: "The only way to make a splendid cup of tea is to place the teabag in the cup and pour boiling water over it. Let the teabag steep for only three minutes!"

What a great evening to decorate the house, she thought, watching the snow steadily turn her yard into a winter wonderland, but who's going to lug that tree from the basement? The roads were treacherous. Calling Jake tonight to help with the lifting was out of the question. She thought of all the seemingly insignificant chores Eli did for her. He even gave me a bell to ring when I was bed-ridden the last month before the twins were born. I should've thanked him more.

The tea kettle whistled and made her jump. She pulled her favorite mug from the cabinet and poured the hot water over the teabag. She stared longingly at the mug that Eli helped Luke and Leila create at a local ceramics store when the twins were in first grade. Leila drew a one-humped camel, and Luke drew the sun and a palm tree. Eli printed for them the neater words spelled correctly that proclaimed, "Mom is an oasis in the desert."

Curling up on the couch, she tucked the mug close under her chin to keep warm. The snow kept falling hard and steady as the pond between the house and the road began to freeze over. The house lay in solemn stillness. She cast a longing look toward the hallway. Her gaze lingered. She was hoping to hear Luke and Leila's voices, hear their music, and watch Leila practice her routines. Ava didn't realize that she was crying until she felt her face warm and wet. Wiping her face with the back of her hand, she jumped up to answer the phone. She cleared her throat before she said, "Hello."

"Ava, I'm watching the weather report. It looks pretty bad for Western Pennsylvania. Stay close to home."

"I know how to weather a storm, Jim."

"You're touchy tonight. Is something wrong?"

"Nothing's wrong. I just don't like being so needy around this house."

"What do you need?"

"I can't even lift a Christmas tree by myself, and I don't want Jake to die in this blizzard helping me."

"Look! If it's that important to you, I can cancel the Florida trip. I can golf any time. I'll come to New Castle, and we'll do Christmas things, okay?"

She loved him for always being sensitive to her needs, but she stopped him before he finalized his plans to cancel his trip.

"No, Jim. You made plans to be with your brothers, and that's where you need to be. Besides, you just warned me about a blizzard. The last place you should be is on a road that leads here." More composed, she said, "Besides, I don't want you to start scheduling your life around my bouts of sadness. That would make me even sadder. Catch your flight, and kiss everyone for me."

"Ava, I'm a phone call away. I love you."

***

O'Brien arrived at Ava's house the following weekend bearing an early Christmas gift: a large box wrapped with bright red paper and topped with a bright green ribbon and bow. Most of her house was decorated, but conspicuously missing was the main Christmas tree. He toured the house and marveled how each room seemed to depict a special aspect of the season. There was a smaller five foot tree in the sun room accented with a myriad of unique Santa Clauses. Ava collected Santa Clauses that bowled, played tennis, and rode motor cycles. There was a journalist Santa leaning on a newspaper dispenser, a Santa riding a camel in the desert, and a Santa surfing a wave. O'Brien chuckled at the sight of a soused Santa that sat in a martini glass sucking on an olive.

"Sean needs to own this jocular guy," he quipped.

The decorations in the dining room displayed more sophistication. An Ebenezer Scrooge and Jacob Marley collector's plate sat on top of her antique China cabinet. A collection of the major characters in *A Christmas Carol* graced the top of the lighted curio cabinet, while a three foot metal tree filled with beautifully crafted handmade ornaments depicted her favorite novels and poems.

"This tree is an odyssey through the annals of literature," she said, filled with pride.

Nodding, he asked, "How long did it take you to create it?"

"I worked on it throughout the year." Laughing, she said, "It started out as a therapeutic exercise, and it turned into this wonderful decoration."

She rearranged some of the ornaments to make them more noticeable. Pointing to *The Wizard of Oz* ornament, he said, "Jake made everyone laugh at the graduation reception when he told us you compared me to all three of these characters."

Caressing his cheek, she said, "You are all three of them, sweetie."

He wrapped his arm around her waist and wedged it underneath hers. They moved into the living room in lock step and plopped lazily on the couch. Excitement grabbed hold of him as his eyes beheld a myriad of wise men. There were wise men on camels and on foot throughout the room.

"Before we do anything else, you have to open that gift," he pointed to the box he gave her. "I can't wait to see your reaction."

She slipped from the couch to the floor and knelt hovering over the box. She eyed it with playful suspicion.

"Just unwrap it. I'm saving the explosives for the Fourth."

Narrowing her eyes, she asked, "Why are you in a hurry to have me unwrap this box?" Turning her eyes to the box, she said, "I wonder what's in it."

He scanned the room with exaggeration. "Ha! Now that I'm familiar with the Christmas inventory, perhaps a more practical gift, like 'paranoia pills' would have served you better."

Grinning with self-assurance, she said, "Question my sanity if you want, but just to be sure . . ."

She proceeded with exaggerated caution. She slipped the ribbon off the large box, guarding against unexpected sounds and movements. She discovered three separate large boxes in the main box. With heightened excitement, she told him, "This gift is even fun to open!" She lifted one of the boxes and placed it on the floor. Gently jiggling the lid off, she peaked inside. Her jaw dropped, and her eyes nearly popped out of their sockets when she saw a wise man riding on a camel. Before she even opened the other two boxes, she jumped up, grabbed him, and planted kisses on his face and neck.

"Where did you find these beautiful creations? Oh my gosh! They're riding the most beautiful camels," she squealed with excitement. Before he could answer, she jumped off of him and cleared the large flat area on top of the entertainment center and lay a sheer, creamed colored curtain down to depict sand. Next she strategically spaced the three wise men on the sheer panel.

"I have to find a nativity display that matches these guys." She examined each nativity ornament in the room before she selected the set that Vikki bought her years ago when she and Jake traveled to Rome. "I even have the perfect finishing touch," she announced. A small spotlight stowed away in her closet finally found purpose when she turned on the switch, and the shadows of the wise men washed the walls and filled the room with majesty and awe. She turned to him and planted softer, longer kisses on his lips. Pointing to the display, she said, "Now that scene takes my breath away, Dr. O'Brien!"

Like a leaf swept up in an autumn windstorm, she had whirled around him gathering objects to complete the display. Calm filled him when she gently wrapped her arms around his waist and asked, "What inspired you to buy them, Jim?"

Running his hand through his hair, he said, "Sean's involved. Do you still want to hear the story?"

"So it's going to be memorable," she said, laughing.

"That's an understatement!" Holding up both his hands palms facing her, he said, "Okay. Sean saw them first. He grabbed me and practically shoved me into the display. He actually made a spectacle of himself in the store." O'Brien imitated his brother saying, "'Hey look! Ava's three cousins! I wonder if Ava the Arab is lagging behind.' Then Sean asked, 'Did you ever wonder why God made Ava's mother choose America instead of Lebanon?' I told him, 'No. I'm just glad she chose America.' Sean laughed and said, 'Imagine Ava sitting on top of one of those huge camels toting an automatic . . . red pen I mean . . . correcting every essay across the Arabian Desert! Ava the Ayatollah-teacher!'"

Leaning toward her and planting a kiss on her lips, O'Brien said, "Of course my first impression of the wise men was more sophisticated. They reminded me of the commencement speech I gave the first day I met you."

Ava laughed. "But your brother pointed them out to you, so I owe him."

As she laid her head on his shoulder and stared, mesmerized by the display, he said, "Before it gets any later, let's go find a nice tree."

Ava stiffened. Her response was curt. "We don't use live trees."

Holding her at arm's length, he asked, "Are you kidding? You can't beat the aroma of fresh pine throughout the house at Christmas!"

She pushed his hands away, and said, "Well, we tried it once, and it didn't work."

Changing the subject, she pulled at his sleeve and said, "I'm going to make a nice hot cup of tea and munch on some delicious homemade Christmas cookies. Do you want to share my stash?"

"Yeah, hot tea sounds good," he said, backing off the tree suggestion. He knew he had triggered another memory, but he didn't know what it meant or why. He was used to waiting for Ava to find the right time to tell him the stories that brought her family to life, at least for the time of the telling. He sat at the table and watched her move around the kitchen with the grace of a polished dancer who knew each step of the routine by heart.

"Show me where the tree is in the basement, and I'll haul it up here while you're getting the tea ready."

Ava nodded.

He followed her downstairs to a large room that stocked more seasonal inventory than Macy's Department Store. She pointed out the tree and ran upstairs to brew the tea. He easily slid the box off the shelf and hoisted it on his shoulder. After he switched off the light, he accidentally bumped into a three-foot Halloween monster that shrieked, "It's Halloween, you know!" A strobe light shooting from its gory eye pierced the dark as the monster lifted its head off its shoulders and continued to scream, "Just thought I'd give you . . . a head's up!"

Startled by the doll's unexpected animation, he lost his balance, dropped the box, and yelled, "It's a *Twilight Zone* gone bad down here!"

Ava tore down the steps, turned on the light, and stood in the doorway. He was sitting on a box holding his chest.

"What on earth happened?"

With provocation in his voice, he pointed to the monster. "That thing scared the living crap out of me!" Bewilderment claimed his face. "Don't you know you're supposed to take the batteries out of these toys before you store them?" Running his hands through his hair, he said, "You never warned me that I'd need nitroglycerin pills to help you decorate."

Kneeling down in front of him, she teased, "What is it with you macho men?" Reaching over to turn off the monster's on/off switch, she laughed. "Eli complained about this little guy every Halloween. He tried to sneak in the house late one night. All the lights were out, and I was in bed. He passed the monster, and it screeched at him." Laughing harder, she said, "I jumped up in time to see him grab it by its neck and carry it to the garage because he planned to take it to a dumpster and dispose of it the first chance he got. In the morning, I brought it back into the house. That sweet guy snubbed me for two days."

"So the moral of this story is what? The penalty for being late in the Panetta home is death by cardiac arrest? Or maybe something more benign, like you chose this animated, heart attack generating freak over your husband?" A sinister grin crossed his lips. "I'm going to carry this tree upstairs. You take the batteries out of the love of your life, and keep him away from me." Raising his eyebrows, he warned, "Next time that creature says anything to me, not even your love will be able to save him!"

She lunged for his stomach and made him laugh. Blocking her assault, he held her arms and pushed her away. "Get off me, Ava. I want out of here. This room gives me the creeps."

"You just ordered me to take the batteries out of *the love of my life*." She grabbed for his stomach again and said, "I'm just trying to find your batteries."

He followed her upstairs where she worked in the kitchen, while he assembled the tree. She helped him with the last few branches. He wrapped several strings of white lights around the artificial pine and threw the switch. Even though the lights sparkled, he blurted out, "Do you have a vendetta against color, Ava?"

Hyperbolizing, she said, "This tree is beautiful. It's like gazing into the night sky and seeing billions and billions of bright shining stars stretching from one end of the universe to the other."

Rolling his eyes, he said, "And I thought only Dr. Carl Sagan had that kind of love affair with the stars." Pecking her on the cheek, he asked, "So what part of the Ava Panetta cosmos do we decorate next?"

Ava laughed and brushed his cheek with her lips. She took a few sips of her hot tea and turned to the box labeled *ornaments*.

"These come next."

She lifted the lid and placed it on the couch. "Just be gentle," she cautioned. "Some of the ornaments are irreplaceable."

"I don't want to be responsible for a damaged ornament, Ava. You'll blame me if I wipe away forever a memory of a loved one." With a nervous laugh, he added, "I'm not used to this kind of tree decorating pressure. How about you unwrap and I hang?"

"I bet you've handled more complicated tasks than unwrapping Christmas ornaments, Mr. President."

"No doubt," he countered, "but none as meaningful."

Handing him an ornament, she said, "Work on this one. I have complete faith in you."

Each time a particular ornament caught his interest, she'd tell him the story of its origin. They were close to completion when he discovered an ornament that she had not only preserved in tissue, but she also secured it in a small plastic box. With utmost care, he removed the tissue and found a photograph in a decorative frame; a little boy around three years old was crying. Inspecting the picture more closely, he asked, "What happened here? It looks like the tree toppled on this poor kid."

Ava reached over and gently lifted the ornament from his hands. Her eyes moistened as she stared at the photograph and caressed it with her fingertips.

"This is Luke," she whispered. She took hold of O'Brien's hand and pulled him toward the couch. "Let's take a break, okay?" Pressing the ornament to her heart, she asked, "Can you handle one more story?"

O'Brien gave her a nod and grinned. He grabbed his tea and popped a small chocolate chip cookie into his mouth. He felt like a spectator in a theater who sits back in anticipation of the feature film. He suspected Ava stored volumes of stories within her beautiful mind, and she would reveal each in its own time. Right now, he was on the verge of discovering why the Panettas never decorated live pine trees at Christmas.

Her eyes caressed Luke's picture for several seconds before she looked up.

"One evening, Eli was driving home from work. The snow fell hard all day, much like last week's blizzard conditions. There was a truck ahead of him carrying a load of over-stacked pine trees. One of the trees tumbled off the truck into Eli's path."

Ava traced the rim of the frame with her index finger. Shaking her head, she said, "Eli swerved to miss the tree, but the road was so icy that the car spun in a three hundred, sixty degree circle! Can you imagine that?" She shuddered at the thought of the near accident.

"Probably because of the treacherous driving conditions, there were no cars on this usually busy road when the car spun. When the car stopped spinning, ironically it faced in the correct direction as if nothing happened. The incident unnerved Eli, so he pulled off the road to gain some composure before he started for home again. That's when he caught sight of the beautiful blue spruce lying in the middle of the road." Ava laughed when she recalled how Eli told her he talked to the tree. "I could imagine his voice saying, 'Okay, blue spruce! You almost killed me, so now I own you!' He loaded it in the trunk of his car and brought the tree home for the kids."

O'Brien's eyes brightened. "I see where this story's going."

Ava smiled as she swept her fingers once again over Luke's photograph and said, "No one knows half the trauma this three year old put us through." She sipped on her tea. "We instructed the kids not to touch the ornaments on the tree because the tree was heavy and would hurt them if it fell on them. For several days, they actually listened." Pointing to the picture, she said, "This particular evening, I was preoccupied with baking cookies and Eli was in the garage changing the oil in the car, when I heard a loud crash and blood-curdling screams. I ran and saw the tree toppled over. Luke was on the floor wailing, and Leila was on the couch crying, hiding under a blanket she pulled over her head. She repeated between sobs, 'He pulled El-lee off the tree. He grabbed El-lee.'"

Ava explained how the kids gravitated toward the Muhammad Ali Hallmark ornament that she bought Eli the year before. "They'd squeal with glee when Eli imitated Ali shadow boxing and when he recited Ali's poems, but they couldn't pronounce Ali's name." She said with confidence, "I could tell Luke wasn't hurt; he just lost his balance and got scared. So, thinking it would make a good memory for him, I snatched the camera and just as I snapped this picture for posterity, Eli heard the commotion and ran in to investigate." Tears welled. Her voice was soft and low. "He yelled at me and said I should've calmed Luke down instead of snap a picture of him."

She brushed her cheeks with her hand and said, "I guess I didn't have a knack for protecting my kids back then either."

She stood to signal the end of intermission. Pushing her hair back behind her ear, she searched for a prominent spot on the tree to hang the ornament that captured Luke forever.

Grabbing her from behind, he pulled her close and nestled his chin between her neck and ear. "Just out of curiosity, how often over the years did you, Eli, and the kids laugh at that picture?"

Her face broke into a soft smile. "It was Luke's favorite ornament. It's also an extended family joke. Anytime anyone is in trouble or does something wrong, some smart-aleck Coury or Panetta yells, 'Forget 911! Just make sure Ava snaps a picture!'"

Squeezing her tighter, he whispered, "Really? I guess you have a knack for making happy memories."

***

Their first Christmas season together introduced more magic in Ava's life than she had experienced in years. They shared their time with the Courys, the O'Briens, and the Panettas. New Year's Eve at Emerson-Thoreau University, with some of their family and mutual friends, proved to be a gala event. Ten minutes before the old year ended and the New Year began, O'Brien sought Ava, but she was conspicuously missing. She draped her shoulders with a Christmas blanket and slipped onto the patio. The bright lights, camaraderie, and festive music felt extraneous to her. Searching the cold night sky, she wondered about the larger purpose, why she was in that place at that time.

Spotting her through the French doors, he quietly walked up behind her and gently massaged her shoulders. He drew her close to shield her from the cold. He wished her thoughts were for him, but he felt certain her mind was on Eli and the twins. She turned and placed her hand on his cheek.

"I'm sorry I wasn't with you for the first seconds of the New Year. I lost track of time."

"I understand," he lied. He was disappointed with himself for being jealous of a dead man.

Stepping back, she said, "I bet you don't." Knowing that she caught him off guard, she leaned into his arms. "Do you want to know what I was thinking?"

"I'm not sure," he whispered.

"I intended to question God again, but instead, I surrendered."

She peered over O'Brien's shoulder for a few seconds and studied their family and friends dancing, eating, and playing games. Her eyes shifted back to him. "I could have lived my whole life without ever finding one person to love, trust, and share my life. God blessed me with two of the nicest, and I might add handsomest, men on earth." She moved her lips to his ear and whispered, "Your love warranted braving the frigid night air to say thank you."

He clung to her and closed his eyes. To both her and God, he whispered back, "Thank you."

CHAPTER FIFTEEN

THE New Year proved to be more challenging for their relationship than the previous several months. O'Brien had more university commitments: business meetings, budgets, interviews, seminars, and negotiations. While Ava's schedule was more predictable, she volunteered to chaperone her school's forensic team that earned a berth at the national competition held in Nashville, Tennessee. The complication: when O'Brien was free, she would not be. His busy schedule and the Nashville trip threatened to keep them apart for at least a month. The long separation would test their relationship.

Before Ava boarded the plane, she called O'Brien to touch base.

"If I don't call you by ten each night, you call me. I want to kiss you goodnight every evening, okay?"

"That sounds good, babe. Stay alert."

When the plane touched down in Nashville, the students cheered. The competing teams from across the country reserved rooms in hotels along the main strip. Students and advisors from rival teams mingled and dined with each other in restaurants throughout the area. As the teams congregated at the Dixie Line Country Club at six o'clock in the evening for a welcome reception, Ava quickly detected an odd sensation. The manager's body language was anomalous. Since Ava's team was one of the first to arrive at the country club, Mr. Embree, the club manager, pulled her aside.

"Ma'm, we're sorry to inform you that there must be some error in communication. The Dixie Line Country Club is an exclusive club. Guests must meet specific standards."

Ava's eyes widened. She waited several seconds for the punch-line, because she imagined what he said had to be a joke in poor taste. He wasn't joking. He planned to deny entrance to Micah, a brilliant bi-racial student, and Kate, her co-advisor of African-American descent, because of the color of their skin. When Ava explained the problem to Kate and Micah, they nervously agreed, "Everyone else shouldn't have to suffer because of us. We'll wait out here."

Ava swung around to face the manager and spewed a fiery indictment: "The students and advisors of color aren't suffering because of you, Kate, or you, Michah. They're suffering," she raised her voice, "because of this racist club's bigoted policies!"

While some advisors initially acquiesced easily, word spread that Ava planned to fight the illegal exclusion of students who had a legal, contractual right to be there on that date. A majority of advisors followed Ava's lead. When the police arrived, the gaunt, scarecrow-like manager with bulging eyes cited Ava as an instigator disturbing the peace. As the officer pushed her toward a cruiser, she threw her cell phone to Kate and yelled, "Call my brother Jake. If you can't reach him, call Dr. Jim O'Brien."

Soon after Kate explained the crisis to Jake, he searched for the earliest flight to Tennessee, but even the earliest flight would place him in Nashville by midnight. Ava would have to spend most of the evening in jail and be at the mercy of the Nashville authorities whom Jake believed already bungled the incident. He didn't believe the climate was favorable for Ava, so he solicited O'Brien's help. As Jake, to the best of his knowledge, filled him in on the initial skirmish and subsequent arrest, O'Brien's office phone rang. It was Henry Morgan.

"Are you watching the news, Jim?"

"No, I have Ava's brother on the other line. We have a problem in Tennessee."

"I'll say! The news report says that the high school advisors from across the country protested the Dixie Line Country Club's exclusion policy. It seems that they don't entertain people of color."

"Let me get back to you, okay, Henry?"

"If there's anything I can do to help, I'm standing by."

"I may take you up on that offer," O'Brien told him.

After O'Brien received the information he needed from Jake, he figured if Jake couldn't secure an earlier evening flight, the odds were against him, too. He decided to cut to the chase. He knew that Henry had a pilot's license and owned a small private plane that he enjoyed flying, so he phoned him. "Do you feel like engaging in a rescue operation in Nashville tonight?"

"I can be fired up and ready to go in an hour," he said with enthusiasm. "The news says that some of the advisors are in jail for disturbing the peace, but if the Dixie doesn't pull back, I see a law suit in its future. Even if those assholes find a loophole that exempts private clubs from the Civil Rights Act of 1964, they signed a binding legal document."

O'Brien held his head with one hand. "I don't know what the hell happened down there. I'm just concerned about what can happen if Ava is in the hands of Big Bubba and the boys for any length of time."

"Just drive down to the mini airport on Crawford Boulevard when you're ready. Don't worry about Ava, Jim. Hell, those boys in Tennessee swatted a hornet's nest and forgot to move out of the way."

Laughing, O'Brien said, "I owe you big time, Henry."

By the time O'Brien and Henry landed in one of the smaller Nashville airports, the authorities uncovered the source of the confusion. The problem originated months earlier when national organizers of the high school competition made a serious blunder by booking the competition with the Dixie Line Country Club rather than the Nashville Country Club. Organizers then forwarded the faulty information and arrangement options to schools nationwide. Although Dixie was located in Nashville, a vibrant, diverse and well-respected southern city, its outmoded segregationist policy was a far cry from the respected Nashville Country Club, an organization that hosted conventions and activities from across the country. Few people challenged Dixie's archaic policies because the only people who dealt with them were their own kind. Another breakdown in communication was the country club secretary who booked the high school competition happened to be a young, unaware substitute secretary. Unfamiliar with the rules, she failed to impart the subtle information that Dixie only catered to *exclusive* patrons. O'Brien subsequently learned why Mr. Embree targeted Ava. Her loud scathing assessment of his bigotry drew his ire when she hurled the incendiary suggestion: "Citizens of Tennessee should sue you for defamation of character. You're a coward hiding behind a historical name that embodies character and courage."

As several locals laughed at Ava's cleaver reference to Elihu Embree, the southern, white, wealthy iron manufacturer and ardent abolitionist who lived in Jonesborough, Tennessee in 1819, the manager's face radiated wrath. His eyes full of rage glared at Ava as he stood aloof like an angry buzzard waiting for an opportune time to swoop down and peck out her tongue. When the police arrived, he had to settle for the extraneous pleasure of watching the authorities cart her away in a cruiser.

***

Henry waited in a rented car outside the police station while O'Brien bailed Ava out of jail. They hadn't fingerprinted her, so he assumed their goal simply was to remove her from the property, to scare her. As a police officer escorted Ava to where O'Brien waited, she spotted him and ran into his arms. Once certain she wasn't hurt, he moved quickly to get her out of the police station before they trumped up charges to file against her.

"These people make Henry Morgan look like Mother Teresa! Just get me out of here."

"Stay calm," he whispered. "We made arrangements for a parent chaperone to help Kate guide the students through the remainder of the competition. It's safer if you fly home with us tonight." Before she could protest, he cautioned, "Stay quiet until we're out of immediate danger of retaliation."

She looked at him dumbfounded. "The Constitution's on my side, Jim. They're the ones who should worry."

He pulled her arm harder than he meant to and led her to the door. In a low but emphatic voice, he said, "For once in your life, Ava, listen for a change!"

Directing her attention to who actually helped get her out of the mess she was in, he said, "Henry is waiting in the car. Be gracious, because if it were not for his generosity and friendship, you'd be bedding down in a jail cell until tomorrow evening with these backwoods boys' imaginations running wild."

"What makes you think I want to ride in a car with a bigot like Henry when I just got manhandled by a bunch of bigots? He makes jail seem like a better place to be."

He stopped short of the car and turned her around.

"At first I thought I was dealing with a Mohandas Gandhi; now you're acting like Angela Davis or whoever the hell the Sixties, radical, social activist that you're channeling at the moment." With a calmer voice, he said, "But I'm telling you, Ava, you can't sum up a human being based on one act, one joke, or one flaw. Henry is a good friend, and for some reason, he admires you and has gone out of his way to help you and me get out of this mess. If you can't respect him, at least show some gratitude when you get in that car."

Henry swung the door open to let Ava in. To O'Brien's dismay, she never said a word, not in the car, not when they stopped by the hotel to gather her belongings, not on the flight home, and not when Henry landed his plane at the New Castle Airport. It would take a couple of hours to get the plane ready for the flight back to the university, so O'Brien and Ava had some time to talk. The good news was by the time the story hit the national airwaves, the local officials in Nashville exercised political foresight and placed pressure on the managers of the Dixie Line Country Club to honor the legal agreement they forged with the schools across the country. Justice prevailed.

***

It was in the early morning hours, and Ava was finally home, sitting on her living room couch. Outward signs of false confidence and composure masked her deep seated anxiety. O'Brien attempted to be conciliatory.

"Is there anything I can do for you while Henry is refueling the plane?"

She shook her head and stared out the window. To give her time to collect herself, he contacted Jake to let him know that his sister was home and safe. He suggested that Jake visit in a couple of hours, maybe share an early breakfast with Ava around the time that he'd be leaving to go back to the university. Before he hung up, he told him, "This incident has potential to reach news frenzy, but if we handle it correctly, it will fizzle."

Jake agreed. "Tell her to make a simple statement and stay out of the limelight. She doesn't need to attract any attention from the lunatics out there."

O'Brien hung up and sat across from her and crossed his legs. He watched her sulk for several more minutes. She could feel his stare, and she was both frightened and angry. With frustration in his voice, he broke the silence. At first, he chose more professorial words, as though he were talking to a colleague at the university.

"What you did today was admirable. You have a right to be proud of yourself. I just want you to consider that in the future it would be beneficial to get an opinion or helpful suggestion from people who love you." He paused. "You could have called Jake or me. We would have

115

helped you with language and actions that could have averted your arrest and still provided you with the positive outcome that you desired." The inflection in O'Brien's voice rose at the end of the last statement as though he was asking a question. Relaxing his tone, he said, "The law may be on your side, babe, but you could have gotten chewed up by those boys. Jake and I believe that it's a good idea to make it short and sweet with the media when it starts calling, and it will call. You know how they turn everything into a three-ring circus."

She refused to look at him. He stared at the back of her head as she told him in a cold, robotic voice, "Fine. I don't want to cause you anymore embarrassment."

"Do you really believe my concern is embarrassment, Ava?"

Outside the police station he told her that his initial concern was for her safety, but her rude behavior toward Henry Morgan disappointed and angered him. Still, she had a defiant urge to turn around and yell, yes, you don't want to be embarrassed, but she didn't have the heart or stamina for another confrontation. She continued to stare out the window and seethed at his unrealistic expectation that she should have sought out and engaged in consultations with him and Jake in the midst of the confrontation.

He was direct with her again. "This event will blow over, honey. But while you fought for the rights of others, your mean spirited and ungrateful attitude toward a man who dropped everything on his rather busy plate the moment he knew we needed help is what concerns me right now. Hell, he had to make special late night arrangements at two airports hundreds of miles apart! Yeah! It bothers me to think that you believe it's alright to be so callous and disrespectful to my boss and friend."

Ava turned and glared at him. She had an intolerant smirk on her face when she asked, "Are you saying that after the bigots in Tennessee manhandled me and threw me in jail, you expected me to be gracious to your bigoted, philandering boss and friend who thinks it's funny to insult me and my ancestors at a party?"

He covered his face with his hands for a few seconds then looked at her again and said, "Why do you have such overt animosity toward Henry?"

"I just told you why. I'm sorry, but I can't help how I feel, Jim."

"You're right," he said, half pleading with her. "You can't help how you feel, but you can certainly help how you react. All I'm asking is that you don't trap yourself in baser places where it's easier to rely on emotions to criticize people mercilessly rather than rely on knowledge and compassion to at least see from where they're coming." He whispered, "You're better than that, Ava. That's why I love you."

She was fighting back tears. He wanted to move toward her, hold her, but her body language suggested that she was highly *explosive*. He backed off, kept his distance, and handled her with care.

He told her, "Stop and think why some people can't always do the right thing when you expect them to. You and Jake have a strong moral compass, Ava. You're more fortunate than most. Some people need more help than others; they lose their way more easily, and they don't have love surrounding them, urging them back on track."

Looking at him, she jabbed, "So now you're telling me that Henry is a bigot, and he cheats on his wife, and tells sexist jokes because he needs more understanding?"

Why is she so obstinate, toward Henry, he thought. O'Brien knew Henry to be a man deluged with personal problems but was a fair minded individual in meetings and negotiations with different factions, and he was generous to a fault with his time and money. Ava only knew him peripherally, and therefore to O'Brien's thinking, not at all, yet she openly held such disdain for him.

Among her many unique characteristics, O'Brien learned that Ava liked to view the world in literary and symbolic terms, so he tried one last time to make her see his point by summoning the help of her favorite works of literature. He uncrossed his legs and held his hands together as if he were about to engage in a do or die competition.

"Ava. Try to think of Henry as though he were a character in one of the novels you teach the kids, like Heathcliff in *Wuthering Heights*. Can you do that?"

Her back to him, she shrugged like a high school teenager held against her will, forced to endure remediation. Her juvenile behavior unnerved him, but he drove home his point.

"Remember a few months ago we were at that party where we discussed how people critique works of art, and someone said, 'Beauty and art are in the eye of the beholder?' You were the only one who balked at that philosophy. Your logic swayed most of us because it made sense. You said that people who critique art, especially literature, generally base their opinions on their limited knowledge of the author and the time period in which the work was written. You convinced us that most people criticize in ignorance. You even used the example that if a critic wanted to critique *Gulliver's Travels* in a valid and honest way, he would make an effort to know the history of Restoration England. They'd find that the Rope Dance and the Egg War in the story weren't just silly incidents, but well defined allegories that highlighted major problems in politics and religion that dominated England and the world."

Her refusal to make eye contact made it impossible for him to gauge if his words penetrated the barrier of her self-imposed isolation. Making an attempt to turn her around, he said, "Are you still with me, babe?"

Again, she shrugged.

Straining to hold his anger at bay, he asked, "When your students characterize Heathcliff, does anyone ever believe he's a nice guy? Hell no! We all know he's a disgusting villain, but you make it a point to teach them that when Heathcliff's story unfolds, when the reader sees all the abuse that the world heaps on him—he's an orphan on the streets; he's ostracized in youth; he loses the woman he loves to another man. While Heathcliff is a vile man whose actions cannot be condoned, the reader's knowledge of Heathcliff's past offers insight, and it allows a fair person with a good heart to offer at least some measure of sympathy for this wretched man."

His gentle consideration forced a groundswell of embarrassment that caused her to sink deeper into disappointment with herself. After decades of expecting my students to appeal to the better angels of their nature by adopting lessons from high-minded literature, here I sit, an adult failure forced into remediation! I'm guilty as charged on all counts, she thought.

Still, something deep-seated impeded her from turning around to look him in the eye and admit it. Her mind raced as she sat trapped, snagged on her self-pity, frightened at her inability to verbalize a simple heart-felt *I'm sorry*. She sat paralyzed in her silence, and her silence was driving him away.

Continuing to treat her more gently than she deserved, he asked, "Why can't you see that maybe I'm not defending a bigot and a philanderer? Maybe I know more of his story than you do, Ava. While some of what he does and says defies both our sensibilities, you might consider that when he's sitting alone in a room, he feels the same disgust for himself that he realizes others feel for him."

Mustering enough confidence to engage in a dialogue, she asked, "Do you think the more I know about Henry, the more I'll like him?"

Her tone told him she already rejected the idea.

"I'm suggesting that the more you know about Henry, or anyone else for that matter, the more valid your reason will be for liking or disliking that person." Tilting his head toward her, he added, "And maybe because you possess more intelligence and more sympathy than most people, you'll choose to offer at least some measure of dignity and respect for his position if not his character." He sat back in the chair, crossed his legs, and breathed in deep and exhaled slowly. "Ava, what you did today was good, but you can't go around fighting every injustice you encounter without knowing who you're dealing with. You have to give people room to back down, and you have to show gratitude to people who help you. You have a right to hold unwavering beliefs, but there's always value in listening to the other person's argument."

His authoritative voice chafed her. She was revving up to retaliate when his phone rang.

"The plane is ready for take-off anytime you are, Jim," Henry said.

"I'm leaving the house right now. Give me fifteen minutes."

O'Brien stood. He walked toward Ava and bent down to kiss her good-bye. She yearned for his touch, but a portentous force deep inside her took hold. She jerked her head away. Blinded by tears, she stared out the window. She didn't want him to be angry with her. She didn't want him to believe that she was thoughtless and contentious. Like a wounded child, she longed to wrap her arms around her father's neck, bury her face in his chest, and cry. She missed the way Eli held her and assured her that everything would be alright. They were the ones privy to her weaknesses and loved her regardless. Why did they have to die?

He was tired, frustrated, and angry. Disheartened by his failure to console her, he grabbed his coat and bolted out the door. Alone and consumed by silence, she let her tears pour onto her cheeks. Her blurred eyes followed his car moving down her driveway. She watched him turn and drive up the road until he was out of sight.

***

"Is Ava's frame of mind any better?" Henry asked on the flight home.

"She was out of line for being rude to you, Henry. I actually had to give her a lecture about gratitude."

Henry rolled his eyes. "Thanks. Now what kind of reception do you suppose I can look forward to?"

O'Brien rolled his eyes, and they both laughed. More serious, he said, "She was so unresponsive." He stared straight ahead. "If she doesn't apologize to both of us, neither of us will have to worry about how she receives us." Peering out the side window, he admitted, "Frankly, I don't have the stomach for this kind of drama." Still mystified by her behavior, he turned to Henry. "I don't know what happened."

Henry shook his head. "Things like this happen in every relationship. Realistically, you can't expect everyone to like everyone else." He let out a laugh. "Hell, people in my own family hate me. Give her some time to work it out. Maybe someday she'll be able to tolerate me as well as she tolerates some of her wayward seniors."

"I really appreciate your understanding, but we're not barnyard animals. What confuses me is that she's always sensitive to other people's situations and needs." Trying to convince himself more than Henry, he said, "She's a quality person, and she'll probably come around, but if she refuses to talk about this in some kind of intelligent way . . ." He stared out the window into the pitch black sky. With bewilderment in his voice, he complained, "For God's sake, she shrugged her shoulders like some damn hoodlum hanging out on a street corner after midnight." He looked at Henry. "I swear, the only things missing were chest hair, some brass knuckles, and a baseball bat under the driver's seat!"

Henry laughed. "What about a tattoo that says, 'SPEAK ENGLISH OR GO HOME!'" Checking his flight instruments, he said, "You have to admit, today was certainly extraordinary. Maybe the ordeal overwhelmed her. She has to be tired and scared. Frankly, I don't know too many people who could be as sane, sensitive, and resilient as Ava after losing a whole family in several seconds, so maybe she deserves some room for occasional obstinacy. Hell, that kind of tenacity is what keeps her alive!" He paused. "If she's as sensitive as you know her to be, right about now, she's probably feeling lousy about herself." He glanced over at O'Brien and laughed. "Take it from me, Jim; I've spent many an evening regretting bad behavior."

O'Brien nodded. He wished that Ava could hear Henry's reasonable, sympathetic defense of her.

After Henry landed the plane, they talked for several more minutes.

"I couldn't have pulled the rescue off without you, Henry."

Slapping O'Brien on the back, he said, "I don't mind telling you, you're the closet person I have to a brother. If you need anything, I'll be there. Don't worry about Ava. She's a good person, and she loves you."

***

When O'Brien walked into his kitchen, the answering machine burgeoning with concern from family and friends beeped for his attention. First he touched base with Jake.

"Vikki and I are on our way. She's cooking us breakfast." Laughing, Jake asked, "Is she only angry with you, or do I need to bring a 'taster' along?"

O'Brien let out one quick sarcastic laugh. "She was extraordinarily rude to my friend Henry, and I spent the rest of the early morning dodging flames that shot from her blazing eyes when I suggested she be more selective in her crusades against injustice."

Jake sucked in his breath. "Those were ill chosen words, Jim. Swaying my sister to limit her fight against injustice is as easy as convincing a boa not to squeeze too tight. It's in her nature; it's in *our* nature. We cut our teeth on stories that highlighted the fight for social justice. One of Ava's favorite stories is when my father's best friend contracted tuberculosis. Dad was the only friend who stood by his side. Back then, TB meant banishment to a sanitarium for months. People feared TB like they fear AIDS today. When Anthony came home, everyone shunned him. My parents were the only visitors to Anthony's house, and we were the only ones who welcomed his family to our home. This went on for weeks, until my father had enough. He dragged Anthony to the local pool hall. The guys kept their distance, until my father, engaged some histrionics."

Jake laughed and said, "Ava inherited the theatrics from him."

Telling the rest of the story, he said, "My father yelled, 'Hey, chicken shits! You see Anthony's cup of coffee?' He took a gulp from it! 'You see his mouth?' He grabbed Anthony's head and gave him a smack-a-roo right on his mouth. The guys started hootin' and hollerin' like nothing ever changed. They figured if Charley wasn't afraid of contracting TB, then they didn't have to be either." Laughing, Jake said, "My father wasn't stupid. He banked on the idea that sanitariums didn't release health risks. You may be right, but fighting injustice is in our DNA. Being rude isn't."

O'Brien admitted, "Maybe my own presumptuous attitude warrants an apology."

"No, let her apologize to you. Ava loves you, but she's stubborn. God knows! Even in high school, she'd scratch and claw her way to victory in

121

every argument." Jake laughed and said, "I'll never forget the night we were at a party where Ava argued with the captain of the football team. He was bragging about his full scholarship to the University of West Virginia. She argued that it was unfair to waste money on academically deficient athletes when smart students who proved they could achieve good grades deserved the help. That Monday at school, someone stuck a poem in her locker that made her see how some people perceived her."

"I'd like to get my hands on that profound piece of literature," O'Brien mused.

"Ha! You're in luck, doctor. It was a goofy poem that went something like this."

As Jake recited it, O'Brien jotted it down.

"This is brutal. What was her reaction?"

"At school, she acted like it didn't bother her, but home, she cried in her room. She never talked about it until Leila was having problems with friends. She used the incident to help her daughter understand that sometimes we need to consider the criticisms waged against us, even if the critic's intent is unkind. That's why I guarantee she already knows she's wrong for not being gracious to Dr. Morgan." Jake sighed with relief. "I'm just glad you were there. Give her time to mull it over."

"I'll take counsel's advice. When I left tonight, it wasn't good, so make sure she knows I love her."

"I'll relay your message, and you get some well deserved rest."

Rest was a figment he couldn't entertain at the moment. He called his brother Sean to start the chain phone calls to the other brothers just in case their local news stations picked up the story. He talked to his parents who were proud of Ava. He didn't want their quarrel to cause them undo anxiety, so he cut the conversation short. He pinned his hope on Jake's assessment of his sister. Just as Ava didn't want to live in a relationship where she knew the man she loved couldn't trust her, he didn't want to live in a relationship where the woman he loved was incapable of exercising understanding and compassion for the people in his life who mattered to him.

***

It was six o'clock in the morning when Jake and Vikki knocked on Ava's door. They caught the tail end of a conversation with a news affiliate who badgered her for a statement.

Taking O'Brien's advice, she made the statement short and sweet. "We are blessed to live in a country where the Constitution guarantees all citizens the freedom to live with dignity and respect. The vast majority of Americans abide by the rule of law."

With the phone in one hand, Ava waved her free hand to Jake and Vikki as they entered. She continued her statement. "When some Americans refuse to follow the law, there will always be patriots who remind them that freedom is for every American. Martin Luther King said it first, but my father always taught us, 'To fight injustice anywhere is to fight injustice everywhere.'"

Ava ended her statement and took her phone off the hook. She looked at Vikki and Jake and threw up her hands. "After all this mess, does anyone expect throngs to challenge the Dixie Line Country Club's policy in the future? This fiasco only happened because a substitute secretary didn't understand the bigoted policy!"

Jake said, "It's one more ugly reality. The Dixie is a haven for radical right wing conspirators who want to take their country back from anyone who they think lacks the purity that a true American patriot possesses."

Vikki agreed. "It doesn't occur to them that thousands of graves at Arlington National Cemetery and throughout the country are filled with patriots of all colors who fought and died for freedom." She hi-fived Ava and said, "But, I have to hand it to you, girl! You put them on notice."

Ava showed Jake a copy of the statement she released. She pointed to the 'justice' quote and said, "Daddy ingrained that idea in us."

He read it and nodded approval. He poured a cup of coffee and searched for homemade biscotti that Ava always stored in the freezer.

"Speaking of Daddy, I talked to Jim this morning. I told him the legend of Anthony. Now he has some history as to why we act the way we do."

As Ava scrambled eggs and made toast, she chided, "All of a sudden it's *we*? When did you ever get carted off to jail?" With mock epiphany, she stuck her face in Jake's face and needled, "Oh, I forgot. You're the guy that dresses up in that witch's black robe and *sends* people to jail!"

"You should thank me, Ava! But then I heard you're having a problem thanking people who go out of their way to help you." He shook his head. "Jim told me you shrugged like a stubborn adolescent when he tried to talk some sense into you." With a stern look, he said, "He's right, and you're wrong. He's not asking you to invite Henry Morgan's extended family to

Easter dinner. Just show some gratitude." Jake drank his coffee. "Since when does it defy your sensibilities to say 'thank you'? Jeez! The guy flew his private plane into hostile territory to rescue you. What the hell were you thinking?"

Jake's phone rang. He took the call in the living room. A minute later, he called out, "Vikki, help me reschedule this trip. I don't want any conflicts."

Vikki mimed strangling her husband. Smirking, she said, "Let me go help him."

As Jake's voice filtered to the kitchen, Ava thought of how much her mother and father loved him. After their mother had a miscarriage and then a stillborn baby girl, Jake was born. While they deemed him their miracle baby, he wasn't always the charming, witty, reasonable person his family came to know and love. He spent his formative years as an oppositional, defiant teenager whose sporadic bad behavior resulted in a dossier that would shake the faith of any God-fearing set of parents. He was handsome and towered at a formidable six feet and maybe another inch. His olive skin and dark brown eyes and hair made him an easy target for profilers at an airport. Ava silently laughed when she recalled how indignant airport officials yanked him out of line when he absentmindedly forgot to throw his keys on the conveyor belt. Raising his hands high over his head, he said, "I'm on your side; I'm a judge! Check my wallet." Although fearless, he admitted feeling queasy at airports after that run-in.

Jake's laughter triggered memories of his engaging personality and how he won over legions of voters simply by listening to their concerns. A respected former prosecutor with a brilliant legal mind, his aptitude for law guided him to take advantage of the G. I. Bill and earn a law degree. He passed the bar exam on the first try. There was always talk in political circles that any time he wanted to move up the political ladder, it was his for the asking, but he decided early in his career not to be a game player. He too was his father's child, and he, like Ava, had a difficult time looking the other way when faced with social injustice.

As he wrapped up his phone call, sadness welled in her. She fostered closeness with Jake only after her father died. He was the one who always told Ava what she needed to hear. Their mother died decades later, creating even a stronger bond between them. Two years after the accident, when both sides of the family continued to tiptoe around Ava's fragile emotions,

Jake was the one who sat her down and exhorted her to live and love again. He told her, "You can blame yourself until hell freezes over, but you know, Eli and the kids know, and the whole damn family knows that you loved them, and you would have died for them. There's no disloyalty in laughing and loving again." As though he were wrapping up a summation in court, he persuaded, "Loyalty and faithfulness benefit the living more than the dead. The best way to honor Eli and the kids is to live the life God has seen fit to loan you for a while longer, and love stronger and better."

She remembered his passion as he tried to convince her that the accident wasn't something she chose to happen. Jake's eyes blazed with conviction when he told her, "Stop feeling guilty because you're alive! The real crime is if you choose to waste the love you would have showered on Eli and the kids. Look around, hon; we all need and want your love."

Jake trailed Vikki back into the kitchen. Handing him a plate of cookies, she asked, "Is your problem solved?"

Vikki brushed her hands together. "Done!"

Still miffed at him for offering O'Brien a character analysis of her actions, Ava playfully reprimanded Jake. "Now help me solve my problem," she slapped his hand, "and don't eat all those biscotti. Take some home to the kids." Motioning to Vikki, she asked, "Can't you put that chubs of love on a diet? God forbid his stomach gets as big as his mouth!"

Jake defended himself with mock indignation. "Get real. I'm in better shape than your boyfriend, so stop trying to avoid the subject. Just call him and tell him you're sorry, and while you're on a roll, call his friend and apologize to him, too."

Jake took a drink from his coffee in one of Ava's embossed camel mugs and finished eating his eggs. Looking more somber, he said, "Nashville is actually a really nice place, but it's still the South. Some of those people are prepared to fight the Civil War forever." He shook his head. "Things could have turned ugly on a dime."

Ava began to understand better the range of negative consequences she escaped after she unleashed her unbridled reprimand on the country club manager. She already decided to call O'Brien and Henry, but growing more anxious, she thought, what magical words will wash away the guilt and embarrassment that gag me each time I attempt to verbalize an apology? What explanation could lend reason to my pigheaded rudeness? With a worried look, she said, "I'll call them as soon as you leave."

She stared at the floor and wondered how she let the incident get so out of hand. Tears stung her eyes. "I was so mean and so cold, Vikki. I knew he was right. I even wanted to tell him he was right, but there was something inside me that refused; I refused to budge even an inch." She turned to Jake. "It was like high school all over again."

Frustrated with herself, and still misty-eyed, she ran her hand through her hair and wondered aloud. "What's wrong with me? Now he thinks I'm a loud-mouthed, liberal crusader." Her eyes darted back to Jake. "Thanks to you, now he even has prior history of my unwillingness, or worse yet, my inability to see other people's point of view. Why would any sane man, especially in the sensitive position he's in, ever want to deal with an emotional mess like me again?"

Vikki wrapped her arms around Ava's neck. "Why are you so hard on yourself? You've been through a lot, and you're tired. Don't forget, you did triumph over the bigots!" Holding her steady, Vikki said, "Relax a while, then talk to him. He loves you." Vikki swung her eyes to Jake. "Tell her what he said about loving her."

He eyed his sister. "Right now you *are* too emotional. Cut the pessimism and listen. Remember when Mom gave Daddy the silent treatment for two weeks because he accused her of mismanaging the money? That wasn't Mom's fault. Mom managed money better than a Swiss bank. If Daddy would have apologized at any time in those two weeks, Mom would have hugged and kissed him. End of fight! If they would have extended that quiet war, it could have been damaging to them and to us." With a half grin, he tilted his head. "I'm no therapist, Ava, but I swear there are times you barricade yourself in a fortress. You shrink when you're afraid people won't love and respect you after you do what you believe is right, and it causes trouble." He let out a laugh. "You want people to like you even when you make waves." He pointed his index finger at her. "Don't ever get into politics. Half the people won't like you the moment you open your mouth, and the majority of your supporters won't go out on a limb for you either. We learned a long time ago when you do what's right, chances are you'll be walking that lonesome road all by yourself." With more compassion, he surmised, "It's in our nature to make waves, but we were raised on gratitude, too." He clasped his hands behind his head and leaned back on his chair. "You're stubborn like Daddy. Most of the time, that's a good thing, but Daddy pounded his chest the hardest when he felt most vulnerable. He always put up that tough exterior when we had financial problems." Jake shook his head somewhat bewildered. "Didn't he know that Mom loved him even when things went wrong?"

Ava looked at Jake sideways. "Maybe it's not stubbornness. We all have our own ways of coping with insecurity. It's easy to feel secure when you know your mate loves and respects you despite your flaws, but how many people do you know experience that kind of unconditional love in a marriage?"

Jake and Vikki both nodded.

Jake said, "Still, the sooner you call Jim, the better off you'll be. It benefits no one to extend this battle, least of all you." Jake shook his head and mused, "Vikki's right. This guy really loves you." He teased his sister. "Somehow you've managed to convince him that he's damn lucky to have you." More serious, he pointed at her and said, "I know you'll balk at what I say next, but there's something to consider. It's not far-fetched to imagine Jim in the governor's mansion. That would place *you* in the limelight."

"Whoa!" Ava raised her hand to stop Jake. "Can you picture me as a conservative candidate's wife? The poor guy wouldn't stand a chance!"

"I'm telling you. He loves you and accepts your flaws, and by flaws, I mean your mouth and unfettered social activism. Continue speaking your mind, but practice more tact. Whether he does become a candidate or not, it will serve you well." Jake stressed, "I'm being serious! He's influential, and that places *you* in a position to influence *him* and others in positive ways."

Vikki agreed with Jake. "Your gorgeous brother has a point, Ava. Influential people in Pennsylvania know him well, and they speak highly of him."

As Jake and Vikki stood to leave, he looked at his wife. "I almost forgot to tell her the best part." He turned to Ava. "The last thing Jim wanted me to make sure I told you was . . ." He scratched his head in thought. "Now what the heck did he want me to tell you?" He mocked O'Brien's anxiety over his possible loss of Ava's love. "'Make sure Ava knows I looove her.'"

His theatrics made Ava and Vikki laugh. Ava playfully shoved Jake and said, "Go . . . home . . . now!"

Waving goodbye, she sat at the dining room table, picked up the phone, and dialed O'Brien's number.

***

"Hell-o."

"I want to explain. . ." Her voice cracked.

"Avaaa. You're making this harder than it has to be. I accepted your apology the moment I heard your voice."

"Thank you. But I'm still afraid . . ." Her voice trailed off. No matter how hard she tried, she couldn't complete a sentence without battling tears.

"Just tell me what you're afraid of so we can deal with it," he coaxed.

"Now that you've seen an irrational side of me, I'm afraid that . . ." She choked up.

After a brief silence, he asked, "Do you remember what you told me the day you wrenched Vietnam out of me, when *I* was so afraid to lose *your* respect?"

"I remember," she said, straining to keep her voice steady.

"Let me read you a poem that someone who loves you brought to my attention. It actually captures your warrior instincts rather well." He cleared his throat and read with gentle tease:

> *Ava's a girl who never has doubts.*
> *She gets her point across with silence and shouts.*
> *She knows facts and figures, all the quotes and citations.*
> *She's never short on long explanations.*
> *She'll win every argument no matter which way.*
> *So what if she drives all her friends away?*

Her breath was long and deep. The poem brought back the high school memory when she first learned that periodic attitude adjustments could be beneficial. But here she was, decades later, in need of remediation for the same character flaw.

"Sometimes I wonder whose side Jake is on, but I guess I deserve that. Actually, maybe it will make Dr. Morgan feel better if you recite that poem to him, too."

O'Brien sighed with relief and said, "Jake is always on your side. So is Henry. I'll admit that I was madder than hell last night, but you should have heard Henry defend you on the flight back to the college. When you apologize, he'll be gracious." He added, "For the record, I don't think less of you. I think you're battle weary. The world smacked you around harder than most people get smacked around in a lifetime. It's difficult to be at your rational best when life tosses you around. Fight the world if you need to, but don't fight me. I'm on your side." He reminded her: "You're the lady who taught me to talk about our demons so we can deal with them."

"Is right now a good time to call Henry and apologize? I'll invite him and his wife to your house and cook them the best dinner they've had in a long time. Since I won't be in Tennessee, is this Friday a good time for you?"

"That's quite a gesture on your part. Are you sure you can tolerate a whole evening with him?"

"Jake explained in vivid terms what could have happened had Henry not flown you in to bail me out. I think I need more than words for this apology."

"Not really, but this weekend is fine. I'm high on the irony that this fiasco's dropping you in my arms for three days."

His excitement allayed her anxiety.

"Call me back after you talk to Henry." Before he hung up, he said, "Just so you know, even though Jake assured me you'd call, I wondered what I'd do with my life if you didn't."

"If it's any consolation, I wondered what I would do with my life if you decided not to answer."

CHAPTER SIXTEEN

FRIDAY evening Henry and Lucy Morgan arrived at O'Brien's house precisely at six o'clock. Ava synchronized the meal for seven. The evening unfolded as she orchestrated it. First she whet their appetites with the Middle Eastern cuisine that Henry requested— rolled grape-leaves, fresh Syrian bread to dip in the homemade yogurt, miniature spinach pies, and taboulch. She carried the main course, roasted Cornish hens, on a large platter that her arms seemed barely able to support. Although the presentation teased delectability, Henry, the first to slice into his hen, discovered quickly that the bird was partially raw. His eyes widened. With exaggerated force, he drove his fork into the bird, lifted it high over his head and yelled, "Taster! I demand a damn taster!"

Stunned by her husband's crass behavior, Lucy glared at him. "Put that bird down!" she said in commandant mode.

Henry smirked and plopped the bird back on his plate. By now, the others cut into their hens and inspected the rawness of their own birds.

In an apologetic voice, Ava said, "I can't understand why they didn't cook through." She placed her fork on the plate and looked up at O'Brien. "I don't know what happened."

"Maybe the temperature was too low," he offered.

Lucy admitted, "The same thing happened to me once. I crammed the hens too close together in the roasting pan. My guess is the heat wasn't able to circulate properly."

Henry chimed in, "Forget the damn chickens. They still have enough life in them to petition PETA for protection." With a glint in his eye, he studied Ava. "A more important question: Are you able to brew a pot of coffee that promises not to threaten my life with e coli?"

Hot with embarrassment, she said, "I'll make sure I get the coffee right, Henry."

She whisked the platter of semi-raw hens from the table and hurried into the kitchen. She slid the platter on the table and bolted toward the sink. After a deep breath, she told herself, you've lived through more embarrassing situations than this. Exhaling slowly, she reached for the coffee maker to fill it with water.

Following her into the kitchen, Lucy said, "Are you okay?"

Startled, Ava swung around to face her. "I'm so embarrassed. I felt my face turn into a first cousin to a strawberry out there!" She wrung her hands. "Henry must be starving." She glanced wide around the kitchen and then surveyed the contents of the refrigerator. "There has to be something else in this house that I can cook for him."

"You're joking! Those side dishes were enough to satisfy a tag team of sumo wrestlers." She shook her head and said, "Besides, they're out there talking business and sports, so I thought I'd help you carry the pie and coffee out to the dining room." She eyed Ava and mimicked Henry. "That is if you know how to brew a pot of coffee that won't threaten him with e coli."

Ava covered her mouth with her hands to stifle her laughter. "He was so hilarious. I can't believe he called for a taster." She shook her head. "My brother, Jake, always calls for a taster when he doesn't like the food or he believes someone is mad at him."

"Thank God you think he's funny," Lucy said. "I thought for sure we'd never see another invitation to this house after that Neanderthal display at the table." Admiring Ava's ability to rebound with ease from the minor fiasco, she asked, "How are you able to make adversity seem so much easier than it is?"

Ava glanced over her shoulder then turned back to look at Lucy. "Are you sure you're talking to the right person? The last thing I ever want to do is give the impression that life is easy."

"I'm so sorry. My phrasing was—"

"Gosh! Don't apologize. I know what you mean." Ava asked, "Did you ever read *Macbeth*?"

"Years ago. Why?"

"I like teaching that play because you learn *appearances are deceiving*." She placed the serving tray on the table and said, "I try to find joy in life, but I don't always succeed. I learned early after my family died that people have little capacity or willingness to be around someone who cries all day long."

Lucy said, "I know what you mean. It's as though they believe your bad luck will rub off on them."

"That's the impression I had, too," Ava said. "First my family and friends nudged me to 'get back to normal'; then some of them actually insisted that I get over my sadness. Some of my relatives even grew impatient and acted bothered by my inability to participate in life the way I used to before the accident." Still offended, she raised her eyebrows and said, "Well, they can wait until cannibals become vegetarians, because my life will never be normal again. I'm a different person than I was three years ago. Oh, I look the same. My voice sounds the same. I live in the same house. But like the Zen Buddhists say, 'Consider the river that flows from year to year. It may look like the same river and the same river bank with its rocks and wild flowers, but the water is different water, and the flowers are different flowers.' That's the way my life is. We're all like the river, Lucy." With a slight shrug and a sigh, she said, "I'm just fortunate to have several understanding people around me who don't feel threatened by my sadness and allow me to cry when I miss my family." A shy smile crossed her lips. "Sometimes Vikki, Jake, and my Aunt Halima cry with me."

Lucy's eyes moistened.

Ava raised her hands. "Great! First I ruined the main course. Now I made you cry. Are you okay?"

"I haven't been okay for years," Lucy said.

Ava looked at the pretty woman with natural blond hair and blue-eyes. Her statuesque height lent an element of elegance to her. She was intelligent, sensitive, and personable, yet her husband was dissatisfied and regularly sought the companionship of other women.

Ava wiped her hands on a towel, sat at the kitchen table and said, "God knows, you listened to me ramble about myself. I don't mind listening, if you think I can help."

Lucy sat across from Ava and said, "It's not all Henry's fault that he cheats on me. I'm afraid I haven't given him much reason to believe in our relationship anymore."

She disagreed with Lucy's assumption that it was up to her to keep her husband from engaging in extramarital affairs, but she kept her opinion to herself and listened.

"Few people know that Henry's father left his mother and him when he was two years old. His mother blamed Henry for his father's irresponsibility. Each time she found a different boyfriend, she pawned Henry off on a relative or neighbor. She didn't want the bum she was enamored with to leave because he didn't want the responsibility of a child." Lucy shook her head and said, "Henry was six years old when his mother left him with a neighbor and ran off with her last boyfriend." Her eyes moistened. "She chose a boyfriend over her little boy." She dabbed her eyes with a napkin. "How do you convince a man that he's good, intelligent, and worthy of genuine love when he only defines himself as the product of a deadbeat dad and an emotionally disturbed mother?"

"I guess one way is by doing what you've been doing all these years. Remain a constant in his life."

"It hasn't been easy," Lucy said, forcing a smile. "People believe he's searching for love, but he's really searching for control. He buys into his mother's assumption that it's his fault she left him behind. I'm at a point in my life where I want a wholesome, loving relationship, and I don't know what to do with him, because I want that relationship to be with him."

As Lucy revealed more of Henry's background, Ava felt deep remorse for her obtuse behavior when O'Brien tried to plead Henry's case the evening they returned from Tennessee.

Ava whispered, "Do you love him, Lucy?"

"I know I sound weak, but yes, he's the only man I've ever loved." She added, "Sometimes I wonder why he hasn't left *me*."

Until that night, Ava believed Lucy cowered to Henry. She witnessed a quiet strength emerge, and she admired her for it. She stood and waved her index finger in the air and said, "No, Lucy! After listening to you, I believe you're the *only* woman he loves. That guy is a frightened child in a grown man's body who needs to know you'll love him unconditionally." She checked the coffee and turned to face Lucy still sitting at the table. "The man in him knows he's wrong, but the abandoned boy keeps testing you in the worst way possible." Ava grabbed a bottle of water from the refrigerator and sat at the table. "Unfortunately, Henry will never get over his loss, but that can't be an excuse for his infidelity. Even though life is treacherous, we need to find wholesome ways to live with the pain." She looked down at the bottle of water as she massaged it with her fingertips.

"One of my secrets to emotional survival is to make good memories." She looked up. "Good memories are my stepping stones around the dark pit that can pull me under and swallow me up. The more good memories I have, the easier it is for me to dodge the darkness." She paused to reflect on her struggle to gain stability and peace after the accident. She touched Lucy's hand and said, "Invite him to make more good memories with you."

Lucy picked up a napkin from the floor. She turned to Ava and said with soft surprise, "I can't believe I let it go on this long. I should have made him choose the kind of life he wanted years ago, but I wanted the children to have their father."

Ava wiped spilled water on the counter and checked the coffee again. She turned and pointed at Lucy. "Your guy is capable of making correct choices, and he is *your* guy, Lucy! He chose to be a loving father. He chose to earn a doctorate. He chose to be a wise trustee." With slight embarrassment, Ava eyed Lucy and said, "You must be sick of me acting like I'm a know-it-all psychiatrist. Just shut me up!"

Lucy shook her head. "Goodness, Ava. I came here tonight not knowing what to expect after your run in with Henry. What I found . . . finally . . . is a sincere person who understands pain and is willing to listen to me instead of judge me."

Ava said, "I have one more thing to say if you can stand it."

"Please."

"Remind Henry one last time that you haven't let go of him in ten years, and you don't want to let go of him now. Be honest with him. Tell him that even though the years of infidelity hurt you, choosing not to work on a loving relationship from this point on will be his real crime." As she poured the coffee, she said, "Up until now, he's allowed the little boy in him to make the decisions about his love life." She looked up and smiled. "Maybe it's time that you insist the man in him makes a commitment to you. He owes you that; he owes himself that."

When Ava and Lucy carried the pie and coffee out to the dining room, Henry bellowed,

"What were you two yakking about in that kitchen? When I asked for coffee, I didn't expect you to book a flight to Colombia and back! Hell, Starbucks is only a quarter of a mile down the road!"

Ava set the coffee tray on the table. She refused to allow Henry to unnerve her. Bearing a disarming smile, she locked eyes with him and said,

"We were talking about love and commitment and how fortunate people are if they're able to find people who continue to love them even when they act like a-holes."

Henry's eyes grew large. He stared at Ava then shifted his eyes to O'Brien. Sporting a wide grin, he declared, "I win! You said they were probably talking about shoes and make-up."

"Stop being chauvinistic, Henry. I'm working overtime to counteract your boorish behavior. I want to be invited back."

"Hell, Lucy, Jim made that chauvinistic assertion. I'm just repeating what he said."

Laughing, Ava eyed Henry and asked, "Do you know that Chaucer wrote the whole *Canterbury Tales* with that premise?"

"So I have something in common with the genius Chaucer?" Henry asked with delight.

"I guess you do," Ava chuckled. "Chaucer says in his *Prologue*, I'm going to tell you some raunchy stories, but don't blame me if the sex, lies, and sinful behavior defy your sensibilities. Blame the pilgrims who tell the stories in the first place. They're the ones who are bawdy and ignorant. I'm just repeating word for word what they say, so you don't think *I'm* lying when I tell their stories to you."

Henry's eyes twinkled. "So according to Chaucer, I can tell any dirty joke I want and still be an upstanding citizen, as long as I'm accurately quoting some hog who tells the dirty joke before I do, right?"

Shaking his head, O'Brien said, "There you go, Henry. Who would've thought that our resident social activist would be the one to give you license to be as racist, sexist, and sacrilegious as your cold, callous heart tempts you to be."

"Thank you Ava and Chaucer. You just added a new dimension to Henry's crudeness," Lucy quipped.

"Come on, guys!" Looking at Ava, Henry said, "I'm just trying to get the hostess to insult me one more time tonight. Her apologies are indescribably delicious. Hell, this is the best meal I've eaten in months."

Henry's clowning entertained them, but Ava included some jabs of her own when she said, "Thanks for the compliment, but I believe you just insulted your wife's cooking."

Henry narrowed his eyes. "Hey, Jim, where's that muzzle you bought?"

O'Brien said, "Don't drag me into your sordid argument. I plan to nurture my tender relationship with the cook."

"Let's talk tender," Henry scoffed. "At least my wife knows enough to kill the damn animal before she serves it to people."

"If you don't stop bantering, I'm going to kill *you*," Lucy warned.

O'Brien leaned toward Ava, brushed her cheek with a soft kiss and said, "I personally believe my *Wal-Mart Special* handles herself in mealtime crises rather well." He smiled at her and lifted his coffee mug. "I'd like to toast the hostess. Borrowing the Roman poet Horace's words, 'A host is like a general; calamities often reveal his' . . . in this case, *her* . . . 'genius.'"

Henry nodded approval. He lifted his mug and declared, "Good save!" He turned to Ava. "You just witnessed one reason why we pay lover boy the big bucks."

As the evening drew to a close, Henry looked at O'Brien with the women standing next to him. He pointed at Ava and said in mock seriousness, "It's a good thing we bailed you out of that jail when we did. Those southern boys aren't as tolerant as I am."

Ava and Lucy both rolled their eyes.

With playful exaggeration, O'Brien grabbed Ava's arms and pressed them to her side to prevent her from retaliating. He cautioned, "Lucy! Hurry! I can't hold her back much longer. Now's your chance to get him out in one piece."

She winked at Ava then turned to Henry. "Let's go before I change my mind."

***

O'Brien helped Ava clear the table. He stopped her in the kitchen and held her close.

"This certainly turned out to be a memorable evening."

Her arms around his waist, she pulled back and asked, "Did you know about Henry's childhood?"

"Yeah," he said, with little interest to discuss it further. "If you don't need me down here, I'll be upstairs. No guarantee that I'll be awake. Will you be down here long?"

"I want to store this food. The rest can wait 'til morning."

As he turned to walk away, Ava grabbed his arm. "I'm sorry I let you drive away believing that I didn't care about you or what matters to you."

He pulled her close and ran his hands up and down her back. "It was a rough day for you, for all of us."

"That wasn't the reason." She backed away. "Jake said something about my father that made me realize shutting you out was wrong." She paused to cover some food with plastic as she struggled to make sense of her behavior that she wasn't even sure she fully grasped. She wiped drops of coffee on the counter and turned to look at him. "The truth is after all this time, I'm still afraid to rely on your shoulders and your chest, and . . ." Her voice cracked. He wanted to hold her, but she raised her hand to stop him. She blinked back tears. "The two men who loved me and sheltered me in their arms, even when I did and said some stupid things, died." Her eyes shifted away from him. "I'm afraid I'll lose . . ." Her voice trailed off.

"Come over here." She edged closer and allowed him to reel her in. He whispered, "Everyone dies. But until our last breath, we have a lot of control over how we live. We have power to love with gratitude, generosity, and hope." He massaged her back and reminded her, "Jake and Vikki are here for you; I'm here for you; some good friends, too." She laid her head on his chest and let him run his fingers through her hair. He teased, "No one is going to baby you like your daddy did, but I can come pretty damn close."

She let out a laugh. "My father did spoil me." She kissed his chest and raised her head to kiss his cheek. "I just wanted you to know that it was me, not you."

"Ava, from now on it's *us*."

***

Late Monday afternoon Ava intercepted a florist delivery truck that pulled into her driveway right before she did. The card accompanying the flowers read:

Ava,

Thank you for the wonderful evening. I insisted on a commitment. Henry was actually relieved. He admitted he's tired of hurting me and the kids. He's tired of hurting himself. We know there will be rough times ahead, but we're going to try.

With gratitude,
Lucy

CHAPTER SEVENTEEN

THE first Friday of June, the weekend of their one year anniversary, O'Brien called Ava at five o'clock in the evening with disappointing news.

"I know you expect me to be in New Castle, babe, but the trustees called a series of emergency meetings to take care of some personnel and athletic problems brewing. I need to be proactive here so that things don't get out of control."

"I don't mind driving to ET," she said.

"No. I have to work late tonight, and they even scheduled a marathon meeting for Saturday, so I won't be able to spend any time with you. The trip won't be worth it."

Although she made an attempt to mask her disappointment, he knew that it was her willingness to understand the tentative nature of his business that made their long-distance relationship work. They talked briefly, before he hurried off the phone. "There's a meeting at six with the coaches, so I better get going. I'll call you after the meeting to say goodnight."

"I'm counting on hearing your voice before I close my eyes tonight and dream of you."

"Save the drama, Ava. Talk to you soon."

***

After she dined on a frozen dinner, she called Vikki to make plans for breakfast and a shopping spree Saturday morning. The phone rang several times before Vikki answered.

"What's your Saturday schedule look like?"

"Gee, I'm sorry. I have a hair appointment in the morning, and then I read to the kids at the library in the early afternoon. I thought Jim's supposed to be here this weekend."

"He canceled because of university meetings." Ava mused, "Did I tell you he asked me to move in with him a couple of months ago?"

"Oh my God! What'd you tell him?"

"What do you mean, what did I tell him? I said, no. I'm not some piece of 'rent-to-own' furniture a guy brings into his home to see if he likes it before he buys it." Sighing, she said, "But on weekends like this, living with him seems much more appealing."

Vikki laughed. "Stick to your guns, girl! Hold out for the Hope Diamond, kiddo!"

"The Hope Diamond? What would I do with the Hope Diamond? All I want is Jim or you, and I'm not getting either this weekend." With resignation, she said, "Call me when you're free."

She poured a glass of ice tea and sat on the front porch. Ripples in the pond danced in the sunlight just before dusk. Ducks glided on the surface moving in formation ready to take flight. Restless and eager to engage in some activity that would deflect disappointment, she grabbed her purse and headed for the local plaza to scout out plants she wanted to grow in her garden. Before she had a chance to slip into the driver's seat, the phone rang.

Agitated by the inconvenient timing, she expected to hear the same nagging voice laden with the heavy foreign accent that had pestered her for weeks. The scammers insisted that her computer had every virus known to the technological world. They claimed the only way to rid herself of the scourge was to give them her password so they could prevent the viruses from contaminating all of cyberspace. Filled with indignation, she told them her password was "GET A JOB!" The scammers insisted she lend seriousness to the problem, or she would give them no other option but to block her computer. With as much sarcasm as she could muster, she suggested, "While you're blocking my computer, do me a favor and block my phone calls, too."

"Hell-o!" she barked.

"Hello, Ava. How are you?"

Sighing with relief, she said, "I'm fine, *Aboona* (Father). What a pleasant surprise!"

"Do you have time right now to come to the church and proofread a letter that I need to send to the bishop? I want it to be flawless."

Chuckling, she said, "Well, if you want it to be flawless, Aboona, why are you calling me?"

"My sweet Ava. You always make me laugh. I always call you because you say what I want to say better than I can say it myself."

Rotating her head until she was dizzy, she said, "I don't even know what you just said, Aboona, but God must find you in good stead. I'm getting in my car right now to buy some plants at the plaza, but I'll swing by the church first, okay?"

"I'll be waiting."

As she drove toward the Maronite Church, a flood of memories washed over her: the Sunday school classes where sweet Sister Alvera impressed upon the children, "Always pray to the Blessed Mother. If Jesus won't let you in the front door to heaven, Mary will sneak you through the side window. Jesus will never say no to his mother."

The Maronite Church was where she first encountered a life-sized crucifix. She remembered how one of the more severe nuns reprimanded her for defacing some characters in her brand new catechism book. When she ran home crying, her father intercepted her. He lifted her onto his lap and asked in Arabic, "Why are you crying *habibi* (sweetheart)?" She handed him her catechism and then wrapped her arms tight around his neck and buried her face in his chest. Her father perused the damaged book, and he noticed immediately that Ava only scratched out the Roman soldiers, Herod, and Pontius Pilate. He smiled to himself and patted her on the back to comfort her. Quick to discern the obvious answer, he pointed to a few of the book's culprits and asked anyway. "Why did you only scratch out these people, Ava?"

With child-like simplicity she answered, "They hurt Jesus."

Looking back, Ava didn't know that as her father held her close, he beamed with pride and silently prayed for blessings on his spirited child.

She was acutely aware of how her church was so intricately tied to her, that any milestone or event that was foundational to her character was invariably connected in some way to this special, holy place.

Aboona was sitting on a marble bench when Ava pulled into his driveway. He stood and greeted her European style: first a kiss on one cheek and then the other. They walked into the rectory where he told her to go ahead, that he would meet her in the church. Ava thought it was odd to proofread a letter in the church when the priest's office would be more comfortable than a pew, but she honored his request. She walked through the short hallway leading to the sanctuary. She genuflected in front of the Blessed Sacrament and sat in the front pew to wait.

A person kneeling off to the side of the altar in front of a statue of the Virgin Mary caught her off guard. His head was bowed and his eyes were closed. Ava's heart began to flutter.

She tiptoed toward him, but he was in a contemplative state. Standing behind him, leaning close over his shoulder, she whispered, "I don't know if Mary answers prayers for conservatives who fabricate elaborate stories."

He bent his head backward as far as it would go and laughed. Without turning around, he lifted his arm and reached over his head to grab her by the back of her neck. Pulling her around and kissing her, he said, "You're here, aren't you?"

Elated that he was with her, but confused by his phone call, she asked, "What happened to all those meetings?"

He stood and walked with her to the front pew and sat. He admitted, "All lies, Ava! And you know what I learned? Never underestimate Jake and Vikki Coury." Laughing, he said, "It only took them three minutes after I told them what I wanted to do to devise this plan." O'Brien shook his head. "If I ever run for office, I want that dynamic duo to organize my campaign."

"Please tell me that you weren't with Vikki when I called her a little while ago."

An impish grin crossed his face. "That 'rent a wife to buy' proposition sounds pretty tantalizing."

Ava smacked him lightly on the head. "Be mindful of where you are!"

He shook his head and laughed. She gave him a *teacher stare*, the kind that stops unruly students dead in their tracks. More serious and still puzzled, she asked, "So what's this covert operation all about?"

Caressing her hand, he said, "I'm relieved to hear that you don't want the Hope Diamond, but I hope you want the O'Brien diamond that's resting on the altar."

Ava pulled back. Her eyes grew large. She felt the sensation of her pounding heart rushing blood though her veins. Of the proposal scenarios she imagined, she never dreamed he'd propose in a church. She was keenly aware of how his war experiences left him struggling with religion. In mild shock, she gingerly climbed the three steps to the altar. Her eyes locked on a white gold ring from which even soft, dim candlelight extracted a bright sparkle. Three semi-circular diamonds hugged the large center stone. The symbolism of the three satellite diamonds wasn't lost on her, and immediately her heart overflowed with love for him. Standing high on the altar, she gazed down at him, the one who made her once shattered heart dance in her chest. She picked up the ring and stepped down. He stood and allowed her to open his hand and place the ring on his palm. She gently folded his fingers around it and said, "I don't want to put this on, Jim."

Puzzled by her refusal, he stepped back and stared at her. She held his face with both hands. "No. I mean I want *you* to put this beautiful ring on my finger."

His chest filled with air, and a sigh of relief flowed from him. He slipped the ring on her finger and placed her hand on his chest and held it there.

"Do you feel that? It took me ten years to find someone who could make my heart pound like that." Holding her hands, he said, "I vow in front of all that is holy: I will always love you and protect you the best way I know how." He reminded Ava of her reaction at Easter dinner when her Aunt Halima editorialized about the spiritual deprivation of young people who sleep together without the benefit of God's blessings in matrimony. "You were so uncharacteristically quiet on the subject. I never want you to feel guilty or ashamed about our love."

Her eyes moistened. "I just want to do what's right."

"I know that about you. I'm well aware that you don't possess a flea-market faith. That's why I chose to stand *here*, in front of all the angels and saints, in front of God, to tell you that I love only you. I want to share my life with you."

CHAPTER EIGHTEEN

WHEN the Coury family learned of Ava's engagement, the extended family breathed one collective sigh of relief. Few people in New Castle were unaware of the emotional devastation that ripped apart her life. More than one person wondered if she could survive the impact of such inestimable loss that cast her into those haunted days, weeks, and months of darkness. When rumors of her engagement rippled through the small city, friends received the news like a much needed rainfall on once fertile soil that lay parched and barren for too long.

The O'Brien side received news of his engagement with much the same ardor. His family admired his material success, but they wanted him to know the joy that money could never buy. He was an attentive, loving son, a caring uncle who would often serve as buffer between warring parent and child, and a respected university president who made his school a haven for other people's children as they passed through year after year. Now they delighted in watching Ava bring to his life the kind of love that completes a person, heals the soul, and makes the spirit soar.

The only person who suggested that O'Brien might benefit with less emotion and more logic was his lawyer Zack Carter. During a racket-ball game with O'Brien in the university gym, Zach inquired, "I know you and Ava love each other now, but I've been a part of some nasty divorces. Did you consider the financial repercussions if the marriage fails?"

O'Brien slammed the ball into the wall. "I'm not in the habit of betting against myself, Zach. Are you suggesting a prenup?" Wiping his brow, he asked, "How much is it worth to marry me?"

"Come on, Jim. Look at the guys who get swindled out of millions." He knelt on one knee to tie his shoe. "One day they're as happy as horny teenagers; the next day they're in divorce court with a short leash pulled tight around their necks." The lawyer looked up with a wry grin. "I swear some of these women had prior experience working in a neutering facility. When they get their hands on an alpha dog," he picked up the racquetball and squeezed it, "they know just how to fix him." He shrugged. "I strongly advise you to protect your assets."

Throwing up his hands, O'Brien said, "This game's over!"

Before disappearing into the locker room, he stopped cold. He turned to Zach and said, "I know you're only doing your job. Ava will be here tonight. I'll talk to her and see if we can meet sometime tomorrow afternoon. How's one sound?"

"Good. I'll put a standard agreement together; modify it any way you want."

O'Brien nodded.

As he showered, he grimaced at the thought. How do I convince her that a prenuptial isn't an attack on her veracity? What's it say about me when I resort to a legal document to protect my assets from a woman who I claim I trust?

***

Ava was waiting for him at the house. They planned to have a late dinner with Lucy and Henry. If there was going to be a prenuptial agreement, it would be good to take care of the particulars that weekend, because the wedding was only a month away. He didn't know how Ava would react to the idea, because, oddly, neither of them ever discussed money in any serious way. O'Brien felt certain that *Ava* and *gold-digger* were contradictory terms, but Zach Carter's extensive experience with finances and divorces suggested otherwise.

He entered the kitchen just as she was retrieving a bag of popcorn from the microwave. She wrapped her arms around his neck and kissed him. Running her fingers through his hair, she asked, "What time do we meet Lucy and Henry?"

"Seven."

She eyed him, because he looked like he wanted to say more, but he didn't.

"Anything else I should know?"

He shook his head.

He wanted to have a nice evening with the Morgans, so he decided to delay the prenuptial discussion that threatened to make her angry or sad.

"My lawyer wants us to meet. I'll tell you about it when we get home."

Ava nodded. She munched on popcorn and said, "I'm looking forward to being with Lucy and Henry tonight. I miss them."

"I enjoy being with them, too." He took a bite of his apple. "I have to admit; early on, I was worried you and Henry would never be able to tolerate each other."

Ava rolled her eyes. "Henry reminds me of Ebenezer Scrooge post Christmas Day. He's changed so much. Lucy says that he really works hard to make their relationship strong."

O'Brien pointed his apple at her and asked, "Did you know that Henry credits you in large part for the breakthrough in his marriage?"

She sashayed around the kitchen until she landed in his arms.

"I guess Muhammad Ali and I have something in common. We both—"

"Yeah. You both dance around a lot, and you both can't stop talking."

She pulled back and pretended to be hurt. "I was thinking more along the line of us both being the greatest!"

He perused her from head to foot, winked and said, "Don't forget you're both *pretty*, too."

***

O'Brien was in a garrulous mood. His stories prompted Lucy, Henry, and Ava to laugh so hard that Henry doubled over several times during the meal. At one point, O'Brien lifted his wine glass, took a drink and declared, "If you want entertainment, Henry, you need to experience one of Ava's family gatherings. I'm telling you, my family is wild, but I never saw or heard anything like her brother Jake holding his head in his hands during Easter dinner with a look of wonderment on his face as his wife Vikki asked him with the whole family listening: 'Would you take half my pension if we got divorced?'

"Jake stared at her and asked, 'Why would I want your pension? Your shoes are worth more than your damn pension.' Vikki pressed the issue."

"Why was Vikki concerned about Jake taking half her pension in the first place?" Henry asked.

O'Brien explained, "One of Vikki's friends went through a divorce, and the judge gave the husband half the woman's pension even though it was the husband's fault that they dissolved the marriage." O'Brien laughed and imitated Vikki badgering Jake: "'No seriously, honey.' She calls Jake *honey* while she tortures him with this inane line of questioning. 'Would you take half my pension?' Jake said, 'Vikki, why are we discussing something that will never happen?' Then with this look of futility, Jake palms his hand on his head really hard and tries to show her how absurd she's being: 'If we fly to Venus, Victoria, do you want a one car garage or two?' She tells him to be serious, and he tells her, 'If you want to be serious, let's talk about something that has a possibility of happening, like the Pope being gay or something.'"

Henry, Lucy, and Ava laughed at O'Brien's voice inflections and facial expressions.

"By now all the cousins' kids are yelling, 'Uncle Jake and Aunt Vikki are getting a divorce *again*.' Another aunt says, 'I didn't know the Pope was gay.'" O'Brien paused to drink some wine. He shook his head. "Most kids would be frightened at the prospect of hearing this kind of divorce talk, but these kids know the drill. It's entertainment for them. These are stories they hand down for generations. Then the whole family gathers round and starts to take sides. Meanwhile Charley, Jake's son, tries to take the last piece of cheesecake, and Vikki yells at him saying, 'Charley! I'll break your arm if you touch your father's cheesecake!'

"Charley looks dumbfounded and says, 'Mom, why do you want to give Dad the last piece of cheesecake if he's taking half your pension? Think about it! With half your pension, He can buy all the cheesecake he wants!' That's when Jake yells in complete frustration motioning to Charley to get the hell out of the room. He turns to Vikki: 'See what you do? Now I have to discipline him for being disrespectful.' Then he acts like he had an epiphany and says, 'I'll tell you what. I'll let you keep your damn pension if you take full custody of the kids, too!'"

Henry couldn't contain himself. When their laughter subsided, O'Brien took another drink of wine, looked at Ava with admiration and said, "I never witnessed a family banter so often, so loud, that loved each other so much." He looked at Henry and said, "Geez, the first time I met Jake, he told me that if I hurt his sister, they'd find Jimmy Hoffa before they'd find me. And this guy's a judge!"

Henry's shoulders shook with laughter. Lucy said, "I can't remember the last time we laughed that hard. You could've been a comedian."

When Ava and Lucy excused themselves to go to the restroom, O'Brien noticed a frightened and lost look wash over Henry in a matter of seconds.

"What's wrong with you?"

Henry looked up. "There's no easy way to put this, Jim, but we want you to know. Lucy has breast cancer. She's probably telling Ava about it right now."

O'Brien pulled back. "I'm so sorry. I never would've been so silly."

"No. We needed to laugh tonight."

"Is there anything Ava and I can do to help?"

Henry picked up his drink and said with sarcasm, "Know any miracle workers?" He waved his hand. "I'm sorry. I don't mean to be flippant. It's just that I can't believe we're finally experiencing some friendship and love, and this . . ." His voice cracked. He picked up his glass and drank some more wine.

"What's the prognosis?"

"The doctor wants her to check into the hospital for surgery this week. Lucy doesn't know what the hell to do because I said she needs to get another opinion before she lets them carve her up."

O'Brien winced. "Please tell me you chose kinder words."

Henry ignored the comment. "What I'd really like to do is contact that breast cancer specialist from the University Medical Center in Minneapolis, but I remember insulting him two years ago at a fundraising dinner. Can you believe that I told a damn racial joke, and this cancer specialist is bi-racial.?"

"You're different than you were two years ago," O'Brien reminded him.

"Anyway, he's on vacation. So we're back to square one."

Henry took another drink as Ava and Lucy sat back down at the table. O'Brien could tell from the look on Ava's face that Lucy shared the news. Henry quipped, "Start lighting those votives, sweetheart."

"I will light candles, Henry, but I was telling Lucy not to rush into surgery before getting a second opinion."

"I agree, but the specialist we want is on vacation."

She looked at Lucy. "I'd contact Dr. Ron Belle, from Minnesota before going anywhere else."

O'Brien and Henry looked at each other then turned to Ava.

"Why are you looking at me like that? Belle is the most knowledgeable breast cancer doctor in the country."

O'Brien informed Ava, "He's the one on vacation. Henry met the guy two years ago and insulted him with a racial joke. He's worried that Dr. Belle might remember the joke."

"You two educated men actually believe a man of Ronnie Belle's caliber would let a woman suffer because her husband told a joke he didn't like?"

He patted her hand. "You're talking about the man like he lives next door, hon. What's this *Ronnie* bit?"

Moving her eyes from one to the other, she said, "My high school managed to produce some world class personalities over the years. Dr. Ron Belle is one of them. He and Jake were on the same football team. They're good friends." Then somewhat defensive, she added, "Maybe I get a little enthusiastic at times, but I'm not a *Mighty Mouse* yelling, 'Here I come to save the day!'" She turned to Lucy. "If you want Ron Belle's opinion, we can contact him right now."

Flabbergasted, Lucy looked at Henry and back at Ava.

O'Brien sounded dubious. "Do you know him well enough to contact him eight o'clock on a Friday evening while he's on vacation? High school was a long time ago, babe."

She shifted her gaze to O'Brien. With a hint of arrogance, she said, "I know his whole family. We all grew up together. And thanks for reminding me that I'm old."

Henry let out a sarcastic laugh. He held Lucy's hand and said, "Who would've thought that we'd be trying to locate the doctor who can ensure that we grow even older?"

Turning to Lucy, Ava said, "I'll talk to his sister first. She'll tell me the best way to reach him."

Henry's eyes mirrored his pleading voice. "Sweetheart. Work this magic, and I'll be your slave forever."

A broad smile claimed her face as she said, "I'm against slavery, Henry, but there are times when I still feel guilty about the first time I met you. Before I get hooked into cooking you another apology dinner, let me just tell you right now that I'm sorry for every mean thing I've ever said to you and about you." She rummaged through her purse to find her phone and dialed Jake's number.

"Where are you, Ava?" Vikki asked, delighted to hear from her.

"We're having dinner with Lucy and Henry Morgan. Do you by any chance have a phone book handy to look up Sarah Mahoney's number?"

It only took a minute for Vikki to locate the number and pass it on to

Ava. She dialed Sarah's number, and Sarah answered on the third ring.

"Ava! What a surprise. How are you, honey?"

"I'm fine, Sarah, but I have a friend who really needs Ron's help. I'd feel a lot better if he rendered a second opinion."

"Call him, Ava. I'm sure he'll do what he can for you. He asks about you all the time."

"I feel funny calling him and putting him on the spot. The university said that he's on vacation. Would you give him my number and email address? He'll be able to contact me at his convenience. I don't want to interrupt his dinner. Your brilliant brother probably gets hounded constantly."

Sarah laughed. "Okay. Give me your number, and keep your phone on. He'll probably call you as soon as I hang up."

"You don't know how much this means to me, Sarah. This literally can be a life saver."

"After everything you've been through, honey, we'll help you in any way we can."

Ava's eyes moistened. "Thank you. Tell David and the kids I said hi."

She pressed the corners of her eyes with a napkin and said, "Now we wait."

As they discussed the incredible circumstances of Ava and Dr. Belle growing up in the same neighborhood, Ava's phone rang.

"Ron Belle! Please tell me that I'm not ruining your evening."

"Hey, Ava. You can never ruin anyone's evening. Sarah said your friend needs a second opinion?"

"She does. The doctors want her to have surgery this week, but her husband wants a second opinion from the best surgeon in the country. Two years ago he told a racial joke at a fundraiser; pretend you don't remember."

Henry palmed his face with his right hand, and O'Brien winced. He whispered, "Stick . . . to . . . the . . . point!" He couldn't understand why Ava had to be so incurably honest in every discussion. Still, they were relieved to hear Dr. Belle laugh.

"I don't remember, but he won't be the first or last to insult me."

"Do you want to talk to Lucy Morgan right now? I'm sitting with her and her husband who's really a wonderful man," she said, winking at Henry.

Dr. Belle paused. "You know, that's a good idea. I can tell her the necessary material to gather. Then she and her husband can fly out here, and I can examine her. I'll be back to work in a week. If she wants me to do the surgery, I'll be able to fit her in. It will give her more time to think about her options. I promise to take good care of her for you, Ava."

She handed the phone to Lucy. After Lucy and Dr. Belle talked for several minutes, they scheduled an appointment for the following Monday in Minneapolis. With tears in her eyes, Lucy handed the phone to Ava.

"What just happened? I can't believe you made that happen for me!"

Ava smiled. "No, Lucy. It's for all of us. We need you in our lives."

As they prepared to leave the restaurant, Henry walked up to Ava and planted a soft kiss on her cheek. His eyes moistened. He whispered, "This is the second time you've given me back the only woman who ever loved me." He shook his head and looked lost. "I wasted so much time screwing around when I should have loved . . ."

Ava raised her thumb to the corner of his eye to catch a single tear before it rolled to his cheek. Consoling him, she said, "Henry, listen. Lucy will have the best doctor this world has to offer, and she'll be in one of the best hospitals in the world. After I light my candles, even the angels and saints will join you at her side. Hopefully she will be well again, and you'll have the time to love her well again."

CHAPTER NINETEEN

BACK at the house, O'Brien lagged behind in the garage. Ava kicked off her shoes and dropped onto the couch to wait for him. He was more shaken by Lucy's illness than she was, and the welfare of his finances seemed trivial compared to Henry and Lucy's ordeal. It was late, and he wanted to avoid broaching the topic. He slipped into the den and sat on the far end of the couch. He lifted her feet onto his lap and massaged them.

"That feels good," she whispered.

Staring at her feet, he said, "What a night! I never saw Henry so scared." He raised his head and made eye contact with Ava. "What you did tonight was remarkable. How phenomenal is it to grow up with the leading cancer surgeon in the country?"

"It's nice to be able to have connections that can help save a life," she said, with an air of detachment.

Silence thickened as she lay on the couch for several more minutes while he rubbed her feet.

"What time's our appointment tomorrow?"

Her question sent a slight shiver up his spine. It gave him little choice but to discuss the prenuptial agreement. He glanced at her and said, "One. After tonight, what he wants to talk about seems unimportant. I'll cancel in the morning."

"If your lawyer believes it's something we should take care of before the wedding, then this is as good a time as any to take care of it."

"Trust me, Ava; you won't like how my lawyer thinks."

She lay silent for a few seconds staring at him. He continued to massage her legs and feet as he braced himself for her reaction. She pulled her feet away from his lap, sat up straight, and tucked her feet underneath her. She had an uncanny ability to analyze and dissect complex issues quickly.

"Let me guess." Her eyes narrowed as she cut to the chase. "Did your lawyer suggest that we work out a prenuptial agreement to protect your money from a possible gold-digger?"

With equal candor, he said, "I told you that after tonight, it's trivial to me."

"Really? Aren't you even curious about what my opinion is?"

"Ava, forget I brought it up, okay?"

"No, no! You're worried about your money."

She straightened her legs and lay back down and began to tickle his side with her toes, but he was still more serious than she wanted him to be. With her head propped up by a pillow, she stopped teasing and stared at him from across the couch. "You know there's something inherently wrong with prenuptial agreements, don't you?"

Focusing on her feet, he nodded.

"Still, they're one of those ugly realistic parts of life. It's the same reason why early in our relationship I had major doubts about your ability to be faithful to me." She sat up. "Let's face it; with a fifty percent divorce rate in a culture that confuses sex with love, how does an intelligent person assume that he or she will defy the odds? I admit that it makes me feel bad that your trust in me takes a back seat to securing your wealth, but I can understand why you'd want to protect what you worked hard for all your life."

He looked at her and said, "I want to share everything I have with you."

She nodded. "You're always more than generous, Jim." She lay back down and stretched her legs across the couch and began to tickle his side with her toes again. He grabbed her feet and smiled.

With an air of caution, she said, "Still, the only thing that I can lose that matters to me is your love. You, on the other hand, stand to lose love and a substantial amount of your fortune."

He released her feet and pulled her across the couch. She laid her head on his shoulder as he massaged her back.

"Did I ever tell you about a recurring dream I had before I met you?" he asked.

"Only your war nightmare."

He hugged her tighter. "This one was different. A beautiful, dark-haired, tantalizing woman lay next to me."

"No kidding! We have something in common because I like teasing you, too."

"Tell me about it," he said, with sarcasm. "Anyway, each time I tried to get romantic with her, she put her hand on my chest, like this, and she pushed me away. She told me that she didn't do recreational sex; she only made love." He kissed Ava's forehead. "I don't have the dream anymore."

Caressing his cheek, she mused, "What do you think it means?"

"Do you remember telling me that men put you in a cab and sent you home because you weren't into casual sex?"

She pulled back. Still embarrassed that she was so open with her feelings so soon after meeting him, she defended herself. "You do know that I was exaggerating a little?"

He drew her back into his arms. "You exaggerate a lot!" Kissing the top of her head, he said, "That night in San Diego, the first time we made love, it was the last time I had that dream. She didn't push me away. She trusted me." He held her face and planted a lingering kiss on her lips. "*You* trusted me, Ava, because I made a commitment to you."

Ava stared at him and said, "Look. I believe that pre-nups are ugly, but if it will make you feel better, then I'm okay with it. The only thing that I ever want from you is for you to love me and be faithful to me." She smiled and said, "Where's your crazy brother Sean when you need him?"

"What's Sean have to do with this?"

"I need him to harmonize 'Heart of Gold' with me."

She bent her head down and kissed him on his chest. She looked up and said, "I don't want your gold, Jim. I want your heart of gold. When I lost Eli, all I longed for was a heart of gold." She patted his chest. "I found one, right here." She kissed his chest again and rested her head on his shoulder. "So write that in the pre-nup. Whatever the agreement says, I'll sign it. I don't even plan to read it." She started to sing "Heart of Gold" to him.

Slightly louder than her rendition, he asked, "Why wouldn't you read a legal document before you sign it? What if I diabolically decide to take half *your* pension?"

She stopped singing. "Then I'll get an annulment and join a nunnery. Better yet, I can just get a job!"

All the talk of money and greed reminded her of the time when she was a high school senior applying for a college scholarship. "My father died five months before I graduated from high school, and my family was strapped for money. A local foundation was willing to allocate up to fifteen hundred dollars for my college education. The head of the scholarship committee required me to calculate what I needed for my first semester of college and come back the next day with a figure. I returned and requested only nine hundred dollars. When Jake found out that I didn't ask for the full scholarship, he grew angry and indignant." She chuckled. "To this day, if you bring up the topic of the college scholarship, he'll curse me and swear that someone had to perform a botched lobotomy on me for the way I reasoned."

"What made you request only nine hundred dollars? You knew your family needed the money. Hell, you even harassed that football player for getting the scholarship that you believed people like you deserved."

She shrugged. "I didn't want to be greedy." She looked at O'Brien and with slight irritation said, "And frankly, I'm still mad at Jake for opening his mouth about my high school days. Goodness! Can't a person ever grow up?"

He pecked her on the cheek and assured her. "We never stop growing up." He planted another hard, quick kiss on her head and said, "Let's get some rest."

Before she let him stand, she asked, "Just for the record, this dark-haired lady in your dreams, does she make love better than I do?"

Lifting her off the couch, he held her shoulders and turned her around so that she faced the stairs. "Why don't you go up those stairs and look in the mirror and ask her, Ava?"

***

O'Brien was awake earlier than usual. He exercised, showered, and cooked a light breakfast for both of them. As she stirred sugar in her tea, she asked, "Will we have time to stop at the library on the way home? I need to research for a magazine submission."

"Sure." On his way to the refrigerator, he gently whacked her on the rear. "It's nice to have you here this weekend. It will be even nicer to have you here every day of the week."

She stood at the end of the counter and laughed. "I don't know, Dr. O'Brien. After today, I might be too expensive for you."

"You think so?" he asked, pouring a cup of coffee. Teasing her, he broke out into a parody of John F. Kennedy's inaugural address: "I '. . .

shall pay any price, bear any burden, meet any hardship, support any friend, and oppose any foe . . .' to assure that you are my wife and that you are a well- kept woman."

Ava nodded. "We'll see, Mr. President."

***

When they arrived at Zach Carter's law office, the lawyer had the prenuptial agreement typed and ready to sign.

"Ask questions of clarification and make modifications before placing your signatures on the document," he told them.

Ava, true to her word, picked up the pen and signed her name on the line without reviewing the document.

Zach's eyes darted to O'Brien. "She needs to review the language, Jim!"

"She's like that," O'Brien said, tapping his pen on the table.

The lawyer cautioned Ava. "There will be no recourse once you're married."

She looked at O'Brien. "The only thing I want from you is fidelity."

O'Brien fixed his eyes on Ava as he continued to tap his pen on the table. "Write this down, Zach. I, James Timothy O'Brien love only Ava Coury Panetta and will always be faithful to her. If I prove to be unfaithful, she deserves and can have all of my assets."

Zach Carter threw up his hands and cried, "Come on! This is lunacy! No rational person with your kind of assets does this!"

O'Brien stood, gathered the documents, and tore them in half. He turned to Ava. "Didn't you say you needed to do some research?"

His actions surprised her. Her eyes swung to Zack then back to O'Brien. "Your lawyer has a point."

He nodded. "You're right. He does have a point." He looked at Zack. "I have a point, too. She could have gone after my money the first night we met. Instead, she made it crystal clear that she wasn't going to settle for anything less than what she had with her husband, Eli. I know where her head and heart are." He looked at Ava and said, "You're my wealth."

With reassuring words to Zach, they walked out of the lawyer's office and headed for the library.

***

Ava was back in New Castle when Lucy called from Minneapolis to tell her the good news. "After Dr. Belle reviewed my records and examined me, he determined that the cancer is in its earliest stage, but I opted for a

157

mastectomy. I'm scheduled for surgery tomorrow morning. There may not be any follow-up treatment. My prognosis is a long, normal, healthy life." Lucy laughed and asked, "Did you grow up with any cosmetic surgeons?"

Ava danced around the kitchen. "Give Ronnie a big hug for me, Lucy. Vikki and I will help research surgeons for you. Maybe Jim and I can fly out and be with you for a few days."

Appreciative of the sentiment, Lucy stopped Ava. "I think your fiancé has his hands full at the university right now. Henry and I will be fine. Just stop in and have tea with me next week. I'll be at the wedding if they have to carry me on a stretcher."

"Tell Henry to call as soon as he can to let us know when you're out of surgery. If you need us, we will be there."

Lucy's voice cracked. "The two times I needed you most, you were there. You know, Ava, your brother was right. We're all so fortunate that you chose to love again."

CHAPTER TWENTY

O'BRIEN only made one request of Ava in June when he asked her to marry him: "I know it doesn't give you much time, but I want to be husband and wife before academic obligations force our private activities to take a back seat."

With little time to spare, the day after the engagement, she began to plan the wedding for mid-August. She resigned her teaching position at the high school and was able to secure a part-time position at a community college twenty miles from Emerson-Thoreau University. Teaching college classes would give her the balance that she needed, to interact with students in an academic setting and to fulfill the duties of the wife of a college president. She also took the liberty to move her more valuable and sentimental possessions into O'Brien's house. Her strategically placed pictures and mementoes throughout the rooms transformed his house into their home.

Determined to avoid turning their wedding into an opulent production, they managed to trim the corpulent guest list to three hundred close family members and intimate friends. Ava planned to look stunning in her floor length, off-white, A-lined silk organza gown. It was fitted in the front, plain and elegant. With two-inch straps on the shoulders, the bodice lay flat across her chest, just below her collar bone. The back of the dress was cut out and swooped low like a Vera Wang classic. Several individual, sheer, silk leaves sewn by hand onto the back right edge of the dress cascaded effortlessly and rested on the small of her back. The bottom rear of the dress flared out into a semi-circle to form a train that skimmed the floor as she walked down the aisle. Her only jewelry besides her engagement ring was a pair of charcoal-gray rhinestone earrings and a matching bracelet that her mother bought her for the last birthday she shared with Ava before she died.

Controversy swirled among several aunts and cousins a week before the wedding when Ava insisted on by-passing a traditional veil.

"You'll be inviting bad luck if you allow your future husband to see your face before the vows," her aunt warned, a touch of melodrama in her voice.

Jake finally ended the stand-off with a pronouncement. "The veil Ava wore at her first wedding didn't exactly ward off evil spirits, did it?" He beamed at his sister and said, "She doesn't need a veil; she has a good heart."

Ava blew her brother a kiss, and Jake pretended that it almost knocked him off his chair. The family laughed. Uncle George gazed at Ava with misty eyes and said, "Veil or no veil, Jim O'Brien is a good man, and you're a beautiful woman. I can't wait to dance at your wedding!"

***

O'Brien locked his eyes on the exquisite form that moved closer toward him with each step she took. But with each step toward the man she loved, she reminded Eli, Luke, and Leila that she would never forget them and never stop loving them. Halfway down the aisle, her eyes moistened. When she paused to compose herself, Jake fumbled for his handkerchief, but O'Brien had already moved swiftly up the aisle with his handkerchief in hand. Dabbing her cheeks to prevent the tears from ruining her make-up, he then tucked the handkerchief in her hand. His lips grazed her ear. He whispered, "They're a part of us forever."

She loved him even more for loving them. He turned to walk back to where protocol dictates that a groom stands and waits for his bride, when she grabbed the cuff of his coat sleeve. He felt her soft hand slip into his. He held it secure. Before Jake turned to sit with the family, he clasped both their hands and gave a deliberate nod of approval. Together, Ava and O'Brien walked the rest of the way to the altar. When the priest introduced them as Dr. and Mrs. Jim O'Brien for the first time, applause filled the church.

***

The highlight of the reception was Jake's emotional toast to his brother-in-law for being ". . . a good man whose love is gracious enough, strong enough, and wise enough to calm my sister's wounded heart." He reminded the guests how rare it is to find an individual ". . . who is secure in his own skin, looks beyond superficial character flaws, abides by commitment, and remains constant and unshakable, steadfast like the North Star when life tosses humanity around." He choked up when he silently reflected on the depth of his sister's despair.

Grabbing Jake in a bear hug, O'Brien whispered, "I'll always take care of her. Now take a deep breath and recite the poem."

Jake nodded. He wiped his eyes with his handkerchief and breathed in an exaggerated deep breath. Making the guests laugh, he said, "My brother-in-law asked me to recite a poem by William Shakespeare. He claims that the bard says everything I just tried to say about love a heck of a lot better and shorter than I did!" Jake laughed and threw down the gauntlet. "Let's see if this Shakespeare is as good as people say he is." As the soft laughter faded, a solemn silence filled the room to hear him recite *Sonnet 116*:

> *Let me not to the marriage of true minds*
> *Admit impediments. Love is not love*
> *Which alters when it alteration finds,*
> *Or bends with the remover to remove:*
> *O no; it is an ever-fixed mark,*
> *That looks on tempests, and is never shaken;*
> *It is the star to every wandering bark,*
> *Whose worth's unknown, although his height be taken.*
> *Love's not Time's fool, though rosy lips and cheeks*
> *Within his bending sickle's compass come;*
> *Love alters not with his brief hours and weeks,*
> *But bears it out even to the edge of doom.*
> *If this be error and upon me proved,*
> *I never writ, nor no man ever loved.*

The judge walked back to his seat as some guests dried their eyes with tissues and napkins. They and most of the others were all too familiar with the sadness that burdened Ava and O'Brien, but love guided them to this moment of celebration and hope for the future.

While O'Brien was relieved to relinquish all aspects of the wedding plans to Ava, he maintained control over one event, the song that would highlight the bride and groom's dance. He held his wife in his arms and sang along with Don McClean's "And I Love You So." They both knew the toll that loneliness and living without love could take on a person, and he wanted her to know that her love had set him free.

***

Living together on a daily basis released them from the shackles of wasted time, traveling back and forth on weekends, and on too many occasions, separated for weeks at a time. Still, the long distance courtship taught them to appreciate their marital leisure. They watched *Jeopardy* together at 7:00 o'clock on a Tuesday evening, and made love when he unexpectedly came home early on a Wednesday night. They rendezvoused for lunch on a Thursday afternoon. When O'Brien had to travel and Ava was unable to travel with him, he possessed a sense of steadfastness in what he would find when he returned.

While they respected each other's opposing political views, they gently integrated the other's lifestyle into their own. O'Brien was successful in weaning Ava off the liberal television political roundtables that simply rotated the same talking heads *ad nauseam*, much like the conservative programs and pundits for which he had little use. Ava scored the larger victory though when she hooked him on the ultra liberal *The Daily Show*. She pretended not to notice, but she would laugh when he'd interrupt what he was doing and attempt to make some sense out of liberal satirist Stephen Colbert. The news correspondent for the fake news program would regularly spew his quasi-conservative views on the social and political issues of the day.

Watching the show together one evening, Ava lay curled up in his arms sipping on a glass of wine. He pointed to the television screen filled with Colbert's face. "What is it that attracts you to that whacko?"

Ava sat up and set her glass of wine on the coffee table. She pulled her legs to her chest and gave him a wide-eyed stare. He didn't anticipate her serious response.

"I explained part of the reason the day I met you." She pointed to the television screen where Colbert was bloviating on the merits of the religious right wing politicians. "I swear that funny man saved my life."

O'Brien raised his eyebrows, placed his wine glass on the table next to hers and leaned closer to her. His eyes narrowed, and he looked concerned. "That's one way to get my undivided attention."

She released her legs and reached for her wine glass. She took a sip and fixed her eyes on him. "Remember when I told you that six o'clock in the evening was the worst time of my day?"

He nodded.

"Well, several months after Eli and the kids died, I faced a six o'clock in the evening that I thought I'd never survive. The pain was so deep and dark. I wondered if it was possible to ever find some kind of peace in my life again." She looked down at her wine glass. "I didn't want to survive the night." Her eyes watered. She turned to focus on the television screen. "Jake and Vikki tried to be with me every moment they could, but their own busy lives occupied them." She looked at O'Brien. "I never imagined my life could overflow with people, activities, and objects, yet be so painfully empty."

Filled with concern, he reached out to hold her. He wanted to keep her safe. She put her hand up. "No! I'm okay. You know about my discussions with the priest and an analyst. Losing everyone is a trauma that I'll always need to navigate, but I learned how to anticipate and manage my sadness. I know life is precious," she added with conviction. "There was a time that I didn't want to live, but now I believe I owe it to Eli and the kids and our families to live. I have no desire to enter eternity being responsible for one more death they have to mourn. I reached a point where I was beginning to have more good days than bad when I met you." She raised her wine glass to him and said, "You're the proverbial candle in the dark night that lights up my life."

He pulled her close. "How can I protect you from that kind of despair, Ava?"

With soft assurance, she said, "No one is able to protect people from that kind of despair, Jim. I believe in my case, if I didn't jump that night . . . " Her voice trailed off. She looked at the television screen. "I really don't know why that funny man popped into my head." She turned back to her husband. "Did you know that he was a ten year-old kid when his father and two brothers were killed in a plane crash? He buried himself in books to escape the pain. He's a brilliant, modern day Jonathan Swift." She glanced at the television screen and said with wonder in her voice, "I wanted to die, and he still made me laugh. That's why I love that whacko." She reached for her wine. She took a drink and then slid back into her husband's arms. She kissed his chest and said, "Nothing will ever replace what I lost, but sharing my life with you and loving you restores meaning and purpose."

He rested his chin on her head and stared at the television screen as the comic ended his segment.

***

It was January 9, 2002. In competition for ratings, television stations across the country tried to outdo each other with recaps of the past horrific year that shook the country to its core. Ava called her husband to join her in the den to watch *The Daily Show* recap the previous year in a segment titled "The Year That Was." This brief episode was one more example of his wife's ability to ferret out individuals who understood deep suffering. Seeming to ramble, comedian correspondent Stephen Colbert seized the first benign, mundane nine days of 2002 and provided an apparent witless review of the New Year rather than recall the events in the previous full year that included the horror of the terrorist attacks on September 11, 2001.

When the poignant segment ended, Ava exclaimed, "I can't believe it took a comedy show to teach a nation how to heal."

O'Brien agreed. "The comedian's focus away from the horror of that day is a hell of a lot more palatable than the media's fixation on the towers repeatedly collapsing all day long. They have to know that over-exposure of those scenes causes psychological harm. It's one thing to 'remember' and another to 'dwell'." He brushed her chin with his cheek and conceded, "It looks like we found another *Moby Dick* fan."

"Colbert, a *Moby Dick* fan?" she asked, puzzled.

"Sure. Look how he turned away from the searing images of the towers collapsing. He's like Ishmael right before the Catskill eagle idea warning, 'Look not too long into the face of the fire, O man! . . . There is a wisdom that is woe; but there is a woe that is madness.'"

"That's so true," she said. "Dwelling on the sadness can kill a person as well as a nation," she reflected. "That segment turned our attention to the positives in life, not to what we can't control or change, but to the moments that steady us and fill us with a level of comfort and certainty."

He nodded. "Looks that way to me."

"Geez, Jim! Remember when I described the emptiness I felt around the time that I ate supper with my family, when I wallowed in the deafening silence of the kitchen? Jake insisted I fill that time with positive activities."

"Yeah, I remember."

"In the midst of all this September 11 media sensationalism, behold the village idiot who reminds us that life's predictable moments are what calm and heal us, not floundering in the searing sadness."

O'Brien admitted, "I didn't give that guy enough credit." He grabbed her tightly and said, "Nor you. Long before I did, you recognized his brand of satire changes minds."

Ava brushed her lips against his ear and whispered in a sweet, seductive voice, "No matter how famous Colbert becomes, I'll always love you more."

***

O'Brien came home early one evening and sang out her name.

"I'm upstairs!"

He mounted the stairs like a gazelle full of power and grace, bounding past several stairs at a time until he stood before her waving two plane tickets over her head.

"Is your passport in order, pretty lady? I'm going to light up the English and Irish night skies with you."

Ava gasped. Sensuously, she danced around him, inching herself closer. Both index fingers gently alternated poking his chest.

"I'll go on the trip with you this time, but next time, ask before you finalize plans." With humor in her voice, she held up her finger and wagged a warning. "Don't start taking me for granted, Dr. O'Brien."

His eyes twinkled and played with her. "So my offer to traipse you all over the British Isles is an affront on your autonomy as a woman?"

Before she had time to respond, he clasped her finger and playfully nudged her, pushing her backward until she stood at the edge of the bed. With the tips of his fingers, he shoved her shoulders, and like a giddy teenage girl, she fell back in exaggerated motion. He plopped down beside her, rolled on top of her, and planted a hard, long kiss on her lips.

"Now that you have me where you want me, Mrs. O'Brien, school me in the proper way to invite my wife to share a dream vacation with me." Between kisses, he said, "Remediate me . . . as many times . . . as you wish."

Her laughter filled the room. She curled his hair around her index finger and gently tugged until he voluntarily lifted his head to face her. She stopped laughing and probed his face with her finger, tracing the soft lines that crossed his forehead. Pinned underneath him, she lay soft and subdued. With a wispy air of awe in her voice, she crooned, "How can one man be so gorgeous?"

"Not this time, Jezebel. I won't let you flatter me into submission!"

"Honest! I'm telling you the tru—"

"Shhh," he said, repeatedly kissing her mouth. She pretended to struggle for air. He raised his head and eyed her momentarily. More slowly and with

165

soft precision, he pressed his lips to hers and held still. Taking a breath, he said, "Do I—" He kissed her again. "Have your permission—" Another kiss. "To make love with you?"

She ran her fingertips over his lips and said, "Do you believe sex with love is a lot better?"

O'Brien stopped kissing her. With a slight push-up, he raised his body over hers and stared down. "It has no equal."

She held his face in her hands and pulled him toward her. "Do you still have that dream about the dark-haired lady that pushes you away?"

"No. The dark-haired lady of my dreams never pushes me away."

She caressed his chest. "So we're going to light up the English and Irish skies, huh?"

"Not tonight. Tonight, we're going to light up this room!"

***

The next morning, O'Brien woke before dawn. When he returned from his workout, he sat at the table and watched Ava work at the sink. She glanced at him and said, "You look worried."

He drank some coffee and fixed his eyes on some distant point. He muttered, "I dreamt of Vietnam." He shook his head. "All these years, I still can't make sense of what happened . . . why it happened." His voice oozed futility. "I'll never be free." Looking down at his coffee mug, he said, "I want to be rid of it. The memory fills my conscience with dread, but I don't ever want to forget them." He took a drink and looked up at her. In a low voice, he said, "It haunts me."

Ava dried her hands and stood behind him. She massaged his neck and back. "I know what you mean. The accident still haunts me." She moved in front of him and kissed his forehead. She bent her head lower forcing eye contact. "But you gave me good memories to counteract the nightmare." She slipped in the chair across from him. "You know what might help?"

"Nothing helps, Ava."

"You never tried my idea," she said, smiling with friendly persuasion.

Weighed down with years of skepticism, he cocked his head to one side. "What's your idea?"

"You need a good memory of Vietnam."

He shook his head and pointed at her. "No! It's impossible to make a good memory out of what happened there!"

She slid out of her chair and knelt in front of him. Placing her hands on his knees, she said, "I didn't suggest that you can make what happened in Vietnam good, Jim. We can go back and make kinder, gentler memories of the whole area. Instead of spending all our vacation in England and Ireland, maybe we should spend a few days in Vietnam."

He jerked back and stared at her in wide-eyed amazement. When he realized the full measure of her suggestion, he spoke in a soft, deliberate tone. "You are certifiably insane. Think about what you're saying, Ava. What human being in his right mind wants to go back to Vietnam?" He stood and stared down at her. "I spent a lifetime trying to escape that hell-hole and . . ." His voice trailed off. He looked off to the side for several seconds. Still confounded by her incredulous suggestion, he swung his eyes back to her. "And this is where you believe I want to spend my leisure, where I want to make love with my wife?"

She stood. "That's the problem. You remember it as a hell-hole." She cupped his face in her hands and wheedled, "Let's go back so that you can experience a peaceful Mekong Delta with floating markets, not floating bodies. Let's walk in the sunshine instead of remembering how you had to trudge in the mud and rain. You'll see people smiling, and you'll hear children laughing. Kids won't be wearing hand grenades." Her voice was assuring. "Vietnam's different, hon. Time transforms all of us and everything."

He gently moved her aside. "I don't want—"

She grabbed his arm, pulled him back and wrapped her arms around his neck. "I'm only asking for five days."

"Ava. You're the only person alive who knows how Vietnam sucked the life out of me. How it sucked my soul out of me."

"Maybe it's time to reclaim what's yours," she urged.

He closed his eyes and bent his head back as far as it would go. He wanted desperately to rid himself of the horror that lodged within him for more than half his life. He opened his eyes and held up his right hand with his fingers separated. "Five days," he whispered. "You make the arrangements."

She kissed the palm of his hand and felt his fingers close gently around her mouth. He pulled her mouth close to his and kissed her lips. She whispered, "You have my word."

CHAPTER TWENTY-ONE

THE flight was long with tedious layovers before the plane touched down in Vinh Long Town. Driving a rented car to the luxury Tai Nguyen Hotel located in the upper Mekong Delta, he noticed the city bustled more with friendlier activity than his war-time recollections.

"Let's go for a walk while the sun's still shining," Ava suggested.

"Anything particular you're looking for?"

"We have several hours before supper. Let's scout out tourist attractions."

When she encountered a vendor who spoke English, she asked, "Is there a church nearby?"

The man pointed. "Church five blocks. Close to walk."

She turned to O'Brien. "My mother taught us always to light a candle and say a prayer for the cities and countries we visit."

As they bounded down the church steps and strolled through the streets teeming with life, positive changes captured his attention. After supper, they toured a small art museum. Though the atmosphere was pleasant, he begged off more sightseeing excursions saying, "Jet lag's catching up with me."

Ava acquiesced. No sense in pushing too hard, too fast, she thought. It served them both well to lounge in bed and talk of future plans until they fell asleep in each other's arms. The next day, they accidentally discovered an outdoor concert in a local park. As the trumpet blared out marching music, he turned to Ava and admitted, "There's a striking difference."

Not sure what to expect, her head kept time with the band as she asked, "Any specifics?"

His eyes swung upward. "The sun's still shining." Scanning the park, he said, "I notice two more differences."

She playfully motioned 'come-on' with her hands. "I'm waiting with baited breath."

"Heat from hell isn't suffocating me, and Brobdingnagian insects aren't feasting on my flesh."

She stopped bobbing her head and locked her sober eyes on his. "I'm so sorry, Jim. There's nothing funny about the horrible memories of this place you and other soldiers live with every day of your lives."

"Relax, babe. You're in our league. Your red badge of courage earned you the right to laugh at any part of life you wish."

She nodded.

That evening, they enjoyed a marathon of Marx Brother movies. Walking to their car, he whispered, "I can think of so many other places I'd rather be with you right now." He grabbed her elbow and stopped her in her tracks. "But so far, and I stress, *so far,* this isn't a bad trip."

For a moment she stood breathless. "You caught me off-guard with that one. Still, I have three more days to dazzle you."

A grin danced on his face. "I can suggest several ways to dazzle me."

***

During breakfast on the third day, Ava ventured to the edge of the taboo topic. "How difficult will it be to find the battle areas?"

"Ava, please. This whole country was a battleground."

"I know, but chances are it's going to be transformed like everywhere else we've been."

"Ava, don't!"

She nodded. Her shoulders drooped with disappointment as she watched the torrential rainfall from the window. "I can't believe clouds can hold that much water! We'll need an ark to get out of here."

As heavy rain pounded hard on the window, he said with more spirit, "Well, believe it, sweetheart. It's just one of the less vile reasons why I detest every single thing about this place."

With a twinkle in her eye, she turned to face him. "I resent that." She sauntered up to him and said, "I'm a part of this place now." She motioned, 'come here' with her index finger. Grabbing him at his waist and playfully tugging several times, she said, "Let me help you clear away decades of debris." She touched the tip of his nose as though she were comforting a pouting little boy who didn't get his way. "Look hard enough; you just might spot a rainbow in that storm."

He cradled her in his arms. "If someone would have predicted that I'd be making love with the woman of my dreams in this lousy—" She raised herself on her tiptoes and planted a lengthy, exaggerated kiss on his mouth to arrest his negative thought.

***

O'Brien was reading an American paper, when Ava announced, "I'm going down to the gift shop to buy Vikki a souvenir." She did buy a gift for her sister-in-law, but she also inquired, "Do you know how close to the hotel the fields are, the ones that became graves for many of the soldiers who fought in the war?"

The clerk nodded. "Drive maybe twenty minutes." He gestured saying, "Southwest along river, you be in one of areas *that cover the dead.*"

O'Brien's eyes examined her face when she walked into the room. "Did you find the yellow brick road that leads to the cesspool of my dreams?"

"Paranoia's not a dominant personality trait, is it?" she teased.

"I have good reason to be paranoid in this place, and you still didn't answer my question."

She offered him a stick of gum and swept his hair off his forehead, Smiling, she said, "I guess you know me well."

He bent his head back "I know you well enough to know that you're not going to quit until we do this, are you, Ava? That's the only reason why we're here, right?" Biting his lip, he grabbed the car keys. "Let's get this over with so I can go home."

Despite his protests, Ava wondered if he had a curiosity about the place. What was it like now, that grotesque shapeless sea of sludge that swallowed up his friends, that haunted him for over half his life?

"There's an area that you may recognize several miles southwest along the river," she told him, pulling the keys from his hand. "It will be better to travel in another hour or two. The roads will be drier."

By late afternoon, the rains gave way to hot, near blistering sunshine. Reluctantly, he joined her as they set out to locate the mass grave of his friends.

Along the route, the terrain was mostly level. Small, quaint houses lined the street giving way to several huts, much like the structures he remembered seeing along the roads during the war. As they approached an intersection, O'Brien recognized a towering tree standing in a clearing not far from the riverbank. That tree was indelibly marked in his mind. He remembered how it stood formidable and forbidding as it dwarfed the vegetation and structures around it. Over twenty-five years later, it remained strong, but alone.

He pulled the car over to the side of the road and parked. Gripping the steering wheel tightly, he hesitated. As his eyes slowly canvassed the area, flashbacks: swollen riverbeds; thick, muddy-red water pouring over the banks; pools of deadly mud holes that sucked men under flooded his mind. Ironically, time had transformed the region fraught with blood and bodies into a quaint park bustling with life. People gathered at their leisure. They sat on benches, while others patronized the street vendors selling their wares. Music from one particular vendor selling refreshments across the street filled the air as people casually walked, rode their bikes, and shared intimate conversations and laughter. Despite the radical changes, he instinctively knew this was the place.

Unbuckling his seatbelt, he slipped out of the car. He tread softly, drawing nearer to the clearing close to the towering tree. Unsure of his capacity to remain steady, he crouched over like an old man weighed down by decades of guilt. His head bent downward, he stared at the ground. First he simply grazed the top of the soil with his fingertips without making an imprint. Then, with his index finger, he etched names into the dry earth: Donny . . . Mike . . . Pete. He picked some of the dirt up and reverently brought it to his lips. His shoulders shook. Ava walked over to him, bent down and kissed the top of his head. Covering his face with one hand and pulling his handkerchief from his pocket with the other, in a barely audible voice, he whispered, "It's a better place."

"You know what I think?"

He stood, keeping his eyes transfixed on the names scrawled on the ground. "I always want to know what you think."

She cupped her hand around her ear. "Listen! Your friends are laughing at you."

Puzzled by her comment, he looked at her. "Why would they be laughing, Ava? I'm alive and they're dead."

"Shhh," she said, brushing his cheek with her hand. "You have to listen." She nodded. "Yeah, they're laughing alright. They're saying, 'How did someone who womanized as much as O'Brien hookup with someone as wonderful as that pretty dark-haired woman?'" She looked at him impishly and editorialized. "Your friends think I'm too good for you."

Ava circled him once in a slow, deliberate manner until she faced him again. She stared at the ground, smiled, and explained to his friends. "Guess what guys. He's actually reeeally good." Acting startled, she covered her mouth with her hands. "Oh no! Now they're *really* laughing. They took the phrase 'really good' the wrong way."

His face relaxed with a slight smile. She was lifting him out of the dark gorge, nudging him into the sunny spaces. He leaned close to her and whispered, "Hey guys, sometimes she's crazier than the Vietcong on bad crack, but you're right. She is too good for me." His eyes moistened along with hers. "I promise . . ." He corrected himself. "*We* promise to live and love with vitality, courage, and strength of character. Your spirits . . . Eli, Luke, and Leila's spirits . . . as long as we breathe . . . we'll never let you die."

He wrapped his arm around her waist and after a minute of silence, pointed to the vendor selling sno-cones. "You want one of those?"

Ava nodded.

As the vendor shaved ice to make a second cone, Ava noticed O'Brien's eyes follow a Vietnamese family moving down the walkway toward a shaded bench beneath a tree: an elderly woman, a younger woman carrying an infant in her arms, and a toddler lagging behind. His jaw stiffened. Instinctively, he turned his head to look the other way, but rather than hand the sno-cone to Ava, he turned back and strolled to where the women sat. Ava watched as he pulled dog tags from his pocket, and she listened to him speak Vietnamese to the elderly woman.

"*Tha thú cho tôi.*"

Smiling with warmth, the weathered woman stood and bowed. She reached out and clasped his hand and ran her fingertips over the dog tags. He kept his eyes fixed on her and nodded as she spoke in a gentle but deliberate tone. She ended saying, "*Đi trong hòa bình.*"

Before she turned to walk away, he held up the sno-cone sparkling with a bright rainbow of flavors: cherry, grape, blueberry, and lime. He motioned toward the little boy. The younger woman nodded her consent. O'Brien walked up close to the toddler, bent down and guided the child's hands to form a grip on the treat. The little boy eagerly began to crunch at the brightly colored pieces of ice. Ava watched her husband as his eyes followed the women and the boy until they were out of sight.

Unable to contain her excitement, she sprang from the bench and ran to him. "I didn't know you spoke Vietnamese. What did she say to you?"

Ignoring her question at first, he apologized. "I'm sorry I gave your sno-cone away."

"Forget the sno-cone. What did she say to you?"

Amazed at what transpired and not understanding fully what just happened to him, he tried to explain. "I asked her to forgive me for killing the woman and baby." He shook his head in wonderment and stuttered, "She…she told me…the war is over. 'Go in peace.'"

Ava caressed his cheek and breathed a sigh of relief. "Well, Jim! The Pope forgives you. I forgive you. A representative of Vietnam forgives you." She eyed her husband and challenged, "What do you think?"

He nodded. "What I think is I owe my wife a rainbow sno-cone!"

"Not really," she laughed. "I'm halfway done with your cone. Besides, you owe me a heck of a lot more than a sno-cone, mister!"

More serious than she anticipated, he leaned close and kissed her lips. "What you made happen here . . . ." His eyes looked up and swept across the cloudless sky. His gaze swung back to her. "I can never repay—"

She lifted his hand to her lips and kissed it. "Aren't you the one who put Humpty Dumpty back together again?"

He nodded.

They walked to one of the benches and sat. She crossed her right leg over his left thigh, and he gently massaged her knee. She followed his focus on spirited children playing in the park when he said, "I feel lighter."

Ava gently tugged on his earlobe. "By the way, why did you bring your dog tags?"

He pulled the pieces of metal out of his pocket and traced his finger over his name. He whispered, "I thought they belonged here . . . *I* belonged here."

"Do you still believe you belong here?"

Perusing the park filled with life, he slipped the tags into his pocket. "No. I'm ready to go home."

"Home? I thought you wanted to light up the Irish night sky."

"Do we have enough time to do that?"

She nodded.

He caressed her arm and said, "Ireland sounds good."

She bit into the last chunk of ice and tossed the wrapper into the nearby trash can. As they walked to their car, contentment filled them. One more time, they found a way to make life more bearable for each other.

Though they felt renewed, the fading laughter of children reminded them that there was still a void in their lives, a sorrow neither one of them could relieve.

CHAPTER TWENTY-TWO

THREE years of marital bliss passed uninterrupted until the day O'Brien's teenage niece pulled them into a whirlwind of family adversity. Ava was off on her yearly shopping trip with friends in New York City, while O'Brien remained homebound to fend for himself. His seventeen year-old niece, Hannah, boarded a bus in Connecticut and traveled to her Uncle Jim's house in Pennsylvania. She stood on his porch, rang the doorbell, and waited shivering in the cold. When O'Brien opened the door, he discovered a confused, frightened girl dissolved in tears.

"I didn't know where else to go," she said as a plea. "I wish I was dead."

Gently guiding her into the kitchen, he said, "Tell me what's so wrong, Hannah."

"You'll hate me," she said, shaking with sobs. "Everyone will hate me."

With a crooked grin, he consoled her saying, "The O'Briens have done some crazy things. We still manage to stick together." He rubbed her shoulders to calm her. "Start at the beginning." He winked and said, "I'm sure we'll find a solution."

Avoiding eye contact, her voice was barely audible when she whispered, "I'm pregnant." She shuffled to the end of the counter and said, "Mom wants me to have an abortion before people find out." Blurred with tears, her eyes darted to O'Brien. Whining like a child, she pleaded, "I just want to stay here. Please let me stay here, Uncle Jim. I won't cause any trouble."

"Does your father know about this?"

She shook her head and blew her nose with a tissue. "Mom keeps everything from him. She said she won't ever talk to me again if people find out." Her voice cracked when she said, "I don't want an abortion."

He ran his hand through his hair and said, "We have to tell your Dad."

Panic rose in her. "Please, don't tell Dad, Uncle Jim. He'll hate me; he'll kill me!"

He grabbed her shoulders to steady her. "Listen to me, Hannah. He loves you, and he needs to know. We're talking about his grandchild. The only way he can help is if he knows what's going on. You need to trust him, and you need to trust me." With a reassuring stare, he said, "I know your father, and he's the only one who can handle your mother."

Hannah dabbed her eyes. "It's just easier to let her do what she wants."

"Not this time. This is too important. We're dealing with a baby's life; we're dealing with your life."

"That's why I need you and Aunt Ava. If you loan me money, I can rent an apartment and get a job, and . . . ." Overwhelmed by the prospect of raising a child on her own, she tried to hold back a flood of tears. She covered her face with her hands to muffle a new surge of sobs.

He looped his arm around her waist and guided her toward the stairs. "Right now, let's get you settled in the guest room. Get out of these wet clothes and take a shower. You'll think more clearly after some rest. Stay as long as you want, and I'll help you straighten things out, okay? If you're hungry, there's plenty to eat." A crooked grin crossed his lips. "Aunt Ava bought out the grocery store because she didn't want your favorite uncle to waste away while she was traipsing all over the Big Apple."

Hannah forced a smile. Taking him by surprise, she wrapped her arms around his neck and said, "I love you so much. If Mom won't let me keep the baby, I want you and Aunt Ava to have it."

This unexpected last statement sent a shock through him, and his eyes grew large with a flood of concern for his niece, and the rest of his family, and for himself. It had been years since he entertained the possibility of becoming a father. Now he had the opportunity to save a baby's life and at the same time be a father to a baby that actually shared his family's lineage. He quickly quelled his internal conflict before his niece could sense his racing thoughts.

"Let's take it one step at a time, kiddo. Call if you need me."

***

When Hannah had fallen asleep, he called Ava in New York. She and her friends were ordering lunch. As Ava rambled about the Broadway play they were scheduled to see, O'Brien interrupted her. "Well, sweetheart, who needs Broadway when you have emotionally disturbed in-laws."

"Why? What happened?"

When he told Ava what Marcia had planned for Hannah, her mouth dropped. Vikki stopped talking to the other ladies and mouthed, "What's wrong?"

Ava held up her index finger to signal, "Wait." She asked O'Brien, "What does your brother have to say about it?"

"Marcia's keeping him in the dark."

She heard the distress in his voice when he said, "I'll tell you, Ava; this is a mess, and it's going to get messier. Right after I hang up from you, I'm calling Pat."

Battling the spirited noise level in the restaurant and the loud conversation at her own table, she stood and walked to a quieter place. "Maybe you should stay out of it for now. Let Hannah break the news to Pat so he and Marsha don't accuse you of interfering."

"Hannah already dragged me into it. I'm trying to keep you out of it as long as possible."

"Can you at least wait until I get home?"

"No, I can't wait. My brother doesn't know what's going on. His whole family's been on a life-long cruise, floating on individual boats, through thick fog. When they randomly bump into each other, it causes chaos for themselves and the people around them." He sighed. "Let me do this; I'll talk to you later."

"Marcia will go ballistic if—" The line went dead.

***

When O'Brien dialed his brother's number, *Mad Marcia*, as those who knew her best described her and for the same reason repelled her, answered. With an edge to his voice, he asked for Pat.

"You sound upset, Jim. Is there a problem?"

He wanted to say, yeah, wing nut! You're the problem, but he checked his anger. "I need to talk to my brother, if he's there, Marsha."

Several seconds passed before Patrick greeted him. "Jimmy! How yah doin'?"

"I've been better, he said with a sigh." After a slight pause, he said, "I have to tell you something, Pat, but you have to stay calm."

Pat let out a sarcastic laugh. "I would've been six feet under a long time ago if I didn't know how to stay calm. You'd cringe at what they do to me around here." He braced himself and said, "Let's hear it."

O'Brien knew Marcia was on red alert, so he chose his words carefully. "Hannah is staying with me. She's scared and confused."

Patrick heightened his concern. "Why in the world is she scared? What happened to her? Was she in an accident?"

"She's pregnant, Pat, and she has it in her head that you'll disown her. I convinced her that you love her, and you'll help her any way you can. We'll all help her. It's important to think ideas through before you make a decision that will affect us for a lifetime."

After absorbing the shock of the news, he broke his silence. Pat scowled at Marcia. "Hannah's in Pennsylvania with Jim. Did you know she's pregnant?"

O'Brien heard Marcia say, "I just found out and was trying to think of a way to tell you."

He knew his sister-in-law had no intention of telling her husband that she scheduled to abort his first grandchild, and it filled him with rage.

Patrick reacted to the announcement as O'Brien knew he would: first confusion; then frustration giving way to anger. "I can't believe this! I need time to work this out, Jim. Can Hannah stay with you for a while?"

"She can stay here as long as you want her to stay."

Marcia screeched like a hawk on high zeroing in on her prey. "She can't stay in Pennsylvania! She has an appointment Wednesday!"

O'Brien wanted Marcia to disclose her abortion plan, so he goaded. "Ask Marcia what kind of an appointment Hannah has to keep that's so important she can't reschedule?"

Hell-bent on stopping O'Brien from interfering, she grabbed the phone from her husband and warned, "STAY . . . OUT . . . OF . . . THIS . . . JIM! We've made up our minds!"

Her use of the word 'we' infuriated him. "WE!" he yelled. "Who in the hell are the *we* who made up their minds? Hannah doesn't want an abortion. Your husband doesn't even know about your plan to abort his first grandchild, and our mother and father certainly don't want to abort their first great-grandchild! So who is this damn royal WE who made up their minds to kill this baby?"

Patrick stared at his wife. Opening his hand, he ordered, "Give me that damn phone!" Oozing with sarcasm, he said, "Welcome to my world, Jim." After a short pause, he said, "Just keep Hannah there until I come up with a plan. There's not going to be any abortion." He glared at Marcia. "I can't promise there won't be a murder before the day's over, but no abortion!"

"I'm sorry you had to find out this way, Pat, but I felt certain that you'd never abort a baby." Then he surprised himself by saying, "Go easy on Marcia. Maybe this is an opportunity to get her the help she needs." He ended the call saying, "I love you and your family. I'll help in any way I can."

"You've always been the one who cared the most, Jim. The well-being of the whole family always meant a lot to you. Just make sure Hannah knows we love her, okay? Give me some time to think some ideas through, and I'll talk to you tomorrow."

***

Still in New York, Ava walked back to the table and pulled Vikki aside. She filled her in on the family crisis. "Sometimes I get the feeling that his sister-in-law is possessed. After Jim inserts himself in this drama, she'll make the Arctic wind feel like a heat-wave."

She hailed a cab to the hotel and threw her belongings in her suitcase. She gripped the steering wheel the whole way back to Emerson-Thoreau University, and her muscles ached. Not knowing what to expect filled her with angst. When she finally arrived, the house was empty and quiet. She used the time alone to unpack and check to see that Hannah had what she needed in the guest room. She was relieved to find her husband at least had the domestic areas under control. She relaxed in the den reading a magazine when she heard the garage door open. Her stomach felt queasy as the sound of footsteps drew closer.

Hannah grabbed Ava and hugged her. She buried her face next to Ava's ear and whispered, "I'm so embarrassed. Please don't be mad at me." Her eyes welled with tears.

Ava held Hannah's hand and guided her to the kitchen. O'Brien dropped his keys on the counter and interrupted their discussion. "Hannah, didn't you say you needed to go to the mall to get a few personal items?"

"I can do that anytime you want me to."

"Why don't you do what you have to do right now. It'll give me a chance to fill Aunt Ava in on what's happened so far."

Hannah dried her eyes and blew her nose. He tossed her the car keys. As she shuffled to the garage, she turned to them. "I didn't mean to cause so much trouble."

Ava motioned for her to come back. She gave her another hug.

Thinking of her husband's and her own mistakes, she offered, "We can't change our past mistakes, sweetheart, but we can help you plan a positive future."

Hannah stared at Ava and blinked back tears. "Thanks for being nice to me." With a child's voice, she told Ava, "Ever since Uncle Jim brought you home to meet all of us, I wished that you were my mother. That's why I want you and Uncle Jim to adopt my baby."

Ava was dumb-struck by the teenager's assumption that giving up a baby was as easy as walking away from a puppy or kitten that you learned demanded too much of you. She kissed Hannah's forehead. "We'll talk about it more when Uncle Jim gives me more details. Just stay focused; be careful driving."

Ava motioned O'Brien to follow her to the den. Over-charged with fatigue, she dropped on the couch and massaged her forehead with both hands.

"I'm sorry you cut your trip short," he said, "but I'm glad you're with me."

Ava nodded. Her voice carried sadness. "That poor kid thinks you can just hand over a baby to someone," brushing her hands together, "problem solved!" She shook her head. "That baby, under the best of circumstances, will change people's lives forever."

He was disappointed that Ava dismissed the idea of assuming guardianship of the baby. With a slight grin, he suggested, "Maybe this is one of those times when we should look for the rainbow in the storm that's swirling around us."

"I'm not sure what you mean," she said, covering her yawn.

"Hannah wants us to raise the baby. Maybe we should consider the idea."

Her husband's serious consideration of adopting the baby caught her off guard. She gave him a blank stare. Collecting herself, she said, "It's one thing to leave your heart in San Francisco, Jim, but please tell me that you didn't leave your capacity to reason there, too!" She told him point blank, "This is an irrational discussion, and I'm too tired to humor you any—"

"Ava, listen to me. Don't interrupt until you hear me out, okay? We have a chance to turn this crisis into something positive. How often does a childless couple get a chance to raise a baby who shares their blood line?"

"My God! You *are* serious!" She jumped off the couch. "You're as unrealistic as Hannah, except she's a kid! Right now, she's a scared, confused girl who loves us simply because we're not her parents. Do you have any idea what it would be like, how convoluted it would be, to raise this baby? We'd saddle him with a monstrous identity crisis. He'll call us mommy and daddy and aunt and uncle, and call Hannah mommy! I'm confused just thinking about what our roles would be!" She raised her hand in the air and pointed to high heaven. "And let's not forget the luscious joy of Marcia's venomous attacks at every family gathering." Ava shook her head. With slight terror in her voice, she said, "Oh no! No! No! No! Don't ask me to set myself up for heartbreak when Hannah graduates from college six years from now and marries someone on the West Coast, and she decides that she wants *her baby* after I . . ." She stopped talking and sat back on the couch. She hugged a pillow to her chest and squeezed it. She peered at O'Brien from across the room. "I already lost two kids, Jim. Please! Don't set me up to lose one more."

He slid next to her on the couch and slipped his hand on the back of her neck. "Could you at least keep an open mind about an adoption so that they won't have a reason to consider an abortion? The baby could stay in the family and grow up in a loving, stable atmosphere."

Ava shrugged his hand off her neck. She stood and stared at her husband with vacant wonder. "Why do I need to keep an open mind when you've already made up your mind?" She laughed with sarcasm. "At least when I try to save the world, it causes chaos for a few days; then it's over. You want to raise a baby that isn't yours by usurping your niece's parental rights and your brother's grandparent rights." Filled with accusation, she added, "Just because Marcia is strange doesn't mean that she should lose the right to her grandchild." She ended her opposition with a warning. "Before the O'Briens get overly possessive about this child, you might want to consider how possessive the biological father and his family will be toward *their* child and grandchild."

With an edge to his voice, he countered, "Hannah insists that she doesn't know who the father is. Right now that point is of remote concern. Marcia remains of immediate concern." He paused. More softly, he said, "You know that my sister-in-law is more than *strange*. For God's sake, Ava, emotional disturbance is to Marcia what water is to Niagara Falls. Are you going to stand by and willingly allow a manipulative, emotionally ill woman who scheduled an abortion to rip the life out of her first grandchild raise this baby the best way she knows how?"

Ava replied with a detached tone. "A large percent of the population would be stripped of parental rights if we had the power to determine parenthood based on emotional stability. I'm sure that Hannah, Patrick, and Marcia will figure out a way to work out their own family problems if you let them."

O'Brien restrained himself from sneering, "How about the large percent of the population who abdicates moral and ethical responsibility because they want an easy life? Why else are we fighting to save a baby from abortion?" He stared at his wife and pleaded, "Let's talk about the real issue. I want that baby to live! But I don't want the baby to be a toddler when they decide it's just too difficult to raise the kid, so they give it up, or worse, verbally and physically abuse it because they view the baby as the source of their miserable lives. Then you have another Henry Morgan in the world."

Ava walked around the room rearranging the pillows. She shot him a stern look and said, "As I recall, you eloquently pointed out to me years ago, Henry Morgan did okay despite his handicap. We all have problems that we have to overcome. Most of us even master living with the scars that come from being beaten and battered by life." She threw the last pillow on the couch. Piercing him with volatile eyes, she said, "Or are you so arrogant that you believe your money can shelter this baby from any adverse realities that life has in store for it?"

He covered his face with his hands for several seconds; then he slowly slid his hands down over his nose and mouth. He slipped his hands from his face and placed the tips of his fingers together just below his chin. He studied her for several seconds. With complete authority and definitiveness, so that there was no way to mistake his intent, he told her: "That baby . . . is going to stay in the O'Brien family . . . even if I have to raise it myself!"

At first his declaration shocked and paralyzed her. Within seconds, hurt converted to anger. She knew well that if she gave him space to retreat and time to contemplate what just transpired, reason had a better chance to prevail. Before she allowed him to walk away, against all wisdom, she chose to serve final words of her own. "Now I know where *your* head and heart are."

His face turned scarlet. When he whirled around, she saw his eyes blazing with anger, and she felt the heat of his piercing stare. He stood in the doorway and shouted, "I refuse to let you question my heart, Ava! By now you damn well better know where my head and heart are! I loved you the moment I met you, and each day I love you more than the day before! Everything, and I mean EVERYTHING I have, including my head and my heart, is yours! This is not about how much I love *you*! It's about the welfare of this baby!" He turned and stormed out of the room.

CHAPTER TWENTY-THREE

HANNAH stayed with her uncle and aunt for several weeks. During that time, O'Brien didn't have to worry about Marcia manipulating her into having a late term abortion. Patrick wanted his daughter to come home so that they could make plans for the baby's arrival. It was late August and the baby was due around Thanksgiving. The way things stood, Hannah and her father agreed that the best case scenario for the baby would be to have Ava and O'Brien appointed as its legal guardians. Marcia had little input in the decision, and Patrick insisted that she enter long overdue counseling if she wanted to salvage their marriage. To everyone's surprise and relief, she cooperated. O'Brien's lawyer drew up adoption papers, but he knew well how the best laid plans go awry. Family dynamics were already beginning to turn sour when Ava informed O'Brien that she made plans to spend holidays in New Castle. As hard as he tried, he couldn't persuade her to understand the reasons why he intervened in the events unfolding in his family. Despite the hurt that it caused him, it probably was a good idea that she chose not to be around Marcia. He didn't want to chance Ava laying blame for the upheaval in her own life on Marcia's instability and unwillingness to support her own daughter.

For the month that Hannah stayed with them, Ava remained distant and cool. O'Brien's stubbornness for moving forward on the adoption when he knew she had major misgivings created a schism in their relationship. She resented him for placing her in the position of being the spoiler if she didn't sign the papers, and she resented his plan to become the legal guardian on his own. She couldn't help but wonder how life would have been different had she been able to give him his own child. Maybe he wouldn't be so enthusiastic about raising Hannah's baby.

Because Hannah was in the house, the estrangement was easier for Ava to orchestrate, but now that Hannah moved out, he wondered how Ava would manage to avoid him in the evenings and on weekends. He couldn't believe that for four agonizing weeks, Ava moved through the same house and slept in the same bed with him, yet he could miss her so much. If he would lean over to touch her, she would find some way to move out of his grasp. If he wanted to get romantic, she would say she felt funny being with him with Hannah in the house. He teased, "You didn't feel funny trying to lure me into the shower at my mother's house during Thanksgiving vacation the first time you met my parents." Ava dismissed her behavior, as "a long time ago when I was just silly." He longed for her to be silly again. He hoped by some miracle Ava would embrace the adoption on her own.

Time was running out. He felt like he was engineering a locomotive barreling down the tracks, and he didn't have the ability to slow it down before it rounded the final bend. He didn't want Patrick or Hannah to entertain the idea that the baby was causing a rift between Ava and him. Successful in saving the baby's life, now he wanted to prevent an excuse to adopt the baby out to a family other than his own. It would legitimize the act of sticking their heads in the sand, to act like the baby never existed. His brother wouldn't have a grandchild, and his mother and father would never hold their great-grandchild; he would lose the link to fatherhood that this child had awakened in him, and he would lose the opportunity finally to restore and to nurture a young life.

***

Ava was baking vanilla biscotti dipped in dark chocolate on a rare, leisure Saturday afternoon. O'Brien took advantage of the unseasonably warm autumn weather and surfed through a sports magazine on the patio. Henry Morgan stopped by with some papers that O'Brien needed to sign for the university. As the two men sat and talked, she watched her husband cover his face and shake his head a couple of times. Ava recognized the mannerism as an outward sign of his mounting frustration when he couldn't find a solution to a dilemma. To make matters worse, she knew that she was his problem. In Ava's mind, he had a choice, the welfare of their relationship or the welfare of the baby. Despite her objections, he chose the welfare of the baby. She saw Henry stand and swagger toward the kitchen.

"Hey, Ava! You should market this aroma. What's on the menu?"

"Taste the biscotti and tell me if they're good. If they don't pass your taste test, I'm not letting anyone else eat them."

"Hell! According to that reasoning, I'll tell you that they taste like hemlock so you'll bag them up and give them all to me."

"Remember when I considered serving you a cookie laced with hemlock?"

Henry nodded.

Directing him to the pantry, she said, "Grab a plastic bag and fill it with as many cookies as you want. You remind me of Jake. Every time he visits, he raids the freezer looking for biscotti."

While Henry had his flaws, beating around the bush was never one of them. He took a bite of his cookie and said, "This is about as good as any cookie can ever get."

'Why thank you, kind sir."

Between bites, he stared at Ava. He told her, "I'm not sure of too many things in this world, but one thing I am sure of is that guy sitting on your patio loves you and needs you." Shaking his head, he laughed. "Hell, your husband is one of those rare people who gets people angry when he does the right thing. Some people actually resent being around good people like him. He'd rather do the right thing and get his head chopped off than do the wrong thing and get his soul ripped out."

She wiped her hands on a towel. "Did he send you in here?"

"No, no." He raised his hand toward heaven. "Honest! The aroma of these wonderful creations drew me to your kitchen." He tilted his head and looked at her. "He did tell me that you're unhappy, and it really hurts him. He's just trying to do what's right for everyone concerned. I think he's experiencing battle fatigue."

"Did he tell you why I'm not on board with the adoption?"

Henry nodded.

"Do you have any words of wisdom on the subject?" she asked with a hint of defiance.

"Do you really want my words of wisdom, or are you poised to do battle with anyone who disagrees with you?"

Ava's eyes began to tear up. She started to wipe the counter. "So you disagree with me, too?"

With a half-closed right eye, he offered her a crooked grin. "My, how ironic this conversation is. Remember when you abhorred my opinion? Hell, you would've shoved a firecracker in my mouth and clamped it shut if you could've gotten away with it."

She methodically wiped the same countertop area. "It matters to me now. So tell me what you think."

"Look at me, Ava."

She stopped what she was doing and turned to face him. He stared at her and spoke more introspectively. "What I think is that *I* would have given anything in the world to have a mother and a father who really wanted me and loved me." His smile returned as he picked up another cookie and started to eat it. "You know what one of my favorite novels is? *Frankenstein.*" He recollected with enthusiasm. "Remember the part when the monster escapes, and he's standing by a window swaying to the music he hears filtering through the night?" he jabbed his index finger at her. "I'm convinced that if his creator, his daddy, didn't run away, abdicate his responsibilities to his creation, the monster would still have been one helluvah ugly, big kid, but he would've been a secure and happier kid."

She chuckled at Henry's physical description of the monster.

"Ava, I'm convinced that if they take that kid away from you at age three, five, or fifteen, don't think for one second that he won't always remember that *you* were the one who saved his life. *You* were the one who held him when he was sick. *You* were the one who sang to him and read to him." With more levity, Henry waved the cookie he was eating in front of his face. "While other kids digest sugar cookies that lead to obesity, diabetes, and death, you'll bake that lucky little angel biscotti fit for an Arab-Irish king." Shaking his head, he added, "The way I see it, Jim isn't choosing the kid over you. He's choosing the baby *because* of you." Holding a small piece of the cookie in his hand, he motioned toward her. "Hell! If it weren't for you, and how you loved your kids, and how you love him, he'd still be stuck in the crazy notion that it's just easier not to make commitments. Just don't get involved and you don't get hurt." He popped the last bite into his mouth. "End of lecture, sweetheart."

He was about to step onto the patio when Ava dangled the bag of cookies and called, "Henry! You forgot your doggie-bag."

Making a quick about face, he jogged back, snatched the bag, and said, "I'm going nowhere without these!"

Before he turned to leave, she said, "Your mother must look down at you with solace and pride. You turned out to be a wonderfully wise and good man, the kind every mother and wife longs for."

Henry raised his eyebrows. He pointed a playful finger at her, yet he spoke with gravity. "That may be the nicest compliment I've ever received." He kissed her cheek and danced his way onto the patio.

***

After Ava baked for most of the morning and early afternoon, she took quality time to scrub down the kitchen. Exhausted by late afternoon, she joined O'Brien on the patio and asked, "Would you consider going to Mass with me tonight instead of in the morning so we could pick up sandwiches for supper afterward? I just don't feel like being in the kitchen anymore today." Before he answered, she added, "If you prefer to stay home tonight, I can bring supper home."

He jumped at the chance to spend time with her. Gathering his magazines, he said, "I'll be ready to go within the hour."

***

The gospel reading was "The Parable of the Mustard Seed." The congregation sat expectant, as the priest climbed the spiral stairs to the platform holding the microphone. O'Brien was uncharacteristically inattentive. As the priest philosophized, he was petitioning saints from A to Z to guide his wife to conversion.

"We can never know the *how* of God's spirit acting in our lives because that is God's realm. Science can *explain* the processes of phenomena, but only God calls life into being and determines the manner it works through its own nature. It's more productive for Christians to ask *why*, for what purpose does an event happen in life?"

Ava gave her head a slight shake. Silently she said with smug sarcasm, I'm way ahead of you on this one, Father. According to my calculations, and some fair-weather family and friends, I've wallowed in *why* for too long. She sat straighter and pushed her shoulders back. Okay, she thought, with a hint of indignation. Let's hear your reason *why* our merciful God kept me alive while I had to bury my whole family.

The priest explained, "When a person asks *why*, he learns to understand that life offers opportunities to serve God and one another in ways that maybe we can't understand with *how*, but when we seek the *why*, we can at least have faith in the positive result of our actions.

"For instance, it's futile to ask *how* God selects a specific tiny mustard seed to grow into a sturdy shrub that shelters creatures from the storms of life. It is more productive to ask *why* the shrub is there. What purpose can the shrub serve? Even though we may never be able to know or explain the botanical mechanics of the shrub, we do know that one of its purposes is to offer shelter and sustenance to God's creatures."

On one side of Ava, a mother shifted in her seat as she tried to quiet her fidgeting baby. On the other side O'Brien sat staring straight ahead working his way through the alphabet of saints, invoking each one by name—Anthony, Barnabas, Charbel, Dismis—pleading with them to intercede on his behalf. Ava's interest piqued when the priest referenced married couples.

"The same concept applies to a husband and wife who consummate a marriage and produce a child. One can explain the *how,* the scientific process of conception, gestation, and birth, but asking *why* is more spiritually productive. Why do people bring forth and nurture children? The answer to *why* leads us to understand that God expects those who are blessed with love to share that love. When people love each other in union with God, their love grows like the mustard seed and produces sturdy havens for those around them."

The priest summed up his analysis of the parable by suggesting, "Don't ask *how* events in your life happen. Be more productive and ask *why,* for what purpose do they happen. You will find that love allows you to extend yourself in ways that you never dreamed possible. When we begin to ask *why* we love as we do, we will begin to act the way love dictates us to act. Love leads us to the wisdom of God. When we understand that the *why* of all love is to produce havens and sustenance for all of God's creation, whether it is bringing forth life or sustaining life, offering food, shelter, and friendship to those around us, we understand that all love in union with God's love bears fruit that leads to harmony and peace."

O'Brien had no way of knowing that at the same time the priest descended the stairs, his prayer rose to heaven, and God said, "Yes."

Ava was in the throes of an epiphany. All this time she believed that O'Brien was God's consolation prize, designed to comfort her and help her restore her faith, but now she wondered if she was O'Brien's consolation prize, designed to restore his faith and help him reconcile his spirit so that he would be able to save the baby. A surge of renewal ran through her body as she thought, could this family ordeal be one of God's manifestations of a *why?* Their love was like a *mustard seed.* It grew strong, sturdy, and it endured. It sheltered them and protected them, and it offered comfort to family and friends around them.

After Mass, they drove to a local restaurant near the university. They talked superficially about politics and school, but to his dismay, she seemed distracted, aloof. She didn't broach the discussion of the baby. Disappointed that there was no visible change in her attitude, he wondered if the only reason she invited him to go to church was a matter of convenience. Sarcastic thoughts festered. We probably staged a battle of the saints in heaven. While I was praying for a conversion, she probably was praying that I'd forget the adoption all together. And the winner is . . . He shrugged. No matter how this stalemate ends, he thought, the winner is going to lose big time.

Paying the check, he turned to Ava and said, "Anything else on the agenda while we're out?"

"No. Let's go home. I have a lot to think about."

"If you need a sounding board, I'm your man."

"You can't help me this time, Jim. I have to make sense of what the priest said tonight."

Great! He thought. I didn't listen to the priest. He made an effort to hide his angst by teasing, "Is it a secret? Maybe I can give you a different perspective. I'd really like to hear the ideas you're tossing around in that brilliant head of yours."

"I don't mean to make my thoughts a mystery. I need to be sure of my decision because once I decide; I'm not changing my mind."

His anxiety escalated to internal alarm. The stalemate over the adoption was about to end. He braced himself for the final blow.

***

He followed her into the kitchen. Emotionally drained, *not knowing* grated on him.

"I didn't do much today, but I'm exhausted. I'm going upstairs to read; then I'm turning in. If you want me—"

Ava nodded.

The evening was still cool and pleasant enough to huddle on a patio lounge chair. Her eyes skimmed across the rosy-twilight sky when she caught sight of a bright star that played peek-a-boo as clouds softly tumbled round it. Keeping her eyes fixed on the star, she tossed the homily over and over in her mind. She loved her husband, and even though they fell into complacency for the past weeks, she knew he loved her with equal fervor. She mused, what are the odds of being able to love a man like Eli and a man like O'Brien in the same lifetime? As her eyes stayed locked on the star high in the sky, she remembered their chance meeting. Reminiscence of the gentle current, the soft magnetic force that drew them to each other and refused to let them part sent a slight surge through her body. She silently communed with Heaven: This love was beyond our own from the very beginning, wasn't it?

A dark cloud eclipsed the star, and the sky turned black. She closed her eyes, and her heart dared to ask God that haunting question one more time: Why did you have to take my babies? When she opened her eyes, she caught hold of the star now hanging in lone splendor. This time, the silence didn't overwhelm her with sadness; rather it enveloped her with peace that welled up like spiritual waves topped with crests of wisdom. Their past was unexplainable, but their future was self-determinable. Their union was designed to provide a haven—a place where they nurtured love, acceptance, and forgiveness— a place where Hannah's baby was destined to be. All she had to do was say *yes*.

Ava raised herself from the lounge chair and breathed deep. The swell and fall of her chest came easier. Her heart was full, but she felt light and free as she walked back to the house and rummaged through the kitchen desk for some stationery. O'Brien wouldn't miss the note on the counter when he woke early in the morning to go out for his daily run. She slipped her engagement ring off her finger and placed it in the envelope with his name on it. She wrote, *Dear Jim*, when the phone rang. It was Lucy. Ava carried the phone and the unfinished letter into the den where she sprawled out on the couch to talk. After Lucy filled her in on the preliminary details of Henry's surprise birthday party, they scheduled to meet for lunch in a couple of days to finalize the plans. They talked for over thirty minutes when Lucy had to fumble a "good-bye" because Henry moseyed into the room.

The soft sound of her heels clicking on the tile echoed in the quiet house. Fanning herself with the letter she intended to place in the envelope with the ring, his presence startled her and caused her to lurch backward.

He braced himself with both hands palm down on the counter and kept his eyes transfixed on her engagement ring. His brow was furrowed, and his broad shoulders slumped. Within seconds, she fathomed his repugnant reaction. Her heart sank when she thought of the horrible imaginings that raced through his head. Before she had a chance to clarify the misunderstanding, he confronted her.

"Inviting me to go to church with you before you dissolve our marriage is unique."

Ava's eyes widened. His cold accusation stung her. She reasoned that his grave, negative reaction to her ring on the counter was a culmination of built up anxiety over the weeks of her unwillingness even to talk with him about the adoption. What else was he supposed to think? Still, she thought, he should have known that living through the weeks of contention wasn't exactly like sailing a yacht on the Riviera, sipping a dry martini with an olive floating in it, for me either. Before she defended herself, she bit her lip and arrested her initial hurt and anger at his faulty conclusion.

"First you disregard how I feel and plan an adoption on your own. Then you convict me on circumstantial evidence." She stared him down with stern eyes. "Are you going to give me a chance to explain before *you* walk out on me?"

His penetrating eyes followed her as she moved along the counter, tapping the missive for emphasis. He maintained a stiff jaw when he said, "Go ahead. Tell me the intriguing story behind why my world is about to unravel."

She couldn't bear to watch him hurt a second longer.

"Despite the fact that you demonstrate little faith in me this evening, I'm going to be nice to you." With a glint in her eye, she pointed the letter at him and said, "Your world isn't unraveling." With a hint of levity in her voice, she said, "Actually, the baby will tighten our world up for a while." A playful smirk crossed her lips. "At least a diaper bag is lighter than a golf bag."

He stared at her with his right eye half closed, not fully comprehending the words he waited so long to hear. Her flippant attitude confused him.

"You're supposed to be holding my ring, Jim, but," she waved the letter, "this note was supposed to accompany it." She straddled a stool and explained, "Lucy called tonight about Henry's birthday party, and I finished the note in the den after I talked to her." More apologetic, she said, "I thought you were asleep. Since you're here, I'll just read the note to you, okay?" Unfolding the letter, she read, "I know that this family ordeal hasn't been easy for you, and I apologize for not making it any easier on you." She looked up and teased. "You'll like this part." She proceeded to read in a sweet voice, the kind of voice he missed over the past weeks. "I want you to ask a jeweler if he could place another small satellite diamond around the large diamond. Every day, I want the baby to see his diamond in my ring that represents the bright shining hope and love that he brings to the O'Brien-Coury families and the world." Then using hyperbole to the nth degree, she handed the note to her beleaguered husband and exaggerated, "Loooove, Ava."

He looked down at the ring. He looked up at her. He read the note to himself to make sure he had all the facts straight this time. His chest rose and fell quickly as he tapped the letter on the palm of his hand.

"Do you have any idea how stupid, and sorry, and elated I feel at this moment?"

She nodded. "You of all people should know that I have extensive experience in all three of those emotions."

"Does this mean I get to hold you again?' he asked, his voice filled with hope. "I miss holding you, Ava."

She pushed her hair behind her ear and inched her way toward him. When she stood at arm's length, he seized her, clutched her close, and breathed in the smell of her hair. She felt the wild thumping of his heart. The weeks of alienation sorely frayed their nerves, and this late night reconciliation was a much needed and welcome healing. After a short silent embrace, he let out a heavy sigh. "The end of this civil war definitely calls for a celebration. Share a glass of wine with me?"

She nodded.

They sat across from each other at the table. Bewildered at the turn of events, he asked, "After all these weeks, what changed your mind?"

"Two things. When Henry came into the kitchen this afternoon, he talked about his favorite novel, *Frankenstein*. He wondered what his life would have been like if someone would have read to him and baked him cookies. He told me how his mother and father ran away from him just like Dr. Frankenstein ran from his creation. In both cases, their creators caused so much emotional damage to their creations." She took a drink of her wine. "I don't want the same tragedy to happen to the baby. If you really believe that we're the best hope for little O'Brien, I'll help you raise him or her. If Patrick and Marcia and Hannah fight to get custody some day, I'll find a way to deal with it."

"You said two things changed your mind."

"Did you listen to the homily in church this evening?"

"I have to admit, my mind was preoccupied."

"Well. One of these days I'll tell you about "The Parable of the Mustard Seed" and how it teaches people to ask *why* instead of *how*."

"Really? I have a *why* for you. Why don't we go upstairs and celebrate that—"

"That I'm not dissolving the marriage?" she said, with a condescending nod.

He closed his eyes and dropped his head down on the table. "Ohhh boy." He turned his head sideways and looked up at her. He held his thumb and index finger close together and said, "Please have this much sympathy on me."

"Did you really think I would intentionally hurt you?"

He sat up. "When I saw your ring in the envelope with my name on it," he grabbed his chest, "I felt nauseous. It was worse than the day I walked into my apartment and saw . . ." He looked away for several moments and cleared his throat. His eyes swung back to her. "You know by now I measure everything in my life by *Ava-meters*."

She sat on his lap. "I'll never leave you," she said, gently pressing her forehead on his. "It's a good thing, too! If I were the leaving kind, I'd take the ring . . . the one with all the diamonds . . . and everything else in the house . . . and bank." She poked her index finger in his chest. "Next time, listen to your lawyer," she said, teasing him.

O'Brien laughed. This was the Ava he adored. "I never thought I'd say this to you, babe, but I missed your sarcastic mouth."

"Really?" she mused. She leaned softly onto his chest and raised her lips to his ear and whispered, "See how different we are. If you follow me up the stairs, I'll show you what I missed most about you."

So he did.

***

During the next several weeks, just to be silly, O'Brien would pick up a five pound bag of sugar or flour from time to time. He'd tell Ava, "I can't believe a baby is this small."

Ava reminded him, "Yeah, but don't expect the baby to be that still and quiet."

The day before Halloween, O'Brien sat on a kitchen barstool watching Ava bake bread. He hoisted a five pound bag of flour and teased Ava about her heritage. Cooing to the bag of flour, he said, "I bet you want to be a loaf of Syrian bread for Trick-or-Treat, don't you?"

Ava laughed. She casually threw a black dish towel over the bag of flour and countered, "No. I think he wants to be a loaf of pumpernickel bread." Pointing to the black towel, she narrowed her eyes. "So, how accepting is the O'Brien clan going to be if the baby looks like that?"

He raised his eyebrows and gave her a blank stare. The family made assumptions about the identity of the biological father, but throughout the discussions, Hannah never really divulged any major details. He conceded that this particular thought probably hadn't crossed anyone's mind but Ava's. He told her, "I can think of one or two O'Briens who still have bigoted blood coursing through their veins." He stared at the black towel and bent his head down and kissed it tenderly. "Regardless of what kind of bread you are, you'll be sweet, and we'll love every bit of you."

CHAPTER TWENTY-FOUR

PATRICK Coury O'Brien was born on November 25. Thanksgiving came late that year, so most of the O'Brien clan had already gathered for the holiday. When Hannah went into labor, the family surrounded her with a groundswell of support. Ava congregated with several of the O'Briens in the waiting room, while O'Brien, Patrick, and Marcia were among the first to see the baby after the delivery. The nurse placed the baby in Hannah's arms, and she gently kissed his head. She looked up at her uncle as she lay in bed caressing the baby's cheek and playing with the fine strands of the baby's hair.

"He's going to be yours, Uncle Jim, so maybe you should hold him."

O'Brien sat on the edge of the bed and looked at her with tenderness. "Yeah, but right now that little one needs his mother."

Patrick asked if he could hold his grandson for a few minutes because he had to tell him one of the most important things he'll ever hear. O'Brien looked up at his brother and laughed. He turned to Hannah and Marcia and quipped, "Can you believe it? Grandpa can't wait to coach the kid on how to give me a rough time."

When Patrick cradled his grandson for the first time, his eyes moistened. He looked into the baby's unusually wide-eyed stare and spoke loud enough for O'Brien to hear.

"I love your Uncle Jim more than he could ever know for saving your life."

O'Brien stood. He enveloped his brother and the baby. "I saw so much death in Nam," he whispered. "Everyone in this room opted for life. It feels good to be surrounded by life."

That was the last time an O'Brien would overtly mention that Patrick

Coury's life was in danger. As far as the O'Briens were concerned, he was initiated into the family where he belonged, a part of them forever.

***

The first night that Ava and O'Brien brought Patrick Coury home, he whimpered all night long like a little puppy yearning for the warmth of its mother's side. O'Brien wanted to bring him into bed with them, but Ava lectured him. "Do you want me to read you horror stories of how well-meaning parents roll on top of their newborns and smother them to death?" From then on, he acquiesced to Ava when it came to baby rules and procedures. He figured that a woman who raised twins possessed the knowledge and wisdom of raising one baby successfully. So during the first three weeks that Patrick Coury was with them, when he cried, Ava would be the one who changed him, fed him, and rocked him back to sleep. O'Brien became a quick study and administered the diaper changes and feedings in the early evenings on a regular basis.

One evening, he sat amused watching and listening to Ava rock the baby to sleep. She sang one song after another to him. He shook his head in wonderment. "Why do you always sing Crosby, Stills, Nash, and Young songs to him, Ava? You know so many songs!"

"So he can sing with his Uncle Sean at family gatherings," she whispered as she gently smooched the baby's cheek.

Reaching for the phone and dialing Sean's number, he said, "Listen, Sean. Ava's grooming the baby to harmonize with you. Listen to how she sings the baby to sleep."

Within seconds, Sean recognized the song and began to harmonize "our house is a very, very, very fine house . . ." with Ava. The baby closed his eyes and dreamed.

***

Ava felt mounting frustration a week before Christmas because she was behind schedule in decorating the house. She concentrated her efforts those first weeks of Patrick Coury's life on meeting his every need. As she watched the snow fall hard and steady, O'Brien unexpectedly threw open the door and announced that he wanted her to brave the blustery conditions to help him search for the perfect tree. His request unnerved her. He knows how I feel about live trees, she thought. Before she could argue against his plan, he circled his arms around her and coaxed, "I think it's time to teach Patrick and his Mommy that live trees are like bailouts,

200

they're not all bad! Besides, the baby won't be able to bother it. I want a live tree this year because we're going to radiate life." He pleaded, "Do this with me, Ava. It will be a good memory to balance the bad." She tried to wiggle out of his arms, but he kept a tight hold. He kissed the back of her neck. "Do this with me! We can plant the tree for Patrick, and they can grow together."

"Okay!" she whispered, with her teeth clenched. With silly gesticulations, she struggled to break free. She turned to him and warned, "If anything disastrous happens with this—"

O'Brien placed his hands on his hips. "What on earth do you think is going to happen?" He extended his arms and pretended to stalk her like a monster pursuing its next victim. "Is the tree going to animate and come after you?" He grabbed her and nibbled on her neck. She fought the urge to laugh as she shooed him away. "So much for being a sophisticated university president! If only the trustees could see you now." She shook her head in mock disdain. "You're worse than a kid!" She grabbed her coat and started for the garage. "If we're going to get a tree, let's get this over with while the baby is sleeping and the nanny is here to watch him."

Following her, he said, "Come on, Ava. This excursion should be fun, not an ordeal."

She turned to face him. "Did you ever hear the adage, 'One person's fun is another person's masochistic attempt to make her husband happy'?"

"No. But my grandfather gave me marital advice."

"Oh, I can't wait to hear what grandpa taught you."

"He told me that I should search for a brilliant woman like Helen Keller. She won't see the bad things I do. She won't hear the bad things I say, and she'd be frugal with her criticism of me."

Ava looked at him dumbfounded. "That sounds like advice straight from the gospel according to Henry Morgan!" She warned, "You better watch what you say, Jim, especially in public. People have lost their jobs over less offensive jokes and rightfully so!" After admonishing him, she added, "Besides, you feel bad when I snub you."

"Ava, remember Geoffrey Chaucer? Those are not my politically incorrect words and sentiments. I was quoting my somewhat unburnished Irish grandfather. Blame him, not me!"

"You're blaming Chaucer for your bad joke?" With a chuckle, she said, "That's brilliant, Jim." She added, "You have so much to teach Patrick.

The parent conference meetings that await us in our old age ought to be invigorating."

***

O'Brien gravitated toward the fuller trees, while Ava appreciated the taller, leaner trees. He complained, "I don't want to stare at an anorexic Christmas tree all season long. You need to be more jovial, honey. It's Christmas for Chri–"

She narrowed her eyes and stared as if hot lasers were ready to reduce him to ashes. She warned, "Don't you dare take the Lord's name in vain, especially when you're searching for a Christmas tree!" More relaxed, she asked, "What's gotten into you? First the bad joke, now you're sacrilegious."

He grabbed her finger wagging at him and laughed. His hold on her brought back levity. "If you don't stop teasing me," she warned, "I'll leave you here, get in the car, drive home, and decorate the artificial tree myself!"

He raised his hands in submission. "I have to tell you, Ava. All things considered, you're doing really well on this excursion."

She shook her head, and said, "Don't patronize me. I'll admit that I have some anxiety, but it's only a Christmas tree."

"Oh, but it's more than that. It's our first live tree together."

"This tree means a lot to you, doesn't it?" she asked, appreciating his innocent, childlike, heart's desire.

"It really does, Ava. It's our first Christmas together as a family, and I want this Christmas to represent life in every way possible."

The snow fell steadily around them. The cadence of Christmas music filled the grove as spirited families searched for the *perfect* tree. Moved by a new thought, Ava kissed him on the cheek and said, "All this is nice, but your love makes everything full of life." She held his face in her hands, took a deep breath, as though she was psyching herself for a serious competition. "Okay! You go that way, and I'll go this way."

With new purpose and more determination, she set out to find the perfect tree. After scouring two rows to no avail, she rounded a corner. She spotted it! The tree was tall, and it possessed some fullness to it. Two branches conspicuously stuck out past the bottom branches. This imperfect specimen reminded her of a tree her father brought home one Christmas when she and Jake were teenagers. Everyone expected her dad to cut off the one branch that stuck out from all the others to make the tree more symmetrical, but Ava begged her father to preserve the branch because it lent character to the tree. When her father left the room for a few minutes, Jake picked up the trimmer and placed it on the branch. He was overly eager to cut it off, and Ava started to scream at him.

"Don't you dare cut that branch off, Jake! Daddy agrees with me!"

"It makes the tree look stupid, Ava!" he yelled back.

"No sir! It gives the tree character! You're the only thing that's stupid, so don't touch that branch!"

Her father in an adjoining room was more than annoyed with the incessant bickering of his two children and wanted them both to stop fighting immediately. He yelled one clear directive: "CUT IT OUT!"

SNAP! Without a moment's hesitation, Jake severed the branch from the tree.

For several seconds, the room filled with eerie silence until Ava gasped and let out a piercing shriek. Pandemonium broke loose. She flung a string of lights at Jake, and then she let out a prolonged wail. Her father stood in the doorway of the room and stared at Jake first. Then he turned to Ava who, with a dramatic flair, sat in the middle of the floor with her face buried in her hands mourning the loss of the branch.

"Why do you two always fight?"

He fixed his eyes on Jake again. "Why did you touch the trimmer in the first place? Who told you to do my job?"

Jake pleaded outlaw-wise to defend himself. "You said, 'Cut it out,' Dad. We all heard you."

Ava's father yanked the trimmer from Jake's hands. Bewildered by his son's behavior, he shook his head and said, "Other baby boys, they circumcise. Not my boy." He shoved Jake's head and said, "My boy, they turned upside down and cut out his brain!" He gently placed his hand on Ava's head and said, "Dry your eyes, princess; life as you know it isn't over." He gave them one last directive: "Both of you stay away from the tree until I tell you to decorate it."

***

"I want this tree," she said, smiling at the recollection. "It brings back memories."

"Well, it's yours, pretty lady. I'll trim these branches to make it even."

"No! This tree is *perfect* just the way it is. Those branches give it character. Besides, I don't want it to look like an artificial tree."

"Really!" he said, amused. "You've come a long way, Mrs. O'Brien."

As midnight arrived, they completed the final touches on the tree. They placed their favorite ornaments in strategic spots, and the icicles hung long and loose. The bright, white lights twinkled. O'Brien held Ava close and marveled at what artistry they had accomplished together.

They began to tidy up the room before retiring for the evening, when a feeling of unfinished business gnawed at him. Something about the tree wasn't right. He scoured the branches several times before it occurred to him. Luke's ornament was missing.

"Ava!" he called. "Where's Luke's ornament? I can't find it on the tree."

She didn't answer. She robotically moved toward the stairs.

"Don't go upstairs yet. I can't find Luke's . . ." He glanced over at her sitting on the bottom step with her head resting on her knees. She was gently rocking back and forth. He knelt down in front of her and held her hands. "Hey, don't cry."

She raised her head. With deep remorse, she said, "I shouldn't have taken his picture, Jim. I should have picked him up. I should have held my baby in my arms, and I should have rocked him." Again, she rocked her body to and fro. "I should have kissed him and told him how much I loved him." She shook her head. "I can't put him on that live tree." She apologized like so many times before. "I miss them so much."

O'Brien leaned in and spoke in a low, soft voice. "Listen to me, Ava. It's natural to miss them the way you do. I don't ever want you to forget them. That's why Luke's picture is so important. It brings the whole family so much laughter and joy." He teased her. "Luke was just like you. He looked like you, and God knows, he had a sarcastic mouth like you. That picture records one of the best vintage Coury/Panetta family stories that the families have." She raised her head and stared at him as he talked. "We can't let his story slip away. Luke's cousins have to keep telling his story, and so does Patrick. It's one more sure way to keep Luke and Leila and Eli with us, alive and vibrant."

Ava knew that everything her husband said was true. She nodded, wiped her eyes with her hand, and crawled to where the box of ornaments lay just a few feet away. She retrieved Luke's infamous picture from the layers of tissue and lifted it to her lips and reverently kissed it. Her eyes searched the tree for a special place to hang it, but the tree was already laden with ornaments.

O'Brien held out his hand. Ava handed him the ornament and watched him stretch his arms as high as they would go. "Let's place our handsome guy right beneath the star."

As Ava gazed at Luke's ornament, O'Brien retrieved a small box from a table drawer where he hid it when he first came home from work. Handing the box to Ava, he said, "I was saving this for Christmas, but it feels right to give it to you now. Open it, and we can share it with Eli, Luke, Leila, and Patrick."

She opened the box to find a necklace, a bright shining North Star. It was a large exquisite diamond, almost the size of her engagement ring.

"Oh, Jim!" she whispered. "It's stunning!"

"I wanted to give you a gift that expresses what you are to me. Your strength of character, your resolve to choose life even after all the death; you've been my 'ever fixed mark' from the moment you bailed me out. Ever since that day, my life has been rich and meaningful." He held her and rested his chin on her head.

She nudged him softly with her elbow. "You've done the same for me."

"Maybe, but you trumped me the moment you agreed to help me be a father." He took the necklace from her hand and clasped it on her neck. He turned her around and said, "All the luxuries my money can buy will never compare to the treasure you gave me. That's why it's always been easy to love only you." Her eyes watered. She turned to face the tree and burrowed backwards into his arms.

"I love the wise men you bought when you were with Sean." She turned to face him and asked, "Don't you think we're all like weary wise men? We travel across the treacherous desert of life. We search for something that endures." She paused to reflect deeper into her and her husband's journey. "We get lost; we get mired in our ignorance, bias, and fear. But faith, even if it's as tiny as a mustard seed, bolsters us and moves us forward." After another short pause she said, "It takes so much courage to keep walking, not knowing what's around the bend or up over the hill." Then she added with more conviction, "If we can keep traveling for even one second longer, maybe we'll be fortunate to encounter someone who is willing to journey with us, shelter us, and even love us."

Patrick Coury's cry interrupted Ava's philosophical mood. They walked up the stairs together to comfort him. Ava cradled the baby in her arms, brought him to her shoulders and sang "Bridge over Troubled Water." O'Brien sat in a chair adjacent to them, content just to watch both of them so closely bound that they looked like one person. He invoked a silent prayer to God who lent them life and love, to Love that guided their course and found them worthy to be with each other. He remembered the first time Ava begged for answers from God, questioning why she had to live without Eli, Luke, and Leila. He believed that he saw an answer unfolding before him. He thought of the thousand times they dreamed and asked the Immanent Will for one more chance, to save the Vietnamese baby, to save her children, but their dreams always ended the same way, in death. As Ava crooned to Patrick Coury, it occurred to him that while the Lord of Life didn't permit them to restore the lives that they had a hand in destroying, He was merciful enough to give them an opportunity to save, protect, and nurture another life.

His mind wandered to a poem he read years ago. He lingered on one stanza in particular:

For while the tired waves, vainly breaking,
Seem here no painful inch to gain,
Far back, through creeks and inlets making,
Comes silent, flooding in, the main.[1]

Back then, the theme seemed grotesque and painful, a depiction of life that demanded too high an emotional sacrifice for love's reward that seemed so tentative. He needed something more immediate, more tangible to sacrifice his heart willingly. Ironically, now the message assured him.

Ava was completing the song, singing how she would take their part and ease their minds. Patrick Coury drifted on a sea of warmth and love. Again, cradling the baby in her arms, she stood near the crib. He whispered, "Don't lay him down yet. I want to hold both of you for a minute." He stood behind her and tenderly wrapped his arms around her and the baby and held them carefully close to his heart. He drew in a deep, quiet breath. While nothing could ever wash away the horrific memories etched indelibly in their minds—a man whose spirit was trapped in the death swamps of a war, a woman whose heart was shattered by a moment of distraction on a highway, and a baby whose existence teetered on the brink of uncertainty— there the three of them converged, warm and secure on a cold winter night. Love guided them to this moment filled with more peace than they could

---

[1] Clough, Arthur. "Say Not the Struggle Naught Availeth."

have ever dreamed of possessing. As Ava lay her head back on his shoulder in calm surrender, he vowed that no sacrifice would ever be too great for the love and promise he held in his arms. In one week they would celebrate Christmas, but his heart felt more like Lent had ended. He wanted to celebrate Easter.

ACKNOWLEDGEMENTS

Characters and events in this story are fiction. Only Sister Alvera is real. Thank you to family and friends who helped me create *The Sunny Spaces*:

Sarifa and Charles Abraham—My parents taught us with stories.

David, Jason, Erin, and Andy—My family encouraged me.

Theresa Abraham Smarrelli—My sister taught me how to write my first essay.

Vincent Scialabba—He's the teacher who inspired me to be a teacher.

Harold Gramley—He's the prof who taught me to appreciate literature.

My Friends—They offered valuable feedback.

Nancy Bonk

Carol Colaizzi

Father James Downs

Louise Ferilla

Elaine Hoffman

Father Gilbert Puznakoski

Gina Antognoli—My niece designed the cover and formatted the book.

Vince Bologna—He and his students are computer wizards.

The Laurel Senior High School students I taught— They taught me more.

REFERENCES

To learn more about the novels, poems, songs and quotations in the story Google:

1. Matthew Arnold's poem, "Dover Beach."
2. Emily Bronte's novel, *Wuthering Heights.*
3. Geoffrey Chaucer's *The Canterbury Tales* .
4. Arthur Clough's poem, "Say Not the Struggle Naught Availeth."
5. Don McClean's song, "And I Love You So." You Tube.
6. Herman Melville's novel, *Moby Dick.*
7. Graham Nash's songs, "Our House" and "Wasted on the Way." You Tube.
8. *The New American Bible.*
9. William Shakespeare's "Sonnet 116."
10. Mary Shelley's novel, *Frankenstein.*
11. Paul Simon's song, "Bridge over Troubled Water." You Tube.
12. Jonathan Swift's story, *Gulliver's Travels.*
13. Henry Van Dyke's story, "The Story of the Other Wise Man."
14. "The Year That Was." *The Dailey Show with Jon Stewart.* Comedy Central. Jan. 9, 2002.
15. Neil Young's song, "Heart of Gold." You Tube.

ABOUT THE AUTHOR

Ann Abraham Antognoli was born and raised in New Castle, Pennsylvania. The sixth child of Lebanese immigrants, she learned to love *story-telling* as a child because her parents always told stories to teach life lessons. She earned a Bachelor of Science in English from Edinboro University of Pennsylvania and a Masters in English from Westminster College in New Wilmington, Pennsylvania. She taught high school English for over twenty-five years and lives with her husband David in New Castle, Pennsylvania. She and her husband are the parents of Jason, Erin, and son-in-law, Andy Cleavenger.

95373143R00120

Made in the USA
Columbia, SC
09 May 2018